KUTZE, STEPP'N ON WHEAT

Kutze, Stepp'n on Wheat

THAMES RIVER PRESS
An imprint of Wimbledon Publishing Company Limited (WPC)
Another imprint of WPC is Anthem Press (www.anthempress.com)
First published in the United Kingdom in 2014 by
THAMES RIVER PRESS
75–76 Blackfriars Road
London SE1 8HA

www.thamesriverpress.com

Original title: *Mugifumi Kuutsue*
Copyright © Shinji Ishii 2002
Originally published in Japan by Shinchosha
English translation copyright © David Karashima 2014

All rights reserved. No part of this publication may be reproduced
in any form or by any means without written permission of the publisher.

The moral rights of the author have been asserted in accordance
with the Copyright, Designs and Patents Act 1988.

All the characters and events described in this novel are imaginary
and any similarity with real people or events is purely coincidental.

Printed and bound in Sweden by ScandBook AB.

A CIP record for this book is available from the British Library.

ISBN 978-1-78308-128-8

This title is also available as an ebook.

This book has been selected by the Japanese Literature Publishing Project (JLPP),
an initiative of the Agency for Cultural Affairs of Japan.

KUTZE, STEPP'N ON WHEAT

Shinji Ishii

Translated by
David Karashima

Thames River Press

Chapter 1

On the Surgeon's Table

I knew nothing about stepping on wheat.

I grew up in a seaport town, very much at home with factory smoke, the smell of beer, and haze rising from cobblestone streets, but unaccustomed to the earthy smells of the ground beneath my feet. From time to time, the strong ocean winds would bring unexpected things to our shores—a piece of sailor's underwear, a last will and testament, or a flag from a foreign land. And at night, we'd hear the moans and groans of the monsters that roamed the deep.

In back alleys, sailors would get into fights, with the winners emerging quickly, no such thing as a draw. Mostly it would take only a single punch for the weaker man to fall to the ground unconscious, the victor strutting back to the bar with his chest puffed up. Us kids would seize the moment to prop up the fallen sailor and drag him to another bar, where we'd pour a glass of water over his head. On regaining his senses, the sailor would give us two or three blood-stained coins for our trouble.

I'd just started elementary school when I met Kutze for the first time. I remember it was a hot midsummer night, and I'd woken in the darkness feeling terrible. I rubbed my eyes and looked to the bed on my right, then glanced over to the bed on my left. Dad wasn't there, and neither was Grandpa. Getting up, I circled the room three times, my footsteps the only sound in the house. I peered into the storage room next to the bedroom–not a soul there. I went down the wooden stairs to the kitchen, its stone floor much older than any of our neighbors'. Nobody there. I went into the living room, hoping to find Grandpa in his usual spot on the old couch. Not there. The front door was still firmly shut, the rusty lock in place.

I ran back upstairs and jumped into bed, burying my head under the covers.

Am I alone? I clutched the sheets over my head. *All alone, locked in the house, on this horrible night?* Was I being punished? What if it wasn't only tonight? What if this is the way it was going to be from now on? Or was this the way it always has been? Maybe I never have noticed, but maybe I'd been left by myself every night, all alone in this stone house, in deathly silence, in total darkness. The thought made me shiver. This had to be a dream, I told myself. I lay down, clasping my arms tightly across my chest. I told myself that Dad and Grandpa were, in fact, sleeping on either side of me. I imagined how I'd get up in the morning and go downstairs and Dad would be making me an omelet like he did every day, and then Grandpa and I would go for a walk along the canal like we always did. By morning, this moment would be forgotten, Dad's and Grandpa's absence nothing but a bad dream.

It was at that moment that I heard it.

Ton, Ta-tan, Ton

I strained my ears at once.

Ton, Ta-tan, Ton

There it was. That same rhythm. Then again. And again. It seemed to be coming from outside the house – a sound like something soft being hit. I'd never heard anything like it before. But strangely enough, it wasn't scary. I poked my head out from under the sheets, only to find the room bathed in light—it was morning already!

For a moment, I watched as the golden sunlight poured in through the windows, reflecting off my white bed sheets, the watercolor on the wall and my toy yacht, too. Then I stepped onto the cold floor with my bare feet.

Ton, Ta-tan, Ton

This time, the sound was coming from the window. I walked over to look out. I gasped at what I saw.

Normally, from the window, you could see the canal, sometimes with barges of cargo floating down to port. Those same barges might go past when Grandpa and I were on our morning walks, and sometimes the men on them would throw me candy, toys, balls, and other goodies. If I managed to catch them, the men would whistle and Grandpa would bang his stick on the ground in response.

But when I looked out the window this time, there was no canal. I couldn't believe it. Not only was the canal gone, the whole town was gone. There was nothing but a vast stretch of yellow ground all the way to the horizon. I stared, afraid to blink, and I thought maybe this is how people feel when they see the ocean for the first time.

Ton, Ta-tan, Ton

When the sound came again, I glanced down to find someone standing right in front of our house, wearing an odd outfit. He had on a straw hat with a large brim and a shirt and baggy pants that matched the color of the land. Only his shoes were a different color, with the uppers as black as the soles. The shoes seemed far too big, but that didn't stop the stranger from kicking the dirt in front of our house.

I opened the window carefully, not making a sound, and leaned out to get a better look. The man's eyes were fixed on the ground as he kept kicking up a cloud of yellow dust with his big, clumpy shoes.

Ton, Ta-tan, Ton

"Excuse me, but what are you doing?" I asked, curiosity getting the better of me.

"Stepp'n on wheat," the stranger replied, without lifting his eyes in my direction. His voice was so gentle voice it could have belonged to a man or a woman.

"What's your name?"

"Kutze," the stranger said, continuing to kick the dirt.

"Kutze," I repeated. "Kutze. Is that your family name? Or is it your nickname?"

"Don't know," came the answer, accompanied by that same *tap-tapping*.

4

I watched, transfixed, as Kutze did his wheat stepp'n. The sweet summer air drifted across the golden land as the sun shone, down on Kutze and me, as I found myself tapping on the window sill in sync with the rhythm of Kutze's stepp'n.

Ton, Ta-tan, Ton

The scene seemed so wonderful that I wanted to set foot on the golden land and step on the wheat myself, and right there I decided that when I got older, I wanted to go with Kutze and wheat-step our way to the horizon.

I'll be joining you, Kutze. Just as soon as I get myself a pair of big, black wheat-stepp'n shoes!

Ton, Ta-tan, Ton

Ton—

"Wake up!"

Someone was shaking me.

"Grandpa's gone off for a walk by himself this morning," said Dad, pulling the covers from my head and looking down at me reproachfully, "because you wouldn't get out of bed. Now go and brush your teeth. I'm going out to buy some eggs."

I got out of bed, slowly washed my face, and stuck a toothbrush in my mouth—all the while thinking how the morning sun in the real world wasn't nearly as beautiful as it was in my dream. Then listening to the gurgle of the canal through the open door, I watched children running along the canal as a barge floated by. Finally I gargled, noticing a rusty aftertaste, then licked my lips, bitterness on my tongue.

That was when I thought I heard something above. It wasn't very distinct, but I was sure I wasn't imagining it. The sound seemed to be coming from the attic, above the bed. I dragged a chair over, and using it to climb on top of the closet, I removed a ceiling tile and poked my head into the attic. I was met, right in front of my eyes, by Kutze. He was diminutive, the size of a wine bottle, and he was making slow side-steps that went *Ton, Ta-tan, Ton,* just like in my dream.

For many years after that, whenever I was alone in the house, I would climb onto the closet to visit Kutze in the attic.

"Are you the only one living in that yellow land?" I asked him once.

"It's not a question of whether anyone else is around," he mumbled, without missing a wheat-stepp'n beat, "or whether anyone is around at all. It's a matter of distance."

Ton, Ta-tan, Ton

This was a typical answer from him—mysterious. There were times when I heard his tapping steps outside—when I was waiting for Grandpa at the bar, or when I was walking home from school. Those steps would always be followed by Kutze's flat voice, almost a whisper. Each time I heard it, I would stop in my tracks. But Kutze's voice never betrayed his emotions. Even later, when he predicted the catastrophe that hit the town, the school caretaker's accident, and the final moments of The Mouse Man. He told me a lot of things in that dear voice that only I could hear. And all the while, his wheat-stepp'n didn't stop.

Ton, Ta-tan, Ton

It's been ten years since I first met Kutze. I lie now in the dark on the surgeon's table, and I listen to the rhythm of Kutze's stepping. Each beat brings a vivid memory. *Ton* ... I see my classroom in elementary and junior high school ... *Ta-Tan* ... the golden instruments lined up in the concert hall, the silver cane, the conductor's baton ... *Ton* ... the mice, the seven dogs, the strains of a cello ... *Ta-Tan* ... Wheat-stepp'n wasn't the only thing I knew nothing about then. There were plenty of other things I was ignorant of. Maybe I still am. *Kutze, you think so?*

Ton, Ta-Tan, Ton

The invisible Kutze gives no reply, but I hear his steps echo in the darkness as people dressed in white enter the operating room.

The King of the Band

Grandpa arrived on this island after a week-long journey by ship. It wasn't long before he made his presence felt.

I was still a baby, and one evening after he'd lain me down to sleep he went to ask our landlord about the terrible racket that coming from the docks at the same time every day.

"Oh that," the overweight owner snorted as he flipped through the guestbook. "It's the town's wind band. A battleship is supposed to be coming to port next month, so they're practicing for the welcoming ceremony. If it's bothering you, old man, why don't you join me in a hand of poker to keep your mind off it?"

By the time the owner looked up from the guestbook, Grandpa was gone. People remember Grandpa that day, walking briskly in the rain, clacking his silver cane on the pavement.

"What a sight he was!" the bartender told me later. "He marched past by the bar like a preacher on fire."

"More like a mountain cat," the police officer standing nearby piped up. "A black mountain cat that escaped from a cage. But being that my business is catching humans, I don't bother with mountain cats."

When he reached the docks, Grandpa proceeded directly to Warehouse #2, where the din was coming from. He raised his silver cane high, brought it down hard on the green metal door.

Inside, it must have sounded as if the warehouse were hit by lightning, which someone screamed out, which caused everyone to dive onto the floor.

"Come out of there!" Grandpa's voice boomed. "You guys are a disgrace! You are an embarrassment to music."

In the rain, with his cane banging on the metal door, Grandpa's booming voice echoed throughout the town. It could be heard in the bar, and it even reached and the school grounds, where Dad was busy correcting papers.

"Which factory is making all that noise?" said the principal, disgusted. "And at this late hour!"

"It's my father," said Dad with a tired voice.

"Is he an alcoholic?" the principal asked, suddenly interested.

"No," said Dad, shaking his head, "it's worse than that."

In the warehouse, the butcher—also known as the clarinetist—crawled along the damp floor and bravely pushed open the door. He was met with the sight of Grandpa, soaking wet in his big black coat, looking like something that had been dragged up from the depths of the ocean, seaweed and all.

Dispensing with niceties, Grandpa strode into the warehouse, striking the floor with his cane. "The first thing you deadbeats need to do is tune your instruments," Grandpa said sternly. "Then, work on your long tones. We have a lot of work to do."

With his booming voice and his accent from across the waters, Grandpa instructed the men to place their chairs in a circle around him. Everyone did what they were told as if it were the most natural thing to do, with no man having the wherewithal to speak up. A long tone, as the name suggests, is holding a single note on an instrument for a long time. And from that day on, the members of the brass band were no longer able to touch vinegar or pickled fish for fear of the toll it'd take on their cracked, swollen lips.

"With a single wave of a magic wand, real music found its way into town," recalled the caretaker of the school.

There was also a story in the local paper a year later, penned by a senior journalist, that began as follows:

Up until recently in this town, playing in a brass band has meant nothing more than picking up a trumpet, blowing casually into it, and allowing nonsense to come flooding out of the other end…

Less than two years later, and by the time I'd learned to talk, the town's struggling crew of ten trumpeters had grown to forty-five—enough for a real brass band. A little later still, the band took tenth place in an island-wide music contest, prompting Town Hall to buy each member of the band a new instrument.

From that time on, every arriving ship was greeted at port by trumpet fanfare. One day stands out: when the band played, the ocean winds subsided and the clarity of the brass notes was carried out to sea, causing that same journalist to write:

Those of you who visited the port yesterday may have seen quite a sight when our town's very own brass band commandeered the unruly ocean winds and forced them to subside. Perhaps music has always been just that—having the power to calm unruly ocean gusts with a melodic, brassy breeze.

Though poetic, it was a frivolous comment. It was also a comment that was soon to be proven wrong.

8

Grandpa was the king of the band. He played the timpani—those four kettle drums, each with a distinct tone—and he was always positioned at the very back of the band, in the highest spot in the room. He was passionate about his music, and even during rehearsals he could be found in a black suit and tie, standing by his drums where he could observe the band members' every move. It was he who, when the moment was right, would breathe in softly and nod to the postmaster who would in turn tap his baton and then music would begin to flow. Even through my young eyes I could see the effect of the music. The air took on a different color, the damp warehouse atmosphere suddenly sparkling, like some sort of semi-transparent metal. Those of us sitting on the floor would breathe in this air, little by little, as if it were a precious commodity. And when we did, it felt as if the brightness in the air became part of our bodies.

If the conductor stood where the music emerged, you could say that Grandpa stood where the sound came from. The backbone of a brass band is its percussion, Grandpa would say, and whenever anyone hit a bum note, Grandpa would purposely bang out the wrong note on the timpani, causing the offending band members to wince and look down in shame. The poor horn player spent hours with his eyes staring at his shoes. But it could happen to anyone in the band, and I even saw Grandpa do similar to the conductor.

"We are very grateful," said the postmaster as he wiped the sweat from his baton during a break. "We are getting the same level of training as a first-class orchestra overseas. He is a timpanist with years of experience in leading orchestras! Everyone respects your grandfather. And he can be a gentleman, even when he's at the bar drinking."

When it came to music, Grandpa sought perfection. He could detect the slightest miss in an ensemble, which he sought to correct. This attitude spread to others who, while they might have originally joined the band just to have something to do, soon started setting their sights on winning competitions. Winning competitions, however, was not what interested Grandpa. Music was his passion, and he poured his heart into it. The band's success was a byproduct of this. And so the band became a fixture in the top ranks of contests, and before long a logo bearing a trumpet and drum adorned the entrance to Town Hall.

It was fair to say that Grandpa was a gentleman when he was away from music. You could often find him crisply dressed sitting in a bar. He sat close to the mirror in the back where he could drink and relax without attracting attention. This changed every time I walked into the bar to get him. He'd wave and shout, "Cat, Cat!" Then he'd ask the bartender to line up a couple of glasses up. "Cat, will you play for me?" he'd say.

I'd pick up a cocktail muddler in each hand and hit big and small glasses with a precise 4/4 rhythm. Grandpa would close his eyes in pleasure and say, "Your rhythm brings the chaotic conversations of the bar into line."

If he was in a particularly good mood, Grandpa would wet his long thin fingers and trail them around the rims of the glasses until they rang. I would listen to the vibrations of the glasses, mesmerized by the magic. When the performance was over, the bar would fill with applause. Grandpa leaned over to me and whispered, "You know, there is actually an instrument like this. Sometimes they're used in orchestras. You can make music with pretty much anything in this world if you want."

Percussion for Grandpa was the real root of music, as well as the source of its allure.

"Probably the first music in the world was made by an ape," he said, "maybe pounding bone on stone. Matter of fact, whenever a composer adds something new to a piece for a brass band, it's almost always percussion. Think of rain. Think of wind. Think of horses galloping and whips lashing. Imagine the cries of animals—these things are all percussion!"

Grandpa had called me Cat ever since he taught me to meow as he cradled me as a baby. "How's it going, Cat?" he'd say to me.

Meow, I'd reply.

I'd even be asked to meow during rehearsals. It was embarrassing, of course, but I couldn't not do it. It would be like breaking a sacred bond between Grandpa and me.

Members of the band said my meowing was different from anything they'd heard. "It's not just good, like a cat," one guy said. "It's more like a cat than a cat. To be honest, it's a bit scary."

Sometime later, when I was about to begin elementary school, Grandpa showed me the music for an old marching song where, in the notation, it read, "Cheerful cat voice." I was astonished. To think there really was such an instrument as a cat voice! Grandpa told me that it looked like a tin can. But for bands that really care about the music, he said the percussionist should use his or her own voice instead.

"And your voice is better than any instrument," Grandpa said, flashing his beautiful full set of original teeth. "Someday, you should stand on stage with me. What do you say to that, eh, Cat?"

I just smiled, thinking how I was being raised to be a living musical instrument!

Being the gentleman he was, Grandpa never hesitated to buy a drink for a young sailor he'd never met before. And in the morning, he would often be seen greeting the mothers in the neighborhood and picking up the trash that blew in from the docks. But when it came to music, he was a different person. It was the same with my meowing. I learned that it could bring good times, but also more than a fair share of awful times.

The Highest Spot in the Room

I, too, had experienced being in the highest spot in the room. Since I was quite young, whenever people asked me my age, they'd always seem surprised by my reply. At school, the next tallest kid stood no taller than my chest. And during my elementary school entrance ceremony, I was asked to stand a little away from the rest of the class so that the child in front of me wouldn't start crying. It was the same for morning assembly and sports day, too. Sometimes I'd gaze at the junior high school buildings next to my elementary classes, knowing there'd be taller kids there, but in my heart I knew no one would be as tall as me. The school doctor, whom I saw once a year for a physical, never failed to say with great seriousness that something inside me was being secreted in the wrong amounts and that I should get it checked out properly. But neither Dad nor Grandpa ever seemed concerned.

More than half the children in my school had sailors for fathers. Perhaps that explained why there were so many fights during recess. Not that any of the kids were bigger or stronger than the others. They just fought all the time. But when the caretaker rang the bell, the fights would end, just like that, and everyone would rush back indoors and wash their hands before returning to class. The caretaker was well aware of the fighting, of course. He said once that he thought the children couldn't help it. It was in their blood—that hot-headed sailor blood.

I never got in any of those fights.

My seat was always at the back of the classroom. Whenever the seating arrangements were drawn out of a hat, my name was always kept out of the hat. My place was set, at the back, where I'd absentmindedly look down on those heads in front of me and feel like I was in peeking in from another room through a gap between black curtains. The teacher would call on someone, who'd give an idiotic answer that set the whole class laughing. When the laughing faded away, the class returned to its usual atmosphere of quiet contempt. The classroom was the sea, and I was a lone island with my head and shoulders above the water.

My position did come with advantages, though. From my perspective at the back, I could see when two boys were spoiling for a fight that would take place in the next break. I'd notice if a girl had a sore neck, maybe from sleeping uncomfortably the night before. And I could see how the history teacher treated some children like favorites, as if he were indebted to their parents, or something.

During those days in class, and before I'd begun to hear Kutze's voice, I'd kill time by rearranging the seats in my mind. I'd place that boy next to that girl and watch his spirit sink while the scrawny kid behind them burned with jealousy. I'd bring the most talkative kid to the middle of the room, or place the kid with the worst sight in the back of the room next to me.

"Excuse me, sir," he'd call out, "I can't see the blackboard! Please write in bigger letters!"

"Be quiet!" our English teacher would say. "If you don't have glasses, go get yourself a telescope from a ship in the harbor!"

There was one class where my mind did not wander like this. That was Dad's class. Dad was a math teacher. He'd originally come with Grandpa to this town with the aim of getting a teaching job at the university. They'd lived a poor life in a foreign land where Dad was born and raised, and someone told Dad there was a vacancy for a professor here. But that wasn't true. There wasn't even a university here. I don't think there's one even today. At first, Dad was at a total loss and very disappointed. But the head of education at Town Hall told him about this position at the elementary and junior high school. Dad took the job and found himself teaching math to nine different grades of rough sailors' kids; this didn't excite him at all. But he never talked of returning to where he came from or what life had been like there. Dad never talked about a lot of things.

From my seat at the back of the class, I could see Dad's expression clearly. Under his long hair flecked with premature gray, his face was crisscrossed with wrinkles. And though he'd speak as if a hornet was in his mouth, I knew no one was listening.

"Are we all okay up to now?" he'd say. "It gets a bit more difficult from here."

Every now and then, the class boor, who was reading a comic book, would burst out laughing, and the student sitting next to him would crane his neck to see what was so funny. Dad would carry on with his numbers on the blackboard, while the girls in the class would carry on with their knitting needles. I couldn't stand to see this happening, so I'd focus on my textbook—where numbers lined up alongside weird symbols and pictograms and I was supposed to *prove it, prove it, prove it.*

For almost an hour every day, until the caretaker rang the bell, I'd sit in the back of the room filled with compassion for Dad, but with a hint of twisted shame as well, resisting the urge to rearrange the seating in my imaginary classroom.

The other children didn't tease me about my dad. But that's because none of them ever spoke to me. It wasn't just the students. The teachers acted as if I didn't exist either. I'd spend my recess time alone, wandering between the scrapping pairs of kids. Some time later, Kutze said to me, "When things are big, it's easy for them to catch the eye. When things are too big, they become invisible."

At home, except when he was cooking dinner, Dad would spend most of his time sitting in the middle of the twelfth step in the stairwell, poring over papers overflowing with numbers. We lived in a two-story brick house with our bedroom and a storage space upstairs and the kitchen and living room downstairs. It was built more than a hundred years ago, and the builder must have had a big thing about stairs. In the whole dusty house they were the only thing made of wood, and every inch of the stairs showed the hallmarks of meticulous workmanship. The banisters were engraved with a forest scene, and they were a work of art.

Those numbers Dad was groaning over were part of a famous mathematical problem that was making mathematicians groan the world over. Dad said that if he solved the problem, then he'd be invited to become a full professor at a big university in a big city. When he was having trouble figuring something out, he'd tap the thirteenth step with his ballpoint pen as if he was trying to pinpoint his location in a thick fog. I sat in the living room, doing nothing but listening to this *tap tap tap*.

Grandpa was always at Warehouse #2 in the evening, rehearsing with the brass band. Then he'd go to the bar. But even when I went to pick him up, he wouldn't come back with me until he was sure Dad had gone to bed. It was like he was avoiding Dad, and now that I think about it, I don't remember a single occasion when Dad went to any of the band's contests, or even to the warehouse. As for me, whether I was at home or at the warehouse, I'd always be sitting on the floor, listening to their sounds and feeling them with all my heart. All the while, I'd be holding my knees to my chest hoping to fold this body that was far too big in half.

Dinosaur Tears

Although the members of the band thought Grandpa was a gentleman, no one but the caretaker made an effort to befriend him. True, Grandpa made no effort to befriend the band members either. His passion for music could make him quite intimidating. As long as there was music playing, he would be far from relaxed. That didn't stop the caretaker from talking to Grandpa about music, however. In fact, he talked about nothing else. Ever since they first met, the caretaker had developed a divine respect for Grandpa, the musician. I don't think any of the other four drum members had ever spoken to Grandpa at all outside the warehouse.

One day, the caretaker came up to me and said, "Cat, do you know what your Grandpa is? He is music itself!"

It was difficult to understand the caretaker since he had a lisp that took the consonants from his words and melded them together, like a stretched cassette tape. He was a little younger than Grandpa, but there wasn't a single wrinkle on his face, arms, or legs. He also had no hair on his body. What he did have was eyes and a nose oddly jammed between them, and an awkward way of moving, like a doll with broken hinges. In his youth, he'd been a sailor and traveled the world. But he'd fallen ill on an island in the South Seas, and ever since then, for more than forty years, he'd been living and working at the school as the caretaker.

The caretaker had been in Warehouse #2 the night Grandpa banged on the door. He was the first to hit the floor when someone yelled "lightning!" and he was the last to pick himself up. Perhaps he'd been the last to choose an instrument, too, because drums weren't the easiest things to carry around and the lighter instruments got chosen first.

"That noise in the warehouse," he said, "it brought out the coward in me. There's nothing that scares me more than lightning." Then he went on to tell me how he'd been struck by lightning on that island.

Anyway, because the caretaker was a percussionist, Grandpa was especially strict with him during rehearsals. He'd place a ping-pong ball on the skin of the snare drum; the caretaker was to produce a drum roll without causing the ball to leave the skin of the drum. The caretaker just couldn't do it, the ball bouncing to the height of his head. One hour or two hours later, you'd still find him trying to do it.

If I was walking along the canal, I might hear a rhythmic beat coming from the park and I'd know it was Grandpa teaching the caretaker another lesson in percussion—using an empty can, a bench, an oak tree, or a mailbox. Grandpa said that there's nothing in this world that can't be used for percussion. So off they'd go, Grandpa and the caretaker, roaming around the town hitting this and hitting that. Interestingly, the caretaker's awkwardness seemed to disappear whenever he was drumming. He did exactly as he was told. Grandpa had the power to smooth him out.

"That's the power of real music," the caretaker said.

When the caretaker rang the bell at school, he did it manually. This wasn't an electric buzzer or some sort of machine. It was a rope connected to a large tin bell. The caretaker would walk over to the wooden bell tower, climb to the top, wrap the rope around his hand, push the bell once or twice to give it momentum, then use his whole body to pull on the rope. This would cause the bell to clang loudly. So much so that I worried I'd go deaf if I were too close. The caretaker took care to stuff his ears with an oil-soaked piece of cloth when he rang the bell. Perhaps the sound reminded him of lightning.

It was the sounding of the bell that stopped the fists of the sailors' kids. It also stopped the suffocating pain of math class. The bell was much more than a piece of tin.

After school and during long breaks, I spent a lot of time at the caretaker's quarters. This was the only place where I was treated like a regular student, and it was a lot of fun hearing old sailor jokes and the silly things other band members had done during their childhood. But best of all, the caretaker had a heap of scrapbooks to pore through. One whole wall was taken up by a metal bookcase packed with blue binders—each one brimming with articles and pictures cut from gossip magazines he had gotten from sailors at the docks.

I would lie on my stomach and read through those articles as if possessed. I read about an old dog who traveled 5,000 kilometers to find his master, a comedian who could fart the tunes of popular songs, a mountain town made of ice where yetis lived … It was as if all the mysteries of the world were contained within the pages of those blue binders.

The mystery about dinosaurs was my favorite. As the story went, dinosaurs had been sighted in lakes and oceans around the world. They were the living descendants of those great dinosaurs that had supposedly become extinct thousands of years ago and they were now scattered across distant locations. Occasionally, they would surface in the hope of seeing one of their own kind. The call of a dinosaur was very sad. It would hold up its long neck, look longingly into the distance, then let out a heart-wrenching wail.

The caretaker said that when he was a sailor, the ship he was on came across one such dinosaur in the cold waters up north.

"The fog was very dense," he said, almost in a whisper. "I was up on the bridge, defrosting the antenna. Suddenly there was a foul smell, as if the drunk sailors had eaten rotten fish and thrown up on the deck. It made me dizzy. I looked down, only to find everyone pointing up at me. 'Fools!' I cried, 'I didn't make the stink!' Suddenly I felt a warm breath at the back of my head. And the smell—it was so horrible that I almost lost my grip on the antenna! When I turned around, there he was."

"The dinosaur!" I shouted out, despite having heard the story a thousand times already.

"That's right, a dinosaur," the caretaker said, tilting an eyebrow. "It was black and had a shiny head. I was terrified. I squeezed my eyes shut, sure I was going to die. Nothing happened. A couple of moments later, I dared to open my eyes, and the dinosaur was right in front of me. It was staring at me! It was such a weird thing. I'm such a coward, but I looked straight back into his eyes. His eyes were filled with tears."

"The dinosaur was crying?"

"That's right," said the caretaker, biting his lip. "Then he slowly swam away from the ship and his body melted into the fog until it disappeared. When I got down to the deck, the captain told me to blow the whistle. That was an old tradition among us sailors whenever we encountered something strange at sea. So the sound of that whistle made its way through the fog. Then we heard it! From somewhere in that thick, white fog, a short high-pitched wail, like a siren. I blew the whistle again and waited. Sure enough, there was another reply! So I blew it again and again, and each time he answered back. I don't know how many hours we carried on like that. But eventually, as the fog started to lift, those cries faded, leaving nothing but an exceptionally calm ocean. Later on, we all got together and talked about what had happened and we came to the conclusion that the dinosaur must have thought our ship was his long-lost brother or something. Our ship was black, and it had a very tall mast. So with that tall mast and my body wrapped around the top, we must have looked like a long neck with a head on top!

"After two days, three days, the smell on my jacket was really ripe. I was going to bring it home as proof of my encounter with the dinosaur, but the captain got on my case and I had to toss it into the cold ocean. Without my jacket, the rest of the journey was really cold."

After a story like that, there was nothing you could say. So we sat in silence for a while and let out a sigh simultaneously.

In the corner of the bookcase, there were two files with bright red covers. One contained local articles about the band, and the other one was thicker and stuffed with sheet music. When I first began visiting the caretaker, if he wasn't practicing on the drums, he'd be writing music. He'd learned how to do this from Grandpa, and he wrote at least one piece a week, which he'd then bring to the rehearsals at Warehouse #2. To my ears, they sounded like a racket, with tortuous tunes slamming into shoddy rhythms, and everyone else in the band said they sounded terrible, too. It was as if the caretaker had found a way to transform his awkward physical movements into clumsy musical movements.

As I thumbed through the scrapbooks one hot, humid day, the caretaker was writing music in the bathroom, the paper pushed up against the door as he hummed the tune. I was reading an article on "The Miraculous Reincarnating Man with 3,000 Years of Memories," which was about a man who had, in his various lives, been present at the most important events in history. He'd been assassinated twelve times, been the king of six unnamed countries, served twenty-five warlords, gotten married eighty times and divorced twenty! Also, he was also able to speak languages from all corners of the world.

"It says here this man helped build the pyramids. And that all the workers sang together as they worked," I said as the caretaker came out of the bathroom.

"You know, I wrote some music with that story in mind," he said. "What do you think, Cat? Do you think your grandpa might want to hear it?"

I looked at the three sheets of music covered in little notes that rubbed off on my fingers. At the time, I couldn't read music, and the tunes I'd heard in the warehouse had never been anywhere near as interesting as the stories in those scrapbooks.

"Um, I can't tell what kind of tune it is, but I really like the title—*All Thanks to Teko and Koro.*" The translation was *All Thanks to the Lever and the Pulley*, which the composition became known as.

"The caretaker smiled as he poured me a cup of hot tea with shaking hands.

In this way, various stories from the scrapbooks became music for the band. Not only was there *All Thanks to Teko and Koro*, but there was also a *Serenade for the Weeping Dinosaur*, *The Ensemble of the Yeti and the Mammoth*, and many, many more. The caretaker also used playground scenes as musical inspiration, as in *Fanfare for the Fighting Kids*, but compositions like these didn't get played much in the competitions. They weren't played that much in rehearsals. Maybe it was because the band preferred to play the music of the wind, but in the case of the caretaker's stumbling tunes, the band found it hard to tell where the wind was coming from and where it was headed. I certainly didn't get it, and I wondered how those compositions sounded to Grandpa's refined ears.

But even now, ten years later, I can remember word for word an article I came across one day when I was to meet Kutze. I had an excuse that got me out of gym class—strenuous physical exercise was forbidden because it put too much strain on my heart—so I went to visit the caretaker. The day was very hot, and I remember a cicada lying dead on the windowsill. Here is what the article said:

> *Demise of the Pigeon Lady*
>
> *The circus performer known as the Pigeon Lady met an unfortunate end yesterday as the result of an accumulation of stones in her stomach. Her body was found in her tent by the circus ringmaster, who said the foul smell emanating from there had been "enough to nearly turn my body inside out." Ironically, it was the Pigeon Lady whose body had been turned inside out. It is a well-known fact that pigeons swallow stones to aid their digestion and the Pigeon Lady had been known to have more than seventy stones in her stomach, weighing a total of more than thirty kilograms. According to her colleagues, she would shake her swollen belly so that people could hear the stones rubbing together. In the end, these stones caused her body to split in half, her digestive system clogged from the large intestine to the base of her throat. After her death, after the stones were removed, her body weighed less than twenty kilograms.*

I was so shocked by this article that I read it over and over again. I couldn't help thinking about my mother, although I didn't know what she looked like. She'd died long before we landed on this island, but neither Dad nor Grandpa would say what happened. Whenever I mentioned her at all, they would both seem irritated.

Clutching the article to my chest, I lay my ridiculously heavy body down to think. I closed my eyes and imagined a body turned inside out, my mother's body turned inside out. Then I thought of my oversized body splitting my mother's belly in half. The longer I dwelled on this thought, the more afraid I became even to touch my own body—I pictured it covered in blood.

Dinnnnggg! Dinnnnggg!

The bell sounded the end of gym class. But I couldn't move. My heart was pounding. The vibrations of that huge bell were more pronounced than a lightning strike. My oversized body shook. I felt physically engulfed.

Dinnnnggg! Dinnnnggg!

I still couldn't move. I was trapped on the floor inside this body that had killed mother. My eyes shut tight, my hands clasped above my thumping heart.

Dinnnnggg! Dinnnnggg!

In Concert

Throughout the nine years of elementary and junior high school, my body gathered size like a snowball tumbling down a winter slope. I began to hit my head on the top of door frames. I was called names—pine tree, telegraph pole, giraffe, tower, foreigner from the mountains, shadow ghost ... Note that none of these names suggested I was overweight. I was all height, I grew upward, toward the sky where the ocean winds soared. It was around this time that I acquired the habit of walking with a stoop.

"Don't make fun of him," the gym teacher would say to the students, arms folded, at the beginning of every semester. "You understand, don't you? It's mean to make fun of someone with an illness."

By the time of my second or third year of junior high, the only name I was called was Cat. I was still an outsider. No one engaged me in conversation. I'd walk into the classroom every morning, take my seat at the back, and leave when the bell rang. I'd come back in when the bell rang, and when the bell rang in the late afternoon, I'd go home and meet up with Kutze, or I'd go to the warehouse and listen to the band practicing.

Kutze could pretty much always be found in the attic, wearing the same clothes year after year, come rain or shine. I never did find out how he got to the attic from the yellow land outside and back again, although to be honest, at the time I never really thought about it much. But every time I saw him, his shoes and slacks were covered with yellow dirt, and I could always detect a damp summer smell whenever he stomped his feet.

Ton, Ta-tan, Ton

One pleasant spring day, I visited the attic and curled my outsized body into a ball. "Hey Kutze," I asked, knees under my chin. "Do you think Dad could win the prize this year?"

All through winter and spring, Dad seemed to be in a better mood. You rarely heard him tapping his pen against the stairs and almost every evening he would prepare a new dish for dinner. He said his mind was clear and that he was in the "mood to create." Among the new dishes he created, there was a carrot and flounder salad, a star-shaped steak, and boiled whole onions. Dad didn't seem to care if these new dishes tasted good. He was simply happy that he was being creative in the kitchen. But all the while, the deadline for the math problem was looming.

Ton, Ta-tan, Ton

"There's a black hole in the middle of a herd of sheep," said Kutze, stepping from foot to foot on the ceiling panel. "It's a single back sheep. Now there are two. Oh my, they're really multiplying."

I couldn't help but laugh as I heard his funny comments, like a verse from a nursery rhyme I'd never heard.

"I was asking about Dad's math problem," I said.

Kutze continued to step in place. "A black sheep snowball," he sang.

That was his response. I had no idea what he meant. Instead of asking for a clarification, I changed my question. "Do you have a brass band in the yellow land?" I asked.

"Yes, we do," replied Kutze.

Ta-tan, Ton

"Really? What kind of instruments do they have?"

"Shoes."

Ton, Ta-tan

I looked down at Kutze's big black shoes. "So stepping on dirt is like playing an instrument?"

"And many other things," said Kutze. "We step on dirt. We step on wheat. We step on cats. It's all the same."

"You step on everything?"

"Well, there's nothing that doesn't make a sound here. Nothing. That's music."

Kutze continued stepping, sending tiny particles of dust to dance in the warm sunlight.

Ta-tan, Ton

22

I helped Dad with the cooking.

Once, when I made an omelet, Dad looked at the result and said, "What a horrible color," forcing a smile. "The important thing is how you beat the eggs. That's what makes the color of the omelet. If you're going to place it on a plate next to tomatoes, the omelet needs to be brighter."

Compared to Dad's omelets, mine seemed never to stimulate the appetite. Dad's were always a beautiful bright yellow, while mine always seemed to pale next to the parsley, the red cabbage, or the tomatoes.

One day, after I'd removed a small mound of beans from their pods, Dad asked me how many beans there were, so I spread them out on the table and started to count.

"42, 43 … there's 44," I said.

"44? That's no good!" said Dad, walking over from the sink. "You need to get the number up to either 53 or peel more pods to make it 59."

"Why?"

"Why? Because 44 is not a prime number."

"A prime number?"

"You've learned about prime numbers, haven't you? They're divisible only by one or themselves. They are complete, beautiful numbers on their own. There are two prime numbers in the 50s. There are two in the 60s as well. 61 and 67. How many do you think there are in the 90s?"

"I don't know."

"97, just one!" said Dad, enchanted by it all. "But if we have that many beans, we won't be able to eat them all. So you should settle on a prime number in the 50s."

That spring, the band's rehearsals in Warehouse #2 were going very well. In fact, a lot of people from the town started to show up at the rehearsals, with many of them bringing snacks! Even the foreign sailors would stop by to listen on their way to a bar. For them, it must have felt like a refreshing shower after all that time at sea. They'd sit on the floor and converse in all sorts of languages, but as soon as the band started up, they were immediately quiet and bobbed their heads in time with the trumpets and the drums.

One day, I found an article about the band in one of the scrapbooks.

> *The band's music is so lively this year. It's the result of the band's hardworking members and a good selection of music, but more than anything, it's the beneficial effect of the good weather. The instruments rely on the air to make their sounds, so one could say mastering brass instruments is like mastering the art of air pressure. Right now, the air is helped by spring breezes and optimal humidity drifting in from across the ocean and we're lucky to be blessed by such conditions and by such wondrous music every day. Let's all take the time to visit Warehouse #2 and hear for ourselves how there is nothing more changeable, yet nothing less affected by the human heart than the weather.*

The weather was also good for Grandpa, whose legs didn't hurt when it was warm and the weather was good. I remember being in Warehouse #2 when all the windows and doors were open, watching Grandpa walk up to the stage, dressed in his usual black suit and tie, tapping his cane with every step. The band members were seated and clutching their instruments. Then Grandpa took my hand and climbed up onto the stage.

"How are you today, Cat?" he boomed.

"*Meow!*" I replied after gulping down some spit.

All through the warehouse, the sounds of quiet laughter echoed. But I had long since become accustomed to such a reaction, so I simply backed away and sat back down on the floor.

"Good, good," said Grandpa, moving to the highest spot at the back of the stage and hitting the timpani a few times to check its tuning. Then he lifted his head. "Shall we start?"

Everyone lifted their instrument on cue, the postmaster brought down his baton, and a melody was unleashed that drifted out of the high windows, out toward the port, and along to the town—sparkling and spurred on by the salty sea breeze. For a moment, I sat marveling, and then a foreign sailor poked me in the back and indicated that my large frame was blocking his view.

24

On the day before the competition in the city, the trucks of the grocer and the butcher were packed with instrument cases. Band members, their families, and their friends then boarded the night train. Together there were enough people to fill two whole train cars, and a lively bunch they were. The seating for me, though, was a little too cramped, causing my backside to hurt and my knees to jut into the aisle. So I found a closet where the sheets were kept and I curled up inside it.

This was just my third visit to the city. I remember the trams that rang their bells as they headed this way and that. I remember a motorcycle with two passengers that slowly trundled across the road, and ladies in short sleeves eating corn on the cob as they strolled through the plaza. It was hard to believe that such a place existed on the same island I lived on. Everything was different there except for the sky, which shared the same brilliant shade of blue.

I'd started going along to the competition when I began junior high school. On my first visit the band had taken third place, but it finished in sixth place the year after that. Each time, the band was judged on its performance of two compositions: one that every band was required to play on the first day, and another that the band could choose for itself.

The city bands looked sharp in brand-new black suits, and for the composition of their choosing they played popular tunes or theme songs from movies. The compositions we were the least familiar with were the ones the judges liked most. And though the compositions played by Grandpa's band made the air sparkle at the warehouse, they sounded very dull at the competition. So considering that, the fact that the band finished among the top ten was quite an achievement.

Rehearsals were scheduled for right after lunch, with numerous bands taking the stage at their allotted time to practice their numbers.

"We're missing a cymbal!" shouted the postmaster, right before it was our turn to get on the stage.

"It's not just the cymbal," said the town treasurer, who was also the band manager. "I don't know how it happened, but the large trunk with the small instruments is missing. I know I tied it down in the back of the truck. We don't have the triangle, we don't have the cowbell."

The caretaker started to grumble, but before he could say much, Grandpa jumped in: "We have no time to waste. Just do what you need to do. Do what you can!"

As the manager, who was very upset, ran off to see what he could do, band members took to the stage as Grandpa and the caretaker checked the sound on the timpani, the gong, and the drums. And then the rehearsal began.

The manager ran all over the concert hall that afternoon. He managed to get the band's performance moved to the very last slot in the evening, and he arranged for the band to borrow the necessary instruments, which wasn't too difficult as all bands were using the same instruments for the required composition.

"Tomorrow is a different story, though," the postmaster said to Grandpa. "We'll need other instruments then."

Grandpa didn't respond. He simply bit his lip.

On the final day of the contest, the band always chose to play a composition with heavy emphasis on percussion. It brought our band together in a way that set them apart from the other bands, and the judges and audience alike seemed to look forward to it. It was for this performance that Grandpa and the caretaker always brought in new instruments—the very instruments that were now missing.

On the first evening, before the band took the stage, the postmaster spoke to the group, "We need to play like there's no tomorrow. We need to give it everything we've got. Let's thrill the audience and make ourselves the winners—before anyone plays a note tomorrow!"

Grandpa stood up and nodded, which was the cue for the band to step out onto the brightly lit stage—each member giving the band manager's shoulder a friendly squeeze as they passed him in the wings.

The quality of the performance that evening was fulfillment of the manager's speech. The performance was indeed worthy of first place. It was just like the newspaper said: The crisp night air carried the sounds of the trumpets and drums. Grandpa's band stood apart, right from the start. I stood in the wings and watched the response of the audience. I could almost see goose bumps on their arms. The band was playing the 15-minute-long march that I'd heard them practice so many times before. It was, of course, the same march that all the other bands had performed. But the composition sounded new and different.

Even the cleaning lady, who had come to stand by my side, registered her surprise. "I had no idea this is what the march is supposed to sound like," she said.

On the way back to the hotel that evening, the band was showered with praise and encouragement. Young couples waved at us, and drunken men shouted, "Good luck tomorrow!" "We'll be here!" "We're looking forward to your performance!"

But I knew tomorrow was another, very different day, and I couldn't imagine how the band would manage. If they decided to sit tomorrow's performance out, they'd forfeit. There was no way they could play the same thing they did today, and I knew they wouldn't play the same required composition from the previous year—that would break tradition. No, the performance had to be a percussion-based composition. But it was the percussion instruments that were missing. So what on earth would they do?

Ton, Ta-tan

The tapping sound grew louder and louder. I looked up.

"Lots of people punch the head, the cheeks, the stomach…" sang Kutze.

"What does that mean?" I asked.

Kutze just ignored me and kept singing: "It's painful to be hit, and it's stupid to hit another. But there's nothing more stupid … than to hit nothing at all…"

Ta-tan, Ton

"Just standing there…"

Ton

"… taking no blows."

Ta-tan

Ta-tan, Ton!

Suddenly, I realized someone was knocking at the door. I jumped off the bed and ran over to open it.

"Were you asleep?" asked the band manager.

I shook my head.

"Glad to hear it. Your Grandpa's calling for you. Ah, but he's not in his room. He's in the park across the main road."

There were a few people scattered around the park, illuminated by a full moon. The band manager pointed toward a bright light, from which familiar sounds were carried along the breeze toward me. I walked over, going through bushes, and out onto a dirt field where an array of instruments sparkled as the band members were practicing their parts. I was surprised to see the timpani there, too!

"Cat! How are you doing?" Grandpa called out in a low, peculiar voice from behind the timpani.

Meow! I replied, my voice sounding surprisingly strong and confident despite my bewilderment.

"Good, good."

The band members stole glances in my direction while the manager handed out sheet music.

"I'm afraid we only have ten copies total now," he said, "but I'll prepare one sheet per pair in time for tomorrow."

Grandpa waved me over to stand between him and the caretaker. I was only fifteen and already taller than everyone.

"Listen, Cat. The cue is the drum roll for the snare drum," said Grandpa in a low voice.

"The moment it ends, your part begins. Just do as always. Don't worry, Cat. When you hit the beer glasses at the bar you have perfect rhythm. The caretaker says that the music lives inside you!"

"That's right," laughed the caretaker, poking my chest with a drumstick. "I've been watching you for a long time, every day at school."

A sheet of handwritten music was placed on the stand. It was *Fanfare for the Fighting Kids*! There were red circles drawn here and there, and each circle had a different notation—*Cat's cry: tail stepped on*. Or *Cat's cry: teasing the children*. Or *Cat's cry: gazing at the moon*. Or *Cat's cry: striving to catch the attention of another cat*.

"Shall we start?" said Grandpa. On his cue, everyone picked up their instrument, and the caretaker raised his baton from his place on a ladder. The tip of the baton pierced the moon, and the next moment, the sound of clarinets filled the city sky.

I'd never stood onstage in a concert hall before. But here I was, right at the very back with Grandpa on one side and the caretaker on the other. At first, I'd been worried that they'd never find a black suit for me in time. But in the end, the butcher's wife—who had tagged along for the event—pieced together a respectable suit overnight from three pieces of black curtain.

The atmosphere in the hall was so different from the air in the warehouse. It was serene, yet tense—as if filled with kindling that could catch fire at any moment. It was an atmosphere perfect for the music.

The performance began. First came the cheeky clarinet, bringing up the tempo as it went. Then came the trumpet, and a whole bunch of other instruments, all joining the march. From time to time, the oboe chimed in, then Grandpa's timpani came in gradually, with an effect that seemed to bring the many layers of vibrations together. Then came time for the caretaker's drum roll— the competition was on!

I listened from the back, watching the instruments in action as they seemed to scramble over each other, to fight, to sing from the highest place. Grandpa was on my right, with his shoulders pulled back as he pounded on the timpani. The sounds of the horns and the tuba came crumbling to the ground, making way for the drum roll, and building the music to crescendo. And then. Right then. *Meow*!

All that scramble, all that fighting, all those intertwined notes came crashing down like a breaking ocean wave. Then came the clarinet again, mixing in with ever more brass instruments, ever more percussion. And then, my voice, the cry of a cat, playing with the band, egging them on.

As the music painted pictures in my mind, I could tell the caretaker had been very observant in his job, studying the playground mischief and mayhem carefully before climbing the steps to ring the bell. I could feel the rhythms of the band members, most of them sons of sailors themselves, each holding the power of music within him.

I thought about how I'd spent eight years watching students fighting with each other in school without ever learning a thing. But not today. For today, I was a living, breathing percussion instrument. I'd hit those who hit each other. And I'd hit them hard, with a vibrating growl that started somewhere deep inside my gut. All the way through, the instruments continued to mingle and fight and my cat voice called them out. Everything was in sync, and it was time for my final cry of the cat, which I gave forcefully before deferring to the final, quick clean drum roll that brought everything together and ended the composition.

Applause erupted from the audience, and still I felt all the fighting going on inside my ears. I watched the people standing, clapping vigorously, stomping their feet. The band bowed under this wave of adulation before retreating backstage.

Outside of the view of the roaring crowd, feelings were running high among the band members.

Still, as Grandpa loosened his black tie, his first words were: "The 32nd bar didn't have enough length. And the 45th bar was a little too high. I told you about that yesterday. I'm always telling you, a good instrument needs to have the same sound, always! That's why good maintenance is important!"

"By the way, Cat, how is your heart?" the caretaker cut in from the side.

"Oh, I'm okay."

Seemingly out of nowhere, the band manager came running up to hug the caretaker, laughing and crying at once. The caretaker lost his balance and fell backward. I laughed along with the whole band. The clumsy incident even put a small smile on Grandpa's face.

On the train ride home, all the band members, all their family members and friends, and even total strangers from other cars joined us in celebration. The sound of trumpets and drums could be heard all through the five-car train that ran right through the night, disturbing the cows riding in the last car so much that they kicked holes in their wooden fence.

As we pulled into the station, the entire town was waiting for us. The ships in the port blew their whistles. The butcher, who was also the concertmaster, held out the gold trophy from the train window. The president of the salvage company took it from him and held it high. The caretaker was swept off his feet as he got off the train and hoisted high above the sea of smiling faces. Grandpa—rather against his will—was grabbed by a foreign sailor, who marched off with him toward the harbor with a horde of people in tow. And for me, there were swarms of sailors' sons dangling from my arms like bells.

"How are you doing, Cat? How are you?" they yelled.

Meow! I replied each time they asked. *Meow! Meow!* In a big voice, again and again.

When all the instrument cases had finally been unloaded, they were driven over to Warehouse #2 and lined up neatly in front. The case for the small percussion instruments was still missing. But nobody seemed concerned, apart from Grandpa.

Quickly, the caretaker grabbed his snare drum and ran up to the warehouse stage, leading a surge of the band members, who then broke into another rendition of *Fanfare for the Fighting Kids*. The composition didn't sound so great this time, as most of the band members were a little drunk and my voice had grown hoarse. But the cheers at the end were strong enough to pierce my ears. The whole town had surrounded the warehouse. Once we'd finished playing our triumphant encore, the trophy and a cassette tape of our winning performance were handed over to the mayor.

Afterward, the whole group headed to the bar. I had some beer, happily, but beer was new to me, and around sundown I started to feel pains in my chest. I left Grandpa at the bar and went out for some air. Light pink clouds drifted along the western sky. There were sailors smiling and waving at me, and as I breathed deeply, the pains in my chest subsided. With the cool ocean breeze at my back, I walked along a path through the town and back home.

The house was dark.

"Dad?" I called out, but there was no answer or anything. Just an opened envelope lying on the table.

"Dad, we won!" I called out again in the darkness. "And I performed for the first time!"

Still no answer.

I walked over to the table and looked inside the envelope. Two sheets of paper were stapled together, and though the letter was written in a foreign language, I could see it was addressed to Dad. I tried to read further:

> *Unfortunately, the proof you submitted did not constitute any new solution. In fact, there is a fatal contradiction in your introduction to the problem.*

I understood the words by themselves, but I had no idea what *a fatal contradiction in your introduction to the problem* meant. That's when I suddenly heard Kutze's steps nearby.

Ton, Ta-tan

I fixed my eyes back on the letter and continued to read:

> *Because of the contradiction in your introduction, you have spent a long time attempting to counter the mistake and as a result wasted a lot of effort. To us, it appears that you are veering away from the problem you are meant to be working on. Detrimental gaps created by the fatal contradiction increase exponentially as the proof proceeds to its conclusion. This is only natural because the starting point is flawed.*

Ton, Ta-tan

I paused.

"Black sheep increasing rapidly," Kutze said.

I swallowed hard and returned to the last few sentences of the letter.

> *Thus, you have failed the first screening. We await your submission next year. We acknowledge the passion you have brought to this problem, but if we may be forthright, we question whether you have the intuition of a mathematician and the vision to see the larger picture.*

Ton, Ta-tan

"Snowballing black sheep."

Ta-tan

Ton!

Now this tapping was coming from dark space halfway up the staircase. It was the sound of a ballpoint pen hitting the thirteenth step, a tapping that echoed throughout the room.

Ton Ton Ton

The Black March

From that day on, Dad was quiet, more than he usually was. From early morning until evening, he'd sit hunched on the twelfth step of the staircase, while tapping on the thirteenth. Grandpa asked him to stop, but he ignored him. It was inconvenient for me, too, because I'd have to squeeze past Dad to go up or down the stairs. But each morning, always, there would be a nice golden omelet waiting for me on the table.

It wasn't long after our musical victory that the band started receiving invitations from towns all over the island. Since I had school and the band members, except for Grandpa, had day jobs, we could only accept bookings that allowed us to depart late in the afternoon or that were less than an hour away by train. But sometimes, if there were a holiday, we'd make an overnight journey to perform farther away.

Everywhere we went, the *Fanfare for the Fighting Kids* was a big hit. The caretaker and I were given long ovations, and in response to the cheers, the caretaker would flail his arms and legs about as I waved in a daze. We performed many, many times. After each performance, Grandpa would quickly, unceremoniously, slip his timpani mallets into their leather case and disappear backstage.

"Shouldn't you respond to the calls for an encore?" the journalist who often wrote about our band asked Grandpa. "We understand it can be exhausting to be the leader, but don't you have energy to perform another composition? A man with your experience surely appreciates how much an audience wants to hear one more number."

"One more number?" Grandpa replied. "The audience doesn't need anything more. When the program is done, the band's job is complete. Would a builder stay on site for a day or two more because the customer said it was a job well done?"

The band manager was kept busy with people constantly wanting to join the band—from the cook on the docks, to the twin mechanics, to people who had no musical experience whatsoever. The band was open to anyone who wanted to join, and our ranks grew. And without fail, the new members wanted to know if the huge kid standing in back was really only in junior high school and if the caretaker with shiny skin was really over seventy.

As the band played on, my school offered career counseling for anyone who was interested. I didn't hesitate: I told my homeroom teacher that I wanted to have a career in music and that I wanted to attend the music school in the city, which was where the breakthrough contest had been held, in the center of the island. Had I consulted Dad about it? the teacher asked. I answered that Dad only had numbers in his head, and it made no difference to him. The teacher, whose own field was science, nodded, seeming to understand.

One August day, during band practice in Warehouse #2, Grandpa declared, "Cat, your tone just isn't steady enough." It was the height of summer, but that didn't stop him from wearing his usual black suit. "Out of fifteen cries," he went on, "three are not for human ears. Perhaps you're not taking practice seriously?"

"But I am!" I protested.

Grandpa looked at the band, frowning. "It's not only Cat," he said sternly. "Recently, everyone's sound lacks the right edge. Just because we won a pathetic local competition doesn't mean you can call yourselves musicians. You've got to work hard whether you're performing or not!"

"Take it easy on them," the postmaster intervened. "As the conductor, I'm the one to blame. I promise I'll work harder."

"That's not what I'm talking about!" yelled Grandpa, tapping his cane none too gently. "Doesn't anybody have ears? Brass bands make a single sound by bringing all the sounds of the instruments together. We are channeling wind, literally. But what you're doing is nothing like that. It's more like a drunken sigh or an old dog's cough. I can feel the stink clinging to my ears!"

This insult was injury to the four trumpeters, and it showed on their faces. It was a horrible thing for Grandpa to say.

"Okay, then," said the ruddy-faced postmaster, clapping his hands, trying to rouse everyone's spirit. "Let's start by tuning our instruments."

That night, as I was about to get into bed, I heard steps in the attic. I climbed up the bookcase and removed the ceiling panel. It was pitch black up there, but Kutze's steps were clear.

Ton, Ta-tan

"The black march," said Kutze in the dark. "Small sounds, large sounds. Large sounds echo."

Ton, Ta-tan

"Large things stand out. But when things're too big…"

Ta-Tan, Ton

"When things're too big, they become invisible. And inaudible. The black march."

Ton

I climbed down from atop the closet and got into bed, yawning. Dad was climbing the stairs, mumbling or chanting a spell. He lay down in his bed next to mine and soon drifted off to sleep. Then, just after midnight, I heard a tapping on the stony road. This was replaced with Grandpa's heavy steps making their way up the stairs, and then he too quietly got into bed, coughing into the sheets.

Things started to change with the arrival of one fishing boat. I was on my morning walk along the canal with Grandpa when a sailor asked if we'd heard about it.

"It's about to reach the docks," said the sailor. "Go and see for yourselves."

The dock was packed with people.

"Is the boat here yet?" I asked the butcher's wife.

"Not yet. Look out there," the butcher's wife said as she pointed a rubber-gloved finger to the horizon. "Won't be long. But I don't think you could call something like that a boat!"

She was right. The thing didn't look like a boat. It was more like a white rock drifting on the quiet gray sea.

"Maybe it's an iceberg?" someone shouted.

"No, no. See? I can see movement on it."

I swallowed hard. Maybe it was a baby dinosaur. Now that would be something. Then the mother dinosaur would come to the port too, to get her baby. Everyone in town would be eaten, though. Grandpa, me. And Dad, too.

"There's somebody on it!" yelled the captain of the salvage ship, looking through a pair of binoculars. "The distress flag is up! And it's weird—looks like there's a couple white mountains on the boat."

We watched the small white thing grow in size as it came closer to port. A couple barges went out to guide it in, but without anywhere to attach their ropes, they simply pulled up alongside the thing and proceeded at the same slow pace. On shore we ran over to the tip of the jetty to see better. Sailors were taking out life vests. Three people jumped off the white thing and swam toward a barge, but the white thing continued its slow speed to port. There had to be others onboard.

As the boat and the barges passed in front of us, we realized that the white mountains on the boat were actually an enormous flock of seagulls—on every surface, covering the mast, the deck, everywhere. The birds were filthy, and there were so many of them at the bow that the deck was barely above water.

When the boat finally docked and its engine cut, the captain crawled out from the cabin. He was bald, very pale, and looked like he had an upset stomach.

"Unbelievable," he mumbled after downing a bottle of water someone handed to him. His shoulders slumped over, he gave this account: "When the weather's bad, gulls often alight on boats, but this here's another story. Last Wednesday we passed a funny-looking cloud, and these birds came pouring down from it like rain. They landed on the boat and wouldn't leave. No matter what we did, they wouldn't fly off!"

By now, some of the gulls were fluffing up their feathers, preening themselves, but none seemed to have plans of going anywhere in the near future. They were so crowded next to each other. Some didn't have a lot of breast feathers. You could see their pink skin. Their eyes looked like they were on high alert. Either that or keeping a low profile, waiting for something to blow over. Eventually, when the bird-covered boat was properly secured, everyone left the docks shaking their heads in bewilderment. I went off to school and flipped through all of those blue scrapbooks in the caretaker's room. Finally, in the sixth binder, I found the article I was looking for:

> *Seagull rescue boat comes into port*
>   *Late last night, amidst heavy rain and winds, the foreign vessel* Fox Hunter *approached Jetty no. 6 while carrying a load of more than two hundred seagulls. Fortunately, no one onboard appeared to be hurt. According to the sailors, the cruiser encountered a large typhoon but managed to steer into the eye of the storm. They then followed the typhoon's path, moving slowly eastward. It didn't take long for seagulls fighting the storm to gather on the boat from all directions. The crew welcomed each and every seagull with a silent bow; three racing pigeons were also observed among the refugees. Safeguarding the birds and sailors, the* Fox Hunter *continued at five knots, slowly and anxiously monitoring the movement of the typhoon. When they were ten miles from shore, the ship changed course and courageously headed into the storm. The seagulls, which remained onboard despite the threat of being swept away by large waves, cried encouragement to the sailors who were struggling with the steering. Finally, when the* Fox Hunter *reached Jetty no. 6, the seagulls flapped their wings simultaneously from their perches. "They were applauding us!" said the coxswain. This morning, after the storm passed, the crew returned to the boat under the bright blue sky and found not one seagull there. "Naturally they waited for the weather to clear before flying off," said the captain of the* Fox Hunter. *According to the sailors, one of the pigeons was identified from the registration number on its leg band as the famous Luckiest Lucky—a champion racing pigeon currently enjoying three consecutive wins.*

But why are these birds here not flying off? I wondered. There's no storm now. They can't be afraid of an ocean as calm as this. "Maybe it's the dinosaur," I said out loud, just as the sound of Kutze's steps reached my ears. Then those steps gradually faded into the sound of the caretaker's bell ringing, so I returned the binder to the shelf and made my way to class.

Three days later, the boat in the harbor was still covered with birds. But by then, the birds were no longer jostling with each other. They were sitting there like rocks. As the days went by, the white thing of a boat seemed only to grow in girth, with new birds arriving out of nowhere and settling wherever they could on that feathery white mound. As more birds arrived, the boat began to sit even lower in the water until eventually, from a distance, it appeared to be a large, badly decorated cake.

Around the same time, the winds blowing into port grew stronger and yellow-tinged clouds began to cover the horizon. Soon, people were saying how they'd never felt wind so strong. Each cargo boat and each passenger ship from a foreign land leaned heavily into the billowing winds, and the barges and boats unprepared for rough seas were tied securely to the dock.

By now, the pleasant spring weather was nothing but a dream. People clutched their collars and hats as they walked into the wind, their bodies at an acute angle. The butcher's dog went missing, and the butcher's wife laughed bravely but worried he'd been blown away in the night. The strong gusts brought new things to town, too. A broken mast. A length of a rope. A foreign sailor's hat. I could imagine a shipwreck. I looked up into the cloud-covered sky and saw a small turbulent mass—clothing perhaps, hats, something kicking, maybe the butcher's dog.

Every morning and afternoon, I went to the docks and looked at those eerie clouds. They weren't dissipating at all. In fact they were slowly but steadily covering the sky. My oversized body was constantly harassed by the strong wind, tugging and pushing me like it wanted to carry me far away. In Warehouse #2, there was a constant background roar during the quiet part of the horns' ensemble or when the low roll of the timpani echoed inside the warehouse.

One day, late in the afternoon, a security guard rushed into the warehouse shrieking, "The ocean is on fire!"

Everyone ran outside to see a line of torch-like blue fire on the horizon beyond the heaving waves. It looked like a fleet of bygone battleships was preparing to attack.

"It's a mirage," someone said. "From a distance, the open fires on the fishing boats appear upside down. The air acts like a lens.

First time I've seen it here, but where I come from it happens all the time."

Everyone was relieved.

"It could be the eyes of a herd of dinosaurs!" said the caretaker, leaning close to my neck.

I felt a chill and tossed my shoulders back. I turned around, and the caretaker winked, but even his shiny face was pale.

After staring at the mirage for a while, the band members returned to the warehouse. They were dumbfounded by what they found there. Grandpa was on stage. He was the only one who hadn't gone to the dock. He was standing straight, at the highest spot on the stage, beating on the four timpani in a frenzy.

"Damn it!" he screamed. "Even my timpani sound rotten! Such a horrible sound. Damn it!"

Finally, the band manager announced that the band needed a break. No one disagreed. The reason was clear: The sounds of Grandpa's timpani had made everybody feel ill—which was how everyone's playing had been making Grandpa feel for some time. The younger members of the band ran to the black sea and vomited.

Things had started to become very strange. And when I woke up the next morning, mice were raining down from the sky.

Rains from Paradise

I knew this from articles in the caretaker's scrapbook: Around the world, snails and frogs are falling from the sky after having been swept up by tornadoes into the clouds. In an old article, a farmer abroad complained that snails rained down on his fields and ruined his entire crop that year. There were accounts of tree frogs, lizards, and even northern pike falling from the sky. The downpour of these creatures would never last long—no more than a minute between the first and the last falling creature—but those unfortunate enough to experience it would have then to spend whole days cleaning up the mess.

The downpour in our town was a record breaker. It rained mice all morning long. The townspeople pulled their shutters tight, and school was canceled. A patrol car drove along the streets and backstreets of the town, blasting out static warnings for everyone to stay indoors.

I watched the scene with Grandpa from the second floor of our house. It was just awful. The sky was yellow and gray and filled with black dots that came pelting down in the form of mice. The mice would hit the road and be smashed into blobs. Each blob had a tail sticking out of it—the only clue that it had ever been a mouse.

Of course many mice rained into the canal, and those that survived the impact floated on the surface before they drowned. Some managed to swim to the edge of the canal and climb out onto the road. They scurried away quickly, avoiding the continuing black downpour as they took shelter behind rubbish bins and in the corners of dark alleys.

A little past noon, the sun came out and the rain of mice came to a sudden halt. In the calm, we could see the cobblestone streets marbled with black hair and pink flesh. The Health Department was immediately dispatched to disinfect the town.

Everyone was in a daze. What on earth had just happened? Did the town go through a collective nightmare? People slowly made their way outside, beginning the painstaking cleanup. Seventeen people had died from falling mice. Eighty-three farm animals had died in the same way. And the roofs of one hundred thirty-one houses were damaged.

All this I read in the next day's special edition of the newspaper. When Dad came down the stairs, mumbling, I looked up and saw his eyes dancing with joy.

"They're prime!" he exclaimed. "How amazing! How beautiful! What the mice brought is a prime number."

Of course, there was no way of knowing exactly how many mice had rained down. I do know that the weight of all the mouse carcasses brought to the Health Department came out to a total of thirty-two tons. Thirty-two was divisible by four and so it was not a prime number. Dad was not dissuaded by this. If the measurement had been made to the precise gram, then definitely it would be a prime number, he said. In other words, his mind was committed to "the theory of prime mice." He remained a slave to this theory all the way up to his death. Maybe even longer.

There was one other person in town who was in high spirits because of the raining mice. This was the caretaker.

"They're coming, they're coming!" he cried, flailing his arms and jumping up and down where a ton of mice had been piled in front of the bar.

"Who's coming?" asked the bartender, annoyed, leaning on his broom handle.

"Journalists!" the caretaker shouted. "Magazine journalists! They're all going to come. There's finally going to be an article about this town for my scrapbook. Oh, I can't wait."

Sure enough, the journalists arrived first thing that afternoon. As they flashed their strobes everywhere, they muttered about the horrible sight and the nasty smell. At the Health Department, the truck driver was forced to pose in front of a pile of carcasses. At the hardware store, the elderly proprietress was asked, by a mustachioed writer, how it felt to lose a grandson to falling mice. She responded by throwing a hammer at him.

All the guesthouses in town were packed to capacity with the visiting journalists and people who'd had their roofs ruined by mice. The row houses by the lighthouse hadn't stood a chance against the black rain of mice.

"Tell me more about the disaster!" the journalists would demand.

"What did it sound like in the beginning?"

"Anybody in your family hurt?"

"And where exactly did the mice hit you, ma'am?"

"They were terrible," said the owner of a guesthouse later. "They'd sit together in the cafeteria and laugh loudly. They were laughing at us—at our misfortune! Then they'd brainstorm for some catchy headline and laugh out loud again." She was talking about pathetic stuff like "Splish, Splash, Squeak—Town Hit by Mouse Rain" and "Flying Mice—A Tale of New Migration." "It was so funny to them."

When the sea breezes died down, a strong sun emerged, which heated up the streets and roasted the remains of the mice. The stench was unbearable. But everyone worked hard, lifting the mouse carcass by the tail and scraping the pavement underneath with shoehorns and screwdrivers. They sprayed disinfectant and deodorizer and scrubbed. But still, it stank. The stench had soaked into the very core of the town.

The next morning, the caretaker entertained the journalists. He invited them to his room at the school and to the bar. He introduced them to the staff at the post office and to members of the sailors' union.

I was a witness to one of these conversations. The caretaker, surrounded by three journalists, was holding court: "The question is, where did those mice come from? You know, I worked on a boat once, so I've heard all sorts of rumors, but this one is true. There was a mouse paradise near the equator where the weather is good all year around and there's never a shortage of food. A strong wind blows through the place, so the mice never needed to worry about birds or predators. Their nest ran the whole length of the island and there were thousands of them. I know this is the truth, because a sailor I used to know once drifted to this island. He said there was a Mouse King who wore an old ring for a crown and had a whole legion of servants. But the amazing thing was the Mouse King spoke to my friend in human words: *Do not speak of this island to anyone. If you stay on this island I promise you an easy life. The only condition is that you must live as a mouse.* Then my friend was covered with black coal dust, a rope was tied around his waist, and he started walking around on all fours. After a while, he befriended some mice and even got married to one. The winters were warm, and the humidity on summer afternoons was just right. And come night-time, the whole island was bathed in the sweet smell of fruit. My sailor friend used to say how nice the island was all the time and how the mice were always squealing with joy.

"One day, my sailor friend went to see the King. *Every mouse has been treating me very kindly,* he said, *and I would like to return the favor by doing something only humans can do. My dear King, will you grant me permission?*

What do you have in mind? the Mouse King replied.

I'd like to build a castle for you, dear King. But to do so, I need your permission to chop down a few trees.

Then I hereby grant you permission.

"The mice used their sharp teeth to help with the construction, and in no time the castle was built. On the night before the grand unveiling, the sailor sneaked into the King's quarters, beat the servant mice to death with a stick, and filled his pockets with the treasures they were guarding. He made his way back to the elegant castle, which he flipped over. It was really nothing more than a raft! Under the dark ocean sky, the sailor quickly launched the raft. Suddenly he heard a scratching noise—it was his mouse wife hanging on to the edge of the raft with her front legs. He flicked her off with his index finger and paddled away with all his might."

"Where did you meet this sailor?" asked one of the journalists, stubbing his cigarette out.

"Our boat found him in the raft, floating in the ocean. He looked like he was insane, chewing on the rope tied to his waist. But the moment he saw me—we were old acquaintances—his eyes lit up and he didn't seem like he was out of mind anymore. That's when he started telling me about the mouse paradise. He was suffering from a terrible fever, and he had bites all over his body. He handed me the leather bag with the Mouse King's treasures, saying they were of no use to him, and then he died. I opened the leather bag, and I started laughing. It was full of beer caps and rusted nails. It was just as useless to me, so I tossed the bag overboard."

"So that leads us to the question, why do you think the mice that rained down on this town are from that paradise?" another journalist asked.

"Simple. No other place would have that many thousands of mice. Besides, my sailor friend said the island had a very strong wind. That wind could have turned into a tornado and sucked the mice from whole island into the sky. It's entirely possible."

"Hmm," grunted the third journalist, who then yawned. "Give me some proof. That's all I can say."

"Proof? You want proof?" replied the caretaker, acting like a gambler about to lay down his hand. "Just after the rain of mice stopped, I found this in the school playground. Now, brilliant journalists, do you know what this is?"

The three brilliant journalists leaned forward to see what the caretaker was holding between his fingertips. I took a peek from the next table. It was a ring, an old tarnished ring.

"This is the crown of the Mouse King," the caretaker declared. "This is all the proof you need."

There was a moment of stunned silence before the three journalists burst out laughing hilariously.

"Lunch break!" shouted the bartender behind them, with a mop in hand. "You journalists, I don't want your money, so please leave." When the journalists were out the door, the bartender turned to the townsfolk in the bar. "It makes me sick," he said, "the out-of-town guys teasing an old man like that!"

On the dock, a different cluster of journalists was snapping photos of the ship of gulls as the bald captain looked on, bemused.

"It's awful," said the son of the security guard who played the trombone in the band, pointing to the overloaded boat. "It's like a pressure cooker."

As he explained: When mice started falling from the sky, the gulls on the boat started to crowd together even more. They tried to get below deck, but the place was already packed, so with all that pushing and shoving and squeezing going on, a crack formed on the sides of the boat, extending the full length of it. White feathers were sticking out here and there in the crack.

"It's like a bird pie," said one of the journalists, "except there's only the filling of birds and no crust." No one thought this was funny.

In the end, authorities counted 5,441 dead birds on that boat.

"That's a prime number," said Dad as he scrubbed a frying pan.

I learned from the caretaker later that Grandpa had in the meanwhile decamped to Warehouse #2. It was a practice day after all, even if it was unlikely anyone would show up. They had other matters to tend to—like dead mice. But Grandpa, who wanted to replace the drumhead of his timpani, remained completely focused. "All the more reason," he'd told the caretaker, "because with everything going on around here, we need real music from real instruments more than ever!"

Me, I was at home eating a meal that Dad had cooked. No sound of a pen tapping the twelfth step, just sheets of paper fluttering down.

By the time I'd finished eating, a familiar sound had started up.

Ton, Ta-tan

This time it was Kutze.

"The instrument," he sang. "It's dark in the instrument. What could be in there?"

Ta-tan, Ton

How would I know? I thought.

But Kutze just continued: "In the total darkness, is there wind?"

Ton-ton

"Or is there just darkness? Maybe there's no difference."

Ta-Tan, Ta-Tan

This little monologue was interrupted by a knocking. Not a tapping, a knocking, on the door. It was a quiet knocking, but a very determined knocking.

Ta-Tan, Ta-Tan

We so rarely had visitors, and I couldn't imagine who it was. Dad didn't seem to be coming downstairs to open the old wooden door, so I went and did it myself.

It was the butcher, standing there in his white apron, and behind him stood his wife, her eyes cast to the ground.

"Grandpa's not here," I said. "He's at the bar, or maybe at the warehouse."

The butcher sighed deeply. "We're not here for your grandfather, Cat," he said. "We have a favor to ask of you."

"Me?"

"Yes. We've talked it over with the officials at Town Hall, and we don't know what else to do. Do you think you could help us?"

I stared at the butcher and his wife. They were acting like they were delivering a dark telegram.

"We want you to scare away the mice that have survived. Starting with the ones in our meat refrigerator," said the butcher's wife, making an awkward attempt to smile but failing miserably. "You know, with that big cat cry of yours."

The Call of the Cat

The butcher, who was first clarinet in the band, had been a concertmaster for a long time and he was always self-assured, composed, and had warmth in his voice. It had been his job to break down Grandpa's strict instructions so that those in the woodwind section could actually understand them.

The butcher had started out as a ship's cook. And though he never spoke of his reason for opening up a shop in the town, everyone knew. He'd met his wife on one of his voyages where she'd been in charge of laundry for the crew. In the pocket of his chef whites, she found a love letter. "The wording was so old-fashioned," she'd said, laughing, "and the note was all wrinkly and wasn't addressed to anyone. No woman would fall for that, so I edited it and returned it to him. I was good at cleaning stuff up, you see, because of my job. Then, after a month, he confessed that the letter was meant for me."

The butcher shop's refrigerator was bigger than I was. I stood before it as the butcher cracked open the heavy steel door and a dank odor escaped. I peered in. There were forest critter-sized shadows scurrying about. The carcasses that hung from the ceiling swayed from side to side and the joints had been nibbled away to the bone.

"They got in by chewing through the panel in the back," said the butcher. "And they're not scared of anything. You can throw water at them, hit them with a stick, but still they're not fazed!"

"It's like they're making fun of us, Cat!" the butcher's wife exclaimed. "As soon as we close the door we can almost hear them laughing at us."

As my eyes adjusted to the darkness, I could see more and more mice. They were jumping from one joint of meat to another, setting all the carcasses in motion. As I looked at the mice closely, I thought I could actually make out their expressions. It was like they *were* playing! Like they were so overjoyed to have survived their fall from the sky that they couldn't stay still.

"Cat, can you do your thing, please?" the butcher begged. "Your voice is more cat-like than a cat. Besides, the real cats were all blown away and there are none left in the town. These little creatures might get scared if they hear your voice."

The butcher's wife backed out of the way and I got into position. At first, the tiny mice didn't seem to take any notice of my big looming shadow. They continued to leap and play. For a moment, I could picture the mice clinging onto the side of the canal and scrambling for dear life, and I wondered if they really had all been scooped up and blown away from their paradise. I wondered if the especially big mouse that was scampering across the ham in front of me might be the Mouse King.

"Cat, go ahead!" said the butcher's wife, nudging me.

When I opened my mouth, it was like I'd turned on a tap. From the pit of my stomach, a black tornado of a voice launched in the direction of the mice, causing the carcasses to swing violently and blasting mice onto the floor. There was a powerful ringing in my ears, and I felt as if a huge gaping hole had opened up somewhere in my body, releasing a burst of sound that was flooding into the refrigerator. It was a cry that lasted only for several seconds. Or maybe it lasted closer to a minute. When I came to my senses, my mouth was gaping open, but the noise had come to an end. There were, on the floor of the refrigerator, upturned bodies of mice all over, their four legs pointed skyward and their little tails limp.

The butcher was standing behind me, pale, shaking his head while his wife hung tightly onto his arm. Neither said a word. The butcher's thick hand grasped my upper arm. Then we crouched down and began picking the mice up and dropping them, one by one, into a big linen bag. All trace of life had been wiped from their tiny eyes.

When we'd finished, the butcher's wife asked me if I wanted a bowl of soup. But I just shook my head and set off for home.

When I got there Dad was still awake. "How many did you kill?" he asked.

Although I could have answered, I found myself silent. Dad sucked his teeth for a moment, then he called the butcher to ask him for the number. He put down the receiver in high spirits and frantically scribbled notes onto a little piece of paper.

"I knew it would be prime." Dad's voice followed me as I climbed the stairs. But I was too tired to respond. Too tired even to glance into the attic. I just climbed into bed and pulled the sheets over me, hoping my dry, scratchy throat would feel better in the morning.

Early the next morning, officials from the Health Department came to our house. They were taking me to the recording studio at Town Hall. The studio was small, it was where the daily weather forecasts were broadcast, and clustered at the entrance were several people I was familiar with, including the butcher and his wife. The bartender was complaining that the mice had knocked over and broken all his bar glasses, the band manager was complaining that the mice had nibbled holes in his receipts, and the postmaster was fuming about finding his stamp collection covered in mouse droppings. Everyone looked at me and nodded. My chest felt so tight I thought I might collapse. I walked into the recording studio with my eyes fixed on the ground.

"Cat, how do you feel?" This was the voice of the recording studio staff coming through my headphones. "Are you all right? Would you like a glass of water?"

I shook my head in silence and watched as the red light in front of me came on. Then I opened my mouth. I think my voice was smaller than it had been the night before. Still, a hurricane-like wind came swirling up from the pit of my stomach and blasted out at the microphone hanging from the ceiling. I closed my eyes and let my cry run its course. Then, when no more noise was coming from the center of my being, I opened my eyes and realized that the red light was already off and the studio was filled with a slightly burning smell.

When I got outside, everyone said how amazing it was, how their ears stung. I rubbed my stomach, coughed drily a few times, then drank five glasses of water. Though a little hoarse, my voice slowly began to feel normal to me again.

After lunch, my voice was being broadcast at top volume from speakers all across town. It was so loud that people couldn't hear each other on the street. The whole town was enveloped by my voice. Only, it didn't sound like my voice or even a cat's cry. It was more like:

Gow, ga-gow!

The sound resonated through Town Hall Plaza, bounced through the town center into the night, and echoed through the back alleys.

Gow gow! Ga-gow!

It sounded like the ocean wind. Like the wind from those yellow clouds that had brought the mouse rain to town. It was the wind that had buffeted my body all summer long. In fact, I was sure it was the very same nasty wind. But for some reason the town people thought it sounded like the cry of a cat.

"You're really something!" someone said to me on the street. "More cat-like than a cat. It's the ideal cat voice!"

But I knew that there could be no such thing as an ideal cat. At least not in the world we lived in. Our bodies were perforated with invisible holes made by the sea winds that had pushed through us all summer long. And because of those holes, none of us—myself included—knew how to recognize real sound.

Gow, ga-gow!

As my voice continued to rattle the town, the effect on the mice was immediate and decisive. Those small creatures stranded miles from mouse paradise had nowhere to flee to. They were found shivering, even unconscious, under awnings, in the dark corners of garages, and between piles of construction materials. People used forks, tweezers, or their bare hands to lift the mice by their tails and they threw them in big bags that were then taken to the Health Department.

Beneath the bellowing speakers, the Health Department official noted the mouse count as people held up fingers to indicate the number caught: *I have 17! Here's 31. I've got 23!* The official tossed each bag onto a trolley, which was wheeled over to the incinerator.

Every day, Dad called the Health Department to ask for the count. Of course, there were plenty of days when the number was not prime. But Dad was certain that the final tally would be prime.

"My calculations predict it," he said with confidence. "I can't wait to prove it."

By now, just about everybody in town was busy picking up mice. The ear-piercing sound blasted from the speakers throughout the night, and conversations on the streets had to take place in sign language—with elbows, thumbs, and fingers working hard to convey sentences such as: *The docks still need to be cleaned. We haven't cleaned the warehouse either. Let's go do that tonight. Yeah, let's go there and pick up the mice.*

But despite such intention, nobody chose to step inside Warehouse #2, because Grandpa had forbidden entry to anyone who wasn't there for the purpose of music. I think the postmaster did go there twice, though, and the butcher shop owners once. But during practice, when the postmaster glanced into a dark corner of the stage, Grandpa ordered him to leave immediately.

Every day after school, I pressed my hands firmly to my ears and ran along the cobblestones all the way home. The only place where I couldn't hear my voice was in the attic. I climbed atop the closet and poked my head above the ceiling panel, and when I did, the sound of my voice blowing through town ceased. As always, Kutze was there stepping away, kicking up clouds of dust, and making his yellow shirt wriggle and wave.

Ton, Ta-tan, Ton

"It's the body, the instrument." Another of his opaque comments. "There's something invisible inside."

"Please stop talking," I said. "I just want to hear you stepping."

Kutze fell silent. Then he continued his stepp'n, matter-of-factly.

For three days and three nights, the town used my voice to clear out the mice. Then, on the morning of the fourth day, the newspaper carried a declaration of victory from the Health Department.

Thanks to your cooperation, the town is now officially clear of mice. But even with the incinerator running 24 hours a day, we still haven't managed to burn them all. The battle is won, however, and so we shall be switching off the speakers at precisely noon today.

When the speakers were turned off as scheduled, a strange feeling descended upon the town. Everyone experienced the overwhelming sensation that their heads were spinning, which led them to try to find something to hold onto. All over town, people stood unsteadily in the streets, wobbled along the cobblestone paths, struggled to pull their feet along the ground. They looked like a flock of birds flying through a storm in search of somewhere to rest.

"My head hurts and I feel dizzy," someone said. "There's no sound but I have this echo in my ear. No, not a cat cry. It's this creepy sound. Like there's this thick, gray smoke bellowing inside of me. That's what it sounds like."

There was a rehearsal scheduled for the band that day, and the band members lugged their instruments to Warehouse #2 on unsteady feet. The caretaker was at the warehouse, welcoming everyone back with a big smile on his face, and Grandpa stood at his usual place in the back, waiting for us with a drumstick in each hand. I was there too, fighting a nasty headache, and I watched as everyone climbed the stage, lifted their instruments, and got ready to play.

The postmaster's weak wave of the baton had nothing to do with the clarinet missing a beat, the trumpet sounding muffled, and the oboe being flat. *Boiiinggg, Boiiinggg, Boiiinggg,* boomed the timpani uncharacteristically. Everyone had to have been alarmed to hear such a sound, but nobody turned to give Grandpa a glance. They were in shock. After all, it was a shocking revelation—our entire band had gone tone deaf!

Grandpa tried to rally the band, going over in detail the part each section had to play. Then the rehearsal stage was put away and the music stands were positioned all around the empty-looking warehouse.

"Okay, everyone," boomed Grandpa in the middle of the warehouse, "Let's do it!"

At that moment, the clarinets and oboes let loose a dismally weak *bleep,* the supposedly long tone lasting no more than five seconds. As for the horn and the tuba, they couldn't produce any sound at all!

"Carry on!" Grandpa shouted. "Don't stop!"

His silver cane kept time on the warehouse floor, and the postmaster, three high school students, and I tapped out a rhythm with sticks on old washcloths. One hour went by, then two, and we were still just tapping dully on those washcloths.

"You know it's not good enough to just tap," whispered the caretaker from behind us, with a worried voice. "Our body should be producing the beat from within. You should get to a point that you forget you're making a beat. The core of our body has to become one with the sticks. There's really no other way to do it."

Each of us searched inside ourselves for this elusive core. But without success. Even if there was such a thing inside us, then wherever it was, it wasn't working.

As time went on, the people in town began to appear ever more worn down. Despite the windless autumn sky, nobody was able to take more than three steps in a straight line and people stumbled along the cobblestone paths with eyes hazed over like sailors meandering through alleys. Many people now had developed a fear of stairs, and if they managed to climb them, they collapsed when descending—leaving them no choice but to go down by their bottoms from step to uncomfortable step.

Then there was the issue of the mice. We hadn't seen any in town since the deluge of cat cries, but Dad refused to believe the problem was over.

"They're still around," he mumbled as he pressed an ice cube to his forehead. "They have to be. Otherwise the calculations don't add up."

Dad wasn't alone with his thoughts, as a matter of fact. Plenty of people were saying that they could still sense the presence of the mice. Even I thought I could hear them breathing in the bushes of the park, in the cleaning closet in the school, or deep in the darkness of the drain. Soon enough, you couldn't find a soul who could hold their gaze on a spot in darkness without seeing the dim silhouette of a rodent.

A line in an article somewhere said:

In folklore, from a land in the Far East, there is a saying that describes a mouse as "pure darkness with a tail."

A lot of people must have read the same article because it wasn't long before everyone in town said they felt the presence of dark mice. At school, the kids warned each other about staring into dark corners—because if they did, they'd lock eyes with the dark mice and be abducted into the darkness.

All Kinds of Wheat Stepp'n

When winter came, it was much colder than normal. The town's cobblestone paths were covered in frost, but as in every other season, Dad stayed firmly planted in his spot on the stairs. It was his mathematical paradise, his sanctuary, his kingdom.

"The survivors must be around somewhere," Dad said, having finished his calculations for the day. "I want to know the exact number. According to my theory, it should be a prime number in the fifties."

"But they're invisible," I said, having just read a newspaper article about ghost mice. "Is it possible to count invisible things?"

To my surprise, Dad laughed. "Okay," he began. "You haven't learned this yet, but in math there is a wonderful notion called sets. Even an infinite numerical sequence can be lumped together as an infinite set. We can also lump imaginary numbers together. In that way, we can count them as one set."

I was completely lost.

"What exists or doesn't exist in this world is the same in math," Dad went on, sliding a hot omelet onto my plate. "Don't you understand? Math has the ability to portray a world of absolute beauty."

That night, as always, I climbed onto the closet. Perhaps it was my imagination, but Kutze was looking smaller these days. In fact he was now the size of a pencil rather than a bottle of beer.

Ton, Ta-tan

"What's inside the body?" Kutze said. "What's inside an instrument?"

Ton, Ta-tan, Ton

As I listened to his cryptic words, I noticed how he smelled of warm summer dirt, even with the harsh winter conditions outside.

"Hey Kutze," I said, "you've shrunk quite a bit."

"I haven't shrunk. I don't shrink," sang Kutze. "Small. Big. It's a matter of distance."

The townspeople walked along the paths, letting out gasps of white breath as they did their best to keep their legs steady. In a way, their efforts were not so different from those of the band members, who were hard at work in Warehouse #2. I'd also started to understand that rehearsal didn't have to be so rough-going. You just had to understand that Grandpa's cane was like a metronome that never skipped a beat, not even when he was annoyed or impatient. I believed that his steady keeping of time would lead us back to a place where we could make beautiful music again.

"It's getting much better," Grandpa said after practice as he dabbed a tissue at the beads of sweat on his forehead. "We can fix the sound later. But both the horn and clarinet should focus on capturing their own rhythms. That's the foundation of music—rhythm. It gives order to the world of sound that would otherwise be entirely random. All it takes is a single stroke. Just one. Then, once you grasp that rhythm, you're ready to give birth to music."

I wondered if Grandpa was trying to convince himself of this as well, and indeed, when he stayed behind to practice by himself, the timpani sounded brilliant. Still, Grandpa sighed woefully. "Cat," he said, "we have a long way to go. You can't have a band with just the timpani."

As for me, my sense of rhythm never returned, despite the sacrifice of several old washcloths.

"Can you see?" said the caretaker on more than one occasion. "When I do things exactly as your Grandpa says, my body straightens out! Things will go right for you, too. You weren't always tone deaf, you know. You'll get it back."

The caretaker got his rhythm back, even as his jerky movements and lisp never left him. The physical impediments people were experiencing anew were nothing new to him. "Don't try so hard to talk. Let the words come on their own," the caretaker told fellow drinkers at the bar. "Don't try so hard to walk. Let the legs lead as they please."

All around him, the men in overcoats nodded into their collars.

On the first day of the winter break, I was in the caretaker's room organizing his scrapbooks. The caretaker had clipped articles—about the summer breeze, about the mouse rain, about the decline of the band—and I placed them in the binders. Then I closed the books and lost myself in my thoughts.

"Hey, Cat," interrupted the caretaker, "I can read your mind."

I scrunched my brow and tried to ignore him.

"You're wondering whether I'll be composing something about the rain of mice."

Now that he'd said it out loud, I realized that deep down that's actually what I'd been thinking. "Yeah," I said.

"I knew it," the caretaker gloated, setting a pot of tea on the table. "The problem is, though, the music's not coming to me. I mean, I can picture the mouse rain fine, but it's not music. I mean, what did they sound like coming down? Did we hear their cries as they fell?"

"I don't know," I said. "I was watching from the second floor of my house."

"What a pity. If I could hear something in my head, if I could turn it into a march, maybe it would cure the town's tone deafness. It doesn't even have to be a march. Maybe a short, bright melody. Something to clear their ears. No one was tone deaf to start with. It's from all the psychological stress."

"You know some very difficult words."

"No, no," said the caretaker, turning red. "It doesn't matter what words I know if the music's not coming. Everyone in town's been decent to me. That goes for your Grandpa, too, Cat. I was the only one in town the storm of mice didn't drive crazy, which makes me feel bad. I want to do something for the town. But the music … it's just not coming."

That night, on the way home from the warehouse, I made my way over the canal bridge with my tired arms drooping. There were no stars in the sky, and the only sound was a radio that drifted faintly from the dimly lit barges.

The sailors hadn't escaped the summer's disasters. They suffered from ringing in their ears, and they now got seasick, vomiting off the side of their ships! They were so incapacitated that in order to make a living they were manufacturing fake flowers and embroidery on the barges that never left the docks. In fact, they were so busy doing this night and day that the canal was getting stagnant. It was their radio I was hearing.

Ton, Ta-tan, Ton

I was near the middle of the bridge.

Ta-tan

Kutze's steps echoed through the darkness of the port.

Ton

"Hey Kutze," I asked out loud, "is the yellow land the same as before?"

Without skipping a beat, Kutze replied, "Nothing has changed."

"You mean it's still summer?"

"Maybe."

Ta-tan

"So much has changed here, Kutze. The band's a mess. The town's grown tone deaf. Everyone's walking around like they're sick, and no one has the balance to ride a bicycle or drive a car. Kutze, do you think this will go on forever? Will this town ever see another good day?"

"Good? Bad?" Kutze sang. "Everything's the same. I'm a wheat stepper."

Ton, Ta-tan

"Stepped wheat is wheat that grows. Rotten seeds are fertilizer. Wheat stepp'n Kutze goes the distance, stepp'n the wheat flat along the way."

Ta-tan, Ton

I stared at the dark water of the canal in silence. What does that mean anyway, wheat stepp'n? I'd seen the yellow land when I was seven, and it was a bright warm place that smelled so good. But what if I found myself there tomorrow? How would I feel about it?

Ton, Ta-tan

Suddenly, a shiver went down my spine. I got a tingle in my knees, I got dizzy in my head. But I made it safely across the bridge.

All the accidents that happened after that are documented in the scrapbooks. People died because of their wobbly legs, dizziness, or lack of coordination. One morning, the librarian was found stone cold dead in the park. He'd slipped on the stone steps and hit his head. In fact, there were five older folks who'd died similar deaths.

At the annual New Year's Eve celebration, there was a fireworks tragedy. Instead of being launched high above the barge floating in the port, they were aimed straight at it. Fortunately, most of the fireworks got swallowed up by the sea, but one particularly large affair tore through sailors' lodgings, which caught fire. Twelve charred bodies was the result.

No newspaper said anything about the dark mice. But people sure talked about them. People sensed the presence of them everywhere, but especially when there was a fire or an accident. Some even swore they caught a glimpse of a tail protruding from the darkness.

"In the drains at the sides of stone steps and in ruined accommodations—that's where the dark mice have nests." That was what people said. "They're in there, waiting patiently for us to fall into darkness."

I'm relieved to say now that this didn't prove to be the case at all. Mice are just mice, and every single accident was nothing more than an accident, the result of carelessness. But at that time, all of us were afraid of dark corners. Everyone left their lights on at night, and nobody but the foreign sailors were brave enough to enter dark alleys.

But tragedies happened: In the row houses by the base of the lighthouse where there was no electricity, torches were kept lit all night long. One evening someone knocked over a torch, and the whole place went up in flames.

Each time something like this happened, the band offered to play at the funeral, but we were always turned down. We weren't just out of tune. We couldn't hold a single rhythm, and this threw off the pallbearers. The one time we did play, the undertaker ended up on his knees begging Grandpa to make the noise stop. The band members just carried their instruments solemnly as they followed the funeral procession in silence. Even Grandpa kept his mouth shut as he strode along in his black suit with the dignity of a high priest.

There was no music even for the butcher's funeral. His refrigerator had finally been rewired, and he'd gone inside to check the temperature. For some reason, the butcher's wife followed him in. The door shut on then, and they were trapped. After three days of the butcher not showing up for band rehearsal, we got worried. So the postmaster, Grandpa, and I went to the butcher shop, found a key dangling by the heavy steel door, and opened the refrigerator. Inside, the butcher and his wife were standing frozen among the hanging carcasses, their hands in each other's pockets. I was sure that I heard something rustling in the linen bag in the corner.

There was no hint of spring in the air, but graduation was fast approaching. I was still tone deaf, and there was absolutely no hope of my getting into music school in my current state. The band had continued to practice and not one person quit, but the dismal level of music hadn't improved so the difficult decision was made to have a graduation unaccompanied by live music. I sent my black suit, made by the butcher's wife, to the laundry, and the young clerk who survived the fire at the sailors' lodgings was nice enough to say what a wonderful suit it was.

The Caretaker's Last March

We gathered in the courtyard in the middle of the school buildings, each class standing in line and waiting for the signal to start the procession. When the recorded music started, we began marching, and as we entered the school yard, the music suddenly seemed very loud indeed and I was amazed at how many people were in attendance. Nevertheless, I managed to spot Grandpa immediately— sitting on a chair with his silver cane planted between his knees. It never seemed to matter how far away he was, you could always spot him easily. He was that sort of person, like a beacon.

The students circled the yard before forming into shorter lines. Considering that we were incapable of keeping time, we did quite well. Music, even if it's from a tape recorder, helps. And after all, the recorded music was from the contest when the band was at its best. When the last line of students had gotten into place, I stepped to the right. To those surrounding the yard, I must have looked like a dumbbell lying by the side of a bowl of cherries.

The vice-principal took the stand, and the music came to a halt. Usually, it would be the principal who would speak at graduation, but he'd broken both legs and was resting at home, which meant that everyone could breathe a sigh of relief. We were spared the boredom of hearing his longwinded moral tales peppered with quotes from classical texts.

Twelve years ago, the vice-principal had been an advertising copywriter, writing such catchy lines as *It's the swirly shiny washer that saves you money!* Or *Time to get your ticket to paradise?* They were terrible ads, but because of this training, the vice-principal knew how to keep his speeches short and to the point.

"When I was a little older than you are now and was about to graduate from high school," he began, "I wanted to be the captain of a luxury cruise ship. In the local newspaper there was a help-wanted advertisement for a sailor, but I didn't understand the criteria to be a sailor. So I went to the newspaper that carried the ad and I asked what APPLY WITHIN meant, along with a bunch of other things. The person I met replied, 'Forget about it. You aren't cut out to be a sailor because a sailor wouldn't worry about things like that.' This devastated me, but being young, I believed him. On the way home, I tried to think what kind of job would suit me. A job that would suit the sort of person who gets caught up in the details of help-wanted ads for sailors. Then it dawned on me, and I turned around and ran to the newspaper office. I asked the advertising guy to hire me to write ad copy, and I ended up working at that newspaper for thirty years."

The vice-principal stopped to clear his throat, then continued: "What I want to say is these two things. First, whatever the job, don't take the advertisement for it at face value. And second, remember that one comment can change your next thirty years. Don't miss that comment. That is all I want to say. Congratulations and good luck."

The vice-principal was given a big round of applause. Next up were three teachers who spoke about the past nine years the graduating students had spent in school. Dad was sitting in the row of teachers on the stage, fidgeting. I watched as, every so often, he would take took a small notebook from his pocket and scribble something in it. He never looked my way. In fact, he seemed to have totally forgotten where he was or that there was a graduation ceremony in progress—he kept mumbling "Ah, of course" or "No, that's not right," while tugging at his hair.

It was customary for the concertmaster to climb the stage now and make a short speech. This was usually the butcher, who would tell a not-so-interesting story in his calm voice. This year, however, the cheery pipefitter was invited to speak since he was the trombone player and new concertmaster. He wobbled onto the stage with unsteady feet and mumbled something unintelligible with a voice that sounded like a blocked drain.

Graduation certificates were then handed out. I watched from the back as the students fought their dizziness when they made their way to the front, taking one step at a time. Most of the students were wearing old black suits which were hand-me-downs. But not me. From my lonely spot on the side, I watched Dad, who was now leaning forward on his chair, shaking his head, and writing something in his notebook. Then I looked over to Grandpa. He was digging into the ground with his silver cane, eyes cast downward. It was the first graduation that he wasn't able to perform at.

Sighing, I looked up at the sky, at the sun glistening through thin layers of clouds. A warm breeze with a hint of the sea kicked up the sand in the schoolyard, but on this day it smelled different. It was the smell of an unknown land, of dirt that had been baked for a long time in the sun, and the wind seemed to be coming from all corners of the yard—as if scattered through each illuminated break in the clouds.

Ton, Ta-tan

Kutze? I wondered, looking at the light and narrowing my eyes.

Ton

It's you, isn't it? I asked silently.

Ta-tan

But there was no answer. The steps echoed in my ear as if he was lovingly stepp'n the earth before him, like the proud band members walking into the spotlight. Like the black-suited graduates making their way forward to receive their certificates.

Ton, Ta-tan

I turned toward the direction the sound was coming from. Somewhere around the school building. Somewhere by a line of people.

The bell tower!

I could see feet climbing up the wooden bell tower steps.

Ton, Ton

Each step taken with care. Each step taken with pride. Then, when he reached the top, the caretaker let out one big sigh, turned our way, and waved.

At that moment, I remembered: how the caretaker had scattered his music all over the room, how he'd said, "A graduation without live music? Unbelievable! Unacceptable!"

When I asked him what could be done, he'd responded, "*I*'ll perform live. The march for the town isn't ready, but I'll perform it. I'm the only one left in this town with an ear that can hear. So my performance will be my graduation present to everyone!"

And that was what the caretaker was about to do! He turned to the bell, wound its thick rope around his hand, and gave it a push. Then he waited for the bell to toll.

"Hey, what's going on?" students started saying. Then came a muffled scream. Swallowing hard, I turned back toward the door of the bell tower, which was now an ominous black mass so dark it sucked up the sunlight. A thousand tails stuck out of the mass, which seemed to pulsate! It was the dark mice, thousands of them, huddling tightly together like seagulls on that fishing boat.

"Look!" screamed the postmaster from his seat. "The tower! It's moving!"

Indeed, the tower was moving. It was swaying as if one of its supports of the base had been taken away, and every time the caretaker gave the bell a push, the tower moved, as a crack inched its way along the structure's half-rotten wood.

"Come down!" yelled the vice-principal.

"Come down! It's dangerous!" shouted one student, who was then joined by many.

"Come down!"

"It's not safe!"

"Come down, caretaker!"

"Come down now!" shouted everyone.

For a moment, the caretaker stopped and looked down at everyone in the schoolyard. Then he smiled, waved, and went back to ringing the bell.

"He can't hear us!" someone screamed. "He's wearing his ear plugs!"

I couldn't bear to watch as the caretaker wrapped the rope around his wrinkle-free hand again and pulled it taut.

Booonnggg!

It was the tolling of the bell. It was the splitting of the wood post of the bell tower.

Booonnggg!

The bell tower began to give way, keeling over as if it were bowing, and for a very brief moment I imagined that dinosaur from the distant sea. The only of its kind left in the world, crying out sadly in the fog, hoping to find its long-lost brother.

Holding tight onto the dinosaur's head, the caretaker rang the bell one last time.

Booonnggg!

The sound resonated through the crowd, punctuated with loud cracks as the tower crumbled to the ground. It fell, fortunately, not toward the crowd of people, but instead upon the mass of dark mice. With a dull thud, it hit the ground, sending clouds of dust into the air. It felt as if the earth was rumbling, accompanied by what sounded like the drumroll of huge timpani storming through our being.

We all fell to our knees. Then, as the dust cleared, an infinite number of black specks come rushing, scurrying through the courtyard, and pouring through all open spaces. There were mice everywhere. But they were not dark mice; they were newborn ordinary mice with squinty baby mice eyes.

Once the mice were gone, people slowly got to their feet. We looked at one another, stunned in disbelief. Then we cautiously made our way over to the ruins of the bell tower. But now, no one was stumbling or walking like a drunk. An invisible rod was holding our backs straight, a fresh new wind was starting to blow. And I could hear every sound with the utmost clarity. The blockage in my ears had been blown away.

"We can walk!" the pipefitter yelled, then gasping, he ran to the fallen bell tower, as if pulled by a string to where the caretaker lay.

From that day on, no one was tone deaf. The collapse of the bell tower had come as the caretaker's final performance, a gift to everyone in the form of a mighty sound erupting from his body like a primal howl. It was a performance unlike any other and one that seemed to come from a place high above.

Around the town, we wondered at the mysteries that surrounded us. The dark mice, the breezes from the sea, the wail of my cat cry. There was much we didn't understand, but we knew that the last tolling of the bell by the caretaker marked the end of the reign of dark mice; the birth of ordinary mice was something we could live with. It marked a transformation for the band members, releasing them from the curse of tone deafness and restoring their stature as talented musicians. It marked the ability to walk straight again—even for those who hadn't been present at the graduation but had heard the bell tolling.

For the next two days, Grandpa immersed himself entirely in the band. He played his timpani with unstoppable enthusiasm, not sleeping or even blinking. It was the same for the other band members, who practiced with energy they never knew before.

On the day of the caretaker's funeral, the band, everyone in their black suits, gathered at the cemetery. In the coffin lay the caretaker, wearing a thin layer of makeup. There were plugs in his nose and he was wrapped in the finest black velvet robe.

"Cat," said Grandpa after the vice-principal's short eulogy, "let's give him what he would have wanted."

I tightened my throat and cried my cat cry, letting my voice out naturally. And on my cue, the band began a slow version of *Fanfare for the Fighting Kids* that seemed to float gently in the serene air around us.

As I beat the small drum hanging from my neck with a brush, sometimes gently and sometimes with force, I felt for the first time I understood the meaning of the piece. It's about fighting as a way of connecting. It's about bodies touching, about continuing to fight through music even when your opponent may be invisible. It's about anything being possible as long as there is real music like this.

Halfway through the performance, rain began to fall. It was a warm spring rain and the undertaker rushed to cover the coffin, leaving a small window for us to gaze at the caretaker's kind face. I watched as raindrops fell from the sky, tapping on the coffin, and thought how there is nothing in this world that can't make a beat.

Gimme Candy

It seemed right that I should inherit the mounds of files and sheet music from the caretaker—and it seemed right that I should also inherit his habit of keeping the scrapbooks up to date.

I read, not without a struggle, the many pieces of music he had written, but I didn't know what they might sound like. So, in addition to going regularly to rehearsals at Warehouse #2, I started taking music lessons from the postmaster. I had the hope that one day I too would become the master of the baton.

Dad was having a hard time recovering from the shock of seeing all those mice running around the schoolyard. The mice were living, scurrying proof that the theories and assumptions about prime numbers he'd been working on for more than a year were fundamentally wrong. He'd never believed the stories about the dark mice being evil. He did believe that some had survived my cry, though, and based on some premise, he'd calculated that their number was equal to a prime number in the fifties. But there were far more than fifty mice. In fact, there were at least twice as many mice as people at the ceremony! Dad had also assumed that the mice lived in scattered pockets around town, when it turned out they were living in herds.

"But," I said timidly as I poked at a mess on my plate that was intended to be an omelet, "is it really important to know how many mice there were?"

Dad didn't reply. He got up, threw his uneaten food angrily into the garbage bin, and stormed off to the sanctuary of the stairs.

Later that year, when the yellow sun began to hint at the beginnings of summer, Dad could often be seen in his gray suit, towing a cart of small boxes and crouching in the dark corners of back alleys and parks. He was setting mousetraps, and whatever mice he trapped he took to the schoolyard at night, where he would release them all at once. He did this every day. Over and over and over again.

"I want to recreate that herd," he said. "That enormous herd. I need to check their numbers. You see, according to my calculations, mice form sets of prime numbers naturally."

I didn't understand. Nor did anyone else. After a while people started referring to Dad as 'The Mouse Man" behind his back.

"Grandpa," I once asked after a grueling practice session at Warehouse #2, "do you think Dad understands what he's doing?"

"I don't know," said Grandpa, adjusting the skin on his timpani. "He's always been like this. Once he decides something is so, it can't be anything else. Imagine if we were to take a saw to his head, remove his brains and show them to him saying, 'This is what was inside your head!' He'd just shake his empty head and go off again to catch more mice."

In the time since graduation, Warehouse #2 had regained its former glory. A newspaper journalist wrote that our dedication to practice in winter was starting to bear fruit. But it wasn't our dedication alone. The band had inherited something precious from the caretaker. I'm not sure if everyone in the audience could sense it, but for us on stage we *knew* our sound was clearer than it had ever been—it was like being half-blind for years and then suddenly putting on a pair of prescription glasses.

"We need to get even better," said the pipefitter, our new concertmaster, during every break. "You may have noticed that a steam whistle in the port just put the trumpet out of time slightly there. I heard the fourth trumpet try to compensate by speeding up. But because the second trumpet stayed in time, things got out of sync. So let's start again from just before that note."

No matter how many times we tried, something always went wrong as we worked on a piece. As born-again musicians, we learned to find joy in random musical accidents. After all, there's no such thing as a perfect performance. After a while, the more we heard our accidents, the more they bothered us. But we didn't give up. We were aiming for a goal so far off in the distance that none of us could see it. But at least we knew we were going in the right direction. We carried on, channeling our magical wind in hopes of blowing away the misery from the warehouse and the town, and on to some distant destination.

"That cemetery performance," the postmaster would say to new band members. "That was perfect. It was music itself. During that performance I felt my body melt into the music and become one with it. It was really tough after the caretaker died, but we were able to go on. I don't know how, but we did it. I've become a true believer in the power of music."

That summer, during the two lazy months before music school was to begin, after evening rehearsals in Warehouse #2, I'd go sit on the dock and gaze at the night sea. I'd listen to the sea breezes as they blew their leisurely rhythm onto the land, and I'd watch as the seabirds perched on the pier, huddling together, resting their wings. In the distance, I could hear voices, some cheery, some angry, and everything in-between drifting out from the sailors' lodgings. But the sailors' love of fighting was something that never changed.

One evening I walked over to where the ships came in, to the cargo terminal, which was bathed in yellow light that pushed the darkness aside. Static-riddled announcements in foreign languages spilled out of speakers overhead. There were three cargo ships, and I watched as sailors and officers and dockworkers busily went about their tasks. I recognized a lot of the faces, and thanks to my unusual height many people recognized me, too.

"Hey Cat!" a loud voice boomed. "Over here! Come over here!"

Near a larger container that'd just been lifted onto the dock, a ship's engineer was waving to me. He worked on a foreign-owned ship, and it was his job to blow the trumpet wake-up call when the ship was at sea. Whenever he was in town, he'd come to Warehouse #2 to hear the band practice. He was a fan. I walked over to where he was standing behind a container that had just been lifted off the boat.

"You grow bigger every time I see you," he said as I walked toward him, remembering just how short he was. "If we sent a picture of us standing next to each other, I'm sure a magazine would want to put it on its cover!"

"I wouldn't like that," I said, accepting a pile of magazines from him. "How are you? Anything interesting happen at sea?"

"Well, the captain's parrot flew away. And the captain went mad!" the engineer said, then lowered his voice to a whisper. "It was a stupid parrot. It would fly around the ship saying 'Gimme candy, gimme candy' every time he saw someone. The captain, who was a show-off, loved this parrot so much that he'd give us candy every morning so we'd have something to give to the bird."

"The bird just disappeared?"

"Yeah, but there's a bit more to the story. One night, the watchman says to me, 'You haven't seen that parrot, have you?' I say, nope. The watchman has a smirk on his face and goes on, 'The whole crew's looking for it. Pretty soon you're going to be looking for it, too!' And then he imitates the captain: *You gotta find my parrot, my sweet lost parrot!*

"I sort of laugh. No way! I say. I'm way too busy trying to fix these two engine pistons that are shaking badly. There was also the 'stuff' we have hidden in the vent behind the pistons. We don't want the captain poking around. So I call a meeting in the engineering room, and this young engineer comes up with a brilliant idea.

"The next day during roll call, we hear this voice go 'Gimme candy.' The captain starts running, turning his ropy neck this way and that, running and yelling, 'Where are you? Where are you?' Then this voice comes from somewhere else, 'Gimme candy. Gimme candy. Wherever the poor captain runs, the parrot's voice comes from a completely different place. Soon, the captain is exhausted and about to cry. We're dismissed and go back to our posts, and the whole time we can hear the parrot begging for candy, with some sniggering thrown in. Of course, it was us heartless sailors doing it, and it became a running joke, with more sailors joining in until the parrot's voice could be heard all over the ship—sometimes at the same time! 'Gimme candy.' 'Gimme candy.' 'Wherezme candy.'

"After that, the captain locked himself in his cabin and stopped answering the radio. And then he snapped, He tried to strangle the communications officer, and had to be subdued and confined.

According to the doctor, the captain thought he was being haunted by the ghost of the parrot. Everyone had seen him doting on that parrot, but in his quarters he liked to torture the bird by feeding it thumbtacks. So after the parrot disappeared and we started imitating the parrot, the captain thought the dead parrot was getting revenge. When someone went to his quarters to check on him, there was candy scattered all over the place, and everything—barometer, picture frames, and dishes—was smashed to pieces."

"Did you ever find the parrot?"

"Nope," said the short engineer. "The poor thing probably fell overboard and couldn't fly back on. Maybe 'Gimme candy!' was the bird crying for help, but nobody thought that. So, Cat, if you see this parrot anywhere, can you feed it a grape or something? It's got white feathers and a pink beak. To be honest, it's kind of cute."

"If I ever see him, that's what I'll do," I said. I then handed over three cassette tapes of the band's performances in exchange for the magazines. In just another couple of days I'd be picking up a pile of magazines from another sailor, too.

As I left the port, I glanced back to see a cargo ship sailing into the darkness, with the crests of waves slapping against the hull. I adjusted the magazines under my arm and made my way back toward the dark town.

That summer, I made it part of my daily routine to spread out the magazines on the dining table and cut out articles that caught my interest. As usual, there were dinosaur sightings all over the world, with their siren-like wails directed at ships and lighthouses in the hope that they'd be heard, taken out of their lonely existence, and given a proper place to rest. This, it occurred to me, was like the prehistoric equivalent of the parrot's cries for more candy.

There were a number of magazines that covered the same story about the lighter that had travelled more than two thousand kilometers. About fifty-five years ago a man had escaped some civil war by crossing the border into the next country. One of the cherished things he left behind was a silver lighter passed down from his grandfather. The lighter was shaped like a skunk performing a handstand, and if you pulled down on the tail a flame would dart out from the skunk's rear end. It looked kind of like a toy, but it was far too well made to be just a novelty. So after having used it for many years, the man's father gave it to him on his seventeenth birthday. For that man, it was a truly precious thing, but he'd traveled too far to even consider retrieving it. So instead, the man and his family carried on, boarding a plane bound for another continent.

Some fifty-five years later, the man recounted the following incident in an interview.

I was walking my dog this February. She's an old dog whose eyes have seen better days, but her keen sense of smell more than makes up for it. My sight is failing, too, so she's the perfect partner for me—especially since my dear wife passed away ten years ago and I don't even know where my two daughters are now. Anyway, I was walking in the park as usual when the dog suddenly pulled at the leash. This doesn't happen often. So I followed, allowing myself to be dragged along, until the dog reached the fountain, where a woman about forty years old was sitting. I wouldn't say she was dressed in an especially nice way, but she was wearing a very ostentatious fur coat. In fact, I actually wondered if she might be advertising for customers, if you know what I mean.

"*Can I have a cigarette?*" *the woman said.*

"*Unfortunately I don't smoke,*" *I said.* "*I quit ten years ago.*"

The woman sucked her teeth and looked down at the dog. "*What a large dog. What's its name?*"

"*I call her Skunk.*"

"*Skunk?*" *the woman said, looking surprised.* "*Such a horrible name for a dog!*"

"*All three dogs I've had were named Skunk!*" *I said.*

The woman crouched down and patted the dog, seeming very much at ease with it. When the dog tilted its head and licked her hand—the one with a ring on it—the woman let out a small laugh.

"*You probably won't need this since you don't smoke,*" *said the woman, beginning to rummage through her purse,* "*but let me give you this to honor the dog with the unfortunate name.*" *She then held out her hand.* "*A foreign gentleman gave this to me.*

It's a lighter. Not an ordinary one and not an easy one to use, but it's still a lighter."

I couldn't believe my eyes—it *was* that lighter! Immediately, I pulled down the tail and a flame leaped out. It was exactly as I remembered it *fifty-five years ago! The dog jumped around too, as if it was happy to see an old friend.*

"This kind of coincidence happens all the time around the world," wrote the journalist. "It happens randomly. Sometimes the event is so small we don't notice. Sometimes the scale is so large no one sees it."

Two days before music school began, I finally found the article I'd been looking for. It was a small news column written by one of the journalists who must have visited our town to cover the mouse rain. It was not a happy article, but it brought back warm memories of our dear caretaker.

A Drummer's Death
Yet another accident has hit the town where it rained mice. An old man with disabilities in all four limbs has been sadly crushed by a falling bell. He was the bell-ringer for the elementary school, and he'd intended to ring the bell in celebration at the graduation ceremony. Unfortunately, in his excitement, he didn't see the rot that had spread through the base of the bell tower. As a result, when he rang the bell, the tower collapsed and the old man was thrown to the ground, with the bell landing on top of him. Indeed, the bell tolled for a dear old man, a beloved drummer, and a man of many stories who would send us postcards without fail every month.

Carefully, I cut around the edges of the story and transferred it to its new home in the black binder that contained all the other articles about the town that had made the caretaker so happy. If he'd been able to talk to me now, I'm sure he would have complained a little in his distinctive lisp, but in the end he would have happily allowed himself to take his place among the many tales.

Thanks to a recommendation from the school and a successful audition that involved playing the snare drums, I was accepted to music school and given a scholarship. When school was about to begin, I knew it was time to make a change. Instead of percussion, I was going to study conducting. At first I was worried how Grandpa would react. But he didn't say anything. The day before I was to leave for music school he gave me a leather drumstick case that contained a shiny maple baton alongside four mallets for the timpani.

For my last dinner at home, Dad made me an omelet. When I'd finished it, I went upstairs and listened to the sounds of mice as they scurried inside Dad's many boxes. I had hoped that I could listen to Dad from time to time. But just like he never spoke to Grandpa, he'd spoke to me less and less as well. I turned off the lights and climbed into bed.

A little past midnight, I heard those old familiar steps again. But this time they carried a different type of echo and when I opened my eyes I found myself in a gleaming white room. I jumped out of bed and found myself bathed in the same morning light I'd seen in a dream ten years earlier. Then I turned to my bed, which was the same as always, but without Dad or Grandpa by its side. I stepped over to the window and gazed at the yellow land that stretched out before me. But this time I didn't see Kutze at our doorstep. I looked out far into the distance, beyond where the canal would be, beyond the docks, to where I could see the small shadow of a man stepping along sideways, and I thought of Kutze.

"Big or small, it's a matter of distance."

Kutze had wheat-stepped for quite some distance without my knowledge, with his steps now barely audible and his great black shoes stepping their way to the horizon.

"Hey Kutze," I said, thinking to myself, "there's no such thing as good or bad. That's why you keep going on wheat stepping."

For a moment I thought I saw him pause. Then the calm and quiet stepping continued, strangely close to my ear.

Ton, Ta-tan, Ton
Ton, Ta-tan, Ton

"That's right," said Kutze, lifting his head a little. "There is no right or wrong in wheat stepp'n.'"

I moved away from the window and returned to my bed, where I lay face up as usual and closed my eyes. And from that day on, I stopped hearing Kutze's voice.

Early the next morning—after I'd packed my trunk with clothes, sheet music, and cassette tapes—I climbed up on a chair and poked my head in the attic. Kutze wasn't there. Nobody was. Just the yellow rays of the sun that played cross the dust-covered panels. Then I heard something.

Ton, Ta-tan

Those rhythmic stepping sounds still echoed in my ears.

Ton, Ta-tan, Ton

I grabbed my trunk and went down the stairs, squeezing past Dad on the twelfth step and stepping out into the summer sun. In front of me, I could see a ship that had just returned from a faraway land. On deck were two sailors engaged in a heated argument. When they saw me, they stopped.

"Been years, Cat," yelled one sailor to me, waving. "How's it going?"

"Cat, how are you this morning? Let's hear it!" yelled the other.

Smiling, I waved back to them both. With my trunk in hand, I set off toward the train station, the sound of Kutze's steps keeping time in my ears, and the summer sun, strong enough to melt candy, swimming on the surface of those old canal waters and bathing my oversized body in wonderful warmth.

Chapter 2

The Rickety Old Steam Engine That Couldn't Keep Time

The city at the heart of the island was also the heart of the music scene. Competitions were held there all year round. What's more, the city was known for its string instruments crafted from the maple and teak that grew in the forests around it. Even the shape of the town was musical, stretching long and thin from east to west with a lump in the middle that made it look like an open castanet on a map.

I arrived there on the afternoon of the school entrance ceremony and was met at the station by the younger sister of the postmaster from my town—the conductor of Grandpa's band.

"I wonder how the dates got mixed up?" she said, stroking her double chin. She was about half my height, she must have weighed twice as much as me, and it was a struggle for her to get into her car. As we set off, she stole occasional glances at me, and I wondered if she worried that I was nervous. Then she started to sing a verse from an opera—she had a beautiful soprano—every so often turning the steering wheel sharply.

"Whoopsy-daisy!" she sang. For a moment, I thought that was part of the lyrics, but then she laughed, "I nearly ran over a pigeon!"

By the time we reached her place, I liked her. She showed me into her apartment, which comprised the entire fourth floor and which was covered from wall to wall with a slightly worn, but soft and comfortable light pink carpet. Oil paintings covered the walls.

"Did you paint these?" I asked, very impressed.

"Oh, I just do those for fun," she replied with a hint of shyness. "When you live alone at my age, the one thing you have plenty of is time."

The only oil painting I'd ever seen before that day had been an old, dust-covered painting of a salmon—and a rather unappetizing one at that—which was hanging in the back of the bar back home. These paintings were much better, and I stood admiring them for several moments before the postmaster's sister picked up my trunk and said she wanted to show me my room. She opened the door to a room filled with the warm afternoon sun. A wooden box had been placed at the foot of the bed so as to make it long enough for me. The bay window looked out to the quiet town and a peaceful lake beyond. Then I turned around.

"Wow!" I exclaimed.

In one corner of the room were dozens and dozens of records, and next to them a very impressive audio system.

"I moved these here yesterday from my room," explained the postmaster's sister. Then she picked up a piece of paper that had been sitting on top of one of the speakers.

"All the records are on this list," she said. "I just listen to music for pleasure, but for you, it's something you have to study. Anyway, feel free to listen to whatever you want, and don't worry about making too much noise. If anyone in the building complains, I'll stuff sardine paste into their ears!"

The list of records was accompanied by an incredible level of detail in neat handwriting, including the date and place of each recording and a brief explanation of each piece. The list had been put together by Grandpa and the postmaster, and it contained all of the music they felt I should know. At the bottom of the page was this note:

> *On rare occasions, records can surpass live performances. But to become a true musician, you must continue listening to live music until you develop a ringing in the ears that refuses to go away. Even the poorest of performances can provide the nutrition you need to grow as a musician. When you find your ears suffering from indigestion, you may find these records will help.*

I pasted the list into the first page of my scrapbook. I don't know how many times I've opened the book to reread the list. But in no time at all, I found I was able to close my eyes and recall every single track. That's how often I listened to the records in hopes of alleviating the indigestion my ears were always suffering—during the hours spent in school and the hours spent elsewhere.

The next morning I began my first day of music school. It was only a short walk from the apartment, but I didn't get there before the third period had already begun. I was immediately sent to the headmaster's office where I was told that those who couldn't arrive on time had no business being at this school.

"What do you think music is?" shouted the headmaster while delivering three lashes to my hands with his whip. "It's the art of timing, boy!"

During history class after lunch, the teacher went on and on about the history of the city. If I hadn't been able to hear the sound of violins, I might have thought to wander off to another school. We learned that the city was famous for the clocks it produced, and if you walked around the city you'd see clocks everywhere. You could find the time on the ribs of a bronze statue of a horse, on top of a statue shaped like an ear of corn in the middle of a fountain, and in too many shop windows to mention. On the hour every hour, you could hear chimes all over town, and as the hour approached the teachers would stare at their watches, waiting. It was like the headmaster said about the art of timing—everything in town was precise to the second.

The next class was the study of foreign language. Then came a class on musical theory. Then the day was over—without my seeing a single musical instrument!

"I'm sorry I didn't wake you. I'm very forgetful," the postmaster's sister said as she made dinner. I had just told her about being tardy to school.

"Not your fault," I said. "I overslept."

I did wonder, though, if her forgetfulness was connected to the fact that I arrived in the city a day later than planned. She didn't have a clock or a calendar in her apartment, nothing on the walls except for those beautiful paintings. So maybe I'd thrown her internal clock out of sync. But forgetful or not, she sure could cook. Her stew was so delicious it made my tongue dance!

"There's no secret to making it," she said. "I'm not the sort of person to slave over the stove all afternoon."

After dinner, as we did the dishes together, she broke into an aria. Pretending the liquid detergent was the poison that had killed a princess, she hit the high notes at a volume much greater than the speakers in my room could muster. Later that evening, after she'd gone to bed, I sat in my room listening to records. And as I leaned over to flip the tenth record over, I noticed the early morning sun peering in through the windows.

The students in the faculty of conducting and composition were from all across the country. Two had even come from abroad, though the head of the faculty strictly forbade them from using their native tongue in school.

"There's to be no use of nonstandard language, regional accents, or slang in my class," he said, laying down the law. "You are to speak clearly, and don't slur your words!"

We didn't have to worry about that too much. We hardly spoke—not even during recess, when everyone went through their scores absentmindedly or fiddled with the piano.

There were seven students in this faculty, and all we did the first day was move our fingers back and forth to the beat of the metronome on the piano while the teacher boomed, *Choo-choo, choo-choo!* His finger pointed downward on the first *choo*, upward on each of the next three *choos*. Sometimes his voice was so loud you couldn't even hear the tick of the metronome.

"*Choo-choo*, you're late, frizzy-hair. *Choo-choo*, you're early, mama's boy. *Choo-choo, choo-choo!*"

We repeated this for an entire hour with five short breaks. I pictured a black steam engine with seven pairs of windshield wipers moving in sync.

The teacher chewed on coffee-flavored gum, and if you watched closely, the movement of his jaw was out of sync the metronome. I was quite amazed that he could keep his *choo-choo*s in time with the metronome while chewing to an entirely different beat. Perhaps he'd be less frustrated if he could replace the seven of us with seven little metronomes, I thought. Surely it wouldn't be any more pointless than this stupid exercise.

In composition class the teacher started off by playing us a simple four-bar melody on the piano. Each of us, in turn, was to pick up the melody—on the piano—where the teacher left off.

After the first student tried his luck at this, the teacher slammed his fist on the keys. "That's garbage!" he shouted. The next student then sat down at the piano and played what he could come up with. "That's garbage!" the teacher shouted. Same thing happened with the next student. And the next. Until finally it was my turn.

"What is it?" asked the teacher, looking down his nose at me as I sat dumbly.

"I've never played the piano," I said.

The teacher was stunned. He grasped his head and stomped on the floor while the six other students stared at me, wide-eyed. Everyone in the class had studied the piano from a very early age, but our band back home was piano-less. The teacher stared at me with the disdain a sailor might have for a clump of seaweed caught in his anchor.

"Every one of you here plays like a disaster," the teacher said, teeth clenched.

Again, he sat down and played four bars. "Now this is the only way you can pick up the tune," he said. "Just listen. This is how it should sound."

The class was not an exercise in creativity, I concluded. It was a regular quiz in memorization, where only one answer would do. To make matters worse, the quiz was always from a song the teacher had composed himself or an old song that none of us knew. So with a curriculum consisting only of *choo-choo* and music quizzes, I became notorious for skipping class before even the end of the first month.

This city is dull—and so is the school. It's unbearable.

This is how I began my first letter to the postmaster back home.

> *What they teach at school isn't music. It's more like gymnastics, with each student forced to do exactly as the teacher dictates. Yesterday I had the chance to watch the city orchestra practice. Their instruments and the hall they played in were impressive. But the performance was nothing special.*

I'd run into the cleaning lady that I met during the band competition the year before, and she kindly let me in through the back door. The concert master remembered me somehow, and he asked if I wanted to join in on the snare drum. I was delighted and wasted no time jumping up on stage and standing with the percussion. But not long after we were into the piece, the conductor called a stop to it. Then looking at me, he said, "Looks like the band player from the boonies is no match for us. You're welcome to stay and listen if you like, but please don't interrupt us."

> *Honestly, I feel like a piece of lint caught between the cogs of this clockwork city. I'm just waiting for those clogs to turn and crush me to death.*

Three days later, I received a reply from the postmaster.

> *Don't feel like that, Cat. Repetition is the foundation of conducting. To call those lessons dull is to call conducting a mindless pursuit. How can you expect to meet the demands of a full house if you can't begin by pleasing just a few instructors? You have to grit your teeth and bear it. Go to class and learn the basics well. Only then will you be ready to wave your baton in the wider world. Also, when you write me, please try to select a stamp with an interesting design.*

Then, at the bottom of the letter, there was an additional note in Grandpa's writing.

> *What do you know about music, you fool!*

I had to admit it, the postmaster was right. If I put my mind to it, I could perform the *choo-choo*s while doing handstands. Why not turn myself into a model student—one the headmaster and the teacher would be proud to parade around the school. But my index finger had other plans. The harder I tried to move it in sync with the *choo-choo*s, the clumsier it became, until it was as if my body and index finger were ten meters apart.

"You are messing up our timing!" shouted the teacher. "You! Giant boy! Pick up your chair and go sit in the back where we won't be distracted by your rhythmless finger."

Just like that, I was kicked out of the loop—confined to spending my classes staring at the backs of the six other students who knew how to wave their fingers in unison like a single digital wave.

Choo, choo-choo-choo, choo, choo-choo-choo, the teacher bellowed, pointing his finger downward on the first *choo* and upward on each of the following three *choo*s.

Finally, I thought to myself, *there's a movement that's starting to look like conducting!*

I continued to watch as his finger maintained the precise tick-ticking of the metronome. Then I glanced back to my own finger, which seemed to be poking around the air at random, not even coming close to any kind of rhythm at all.

Eventually, the six students in front of me were allowed to use a baton, leaving me alone at the back of the room chanting *choo-choo* and waving my finger like a half-wit. I realized that I wasn't the piece of lint caught in the cogs of the city after all. I was the rickety old steam engine that was always running behind time.

The Butterfly Man

Since I wasn't allowed to pick up a baton, I picked up a pair of scissors instead. Off I went through the back entrance of the library with scrapbook in hand into a room piled high with newspapers and magazines. The librarian allowed me to do my scrapbooking in the main reading room on several conditions: I was to only cut out articles, to be as quiet as possible with the scissors, and to use just the standing desk in the corner of the room.

I couldn't hang out at the apartment all day because the postmaster's sister—who owned the building and was also its caretaker—was always around. So every morning I'd leave the apartment and drag myself in the direction of school, only to do a ninety-degree turn to the right on arrival and head off to the library instead. I did this a couple of times a week. Actually, to be honest, it was every other day. And although I felt that my truancy was like admitting defeat in class, the mere thought of that stupid metronome made me sick.

In the morning, the library was completely silent. I'd spread out my newspapers and circle with a blue pencil any articles that caught my eye. Then I'd cut out the articles, even if I'd already cut out a similar article from another paper, and paste them into the scrapbook.

Scrapbooking helped me relax. As I filed various incidents from around the world in my book, I forgot about the metronome and the clockwork city. It was fun to read the articles, too. I even enjoyed cutting them out! I got so fully into the task that I'd only realize it was past lunchtime if my stomach growled. Then I'd step outside to eat the sandwiches prepared for me by the postmaster's sister. I couldn't help but feel a little guilty about it, but the sandwiches were absolutely delicious.

When you are cutting out articles for a scrapbook every other day, you start noticing strange coincidences such as unrelated people in different parts of the world experiencing something very similar on the exact same day. Plane crashes, for example. Large ones, small ones. They seemed to happen one after the other. Groundbreaking scientific discoveries seemed to happen all at once, too. On the same day that the electric telescope first captured the true depth of the universe, another astronomer announced a sighting of water vapor on the surface of Mars.

Such coincidences weren't limited to the front page. On the sports page, there was a story of a jockey who fell off his horse and fractured his hip. That same day, in another part of the world, a horse wandered onto a highway and was hit by a motorbike. In that case, it was the horse that suffered broken bones. There was, buried in the front section, a story about the arrest of a cross-dressing burglar. And elsewhere, on that same night, a club for men was burned to the ground, leaving a suspicious collection of ladies' dresses and jewelry among the charred remains. There was also a story, with a photograph, about a baby alligator born in a zoo—complemented by a story in a different town about a circus trainer whom an alligator had attacked and chewed off his right foot.

Whenever I found articles that shared some sort of connection, I pasted them next to each other in my scrapbook. And the more I looked for these kinds of coincidences, the more of them I found. Soon enough, the people, the names of people, the causes of the incidents, and the outcomes all seemed to align.

It's all the same. That's what Kutze said some time ago.

Now, whenever I look through my scrapbook, I am convinced that there isn't a single incident in this world that isn't connected to another. The connection may be small or unimportant. But then, as Kutze said, *Small. Big. It's a matter of distance.* So my scrapbook was a way of bringing together events that would be glad to be linked. At least it seemed that way to me.

One day, as I was engrossed in cutting and pasting in my scrapbook, there came a voice from behind me: "That's a very interesting sound you're making there!"

I turned around to find a man with a shaven head, wearing sunglasses, standing with his mouth slightly open. He was about forty years old, my height, but with shoulders twice as wide as mine, making him look like a bear standing on its hind legs. He was wearing a tank top and his arms were thick with biceps like bowling balls.

I was speechless. The man stepped a little closer.

"That sound," he said. "The one you were making just now."

"Oh, sorry," I said, getting a whiff of his sweat. "I'll stop." I'd been absent-mindedly tapping my pencil onto the newspaper, leaving little blue dots everywhere.

The man opened his mouth, as if he was going to say something, but then he closed his mouth and walked over to the bookshelf, moving like a slow-moving thundercloud. I let out a deep breath and went back to my newspaper, reading a blue-flecked article about a man who jumped off a bridge as a show of bravery. He had a bungee cord tied around his ankle, but when it reached its limit the cord snapped, and the man plummeted thirty meters into the river and drowned. Apparently, he lost consciousness the moment he hit the water.

I was sitting on the bench outside the library having my lunch when the muscle-bound man came over and asked if he could sit with me. His tank-top was drenched in sweat, and he had on his sunglasses, which were quite dark. I nodded noncommittally. The man sat his huge backside down beside me.

"You come here often, don't you?" he said. "Here, to this library."

"Yeah, I guess," I muttered.

"I want to ask you about that sound you were making in the library. What was that?"

"Oh, that…Sorry, I didn't realize what I was doing. It was just me tapping my pencil."

"That was a pencil?" The man looked surprised.

"I use a blue pencil for my scrapbooking."

The man grunted, shaking his head. He was deeply tanned, even his head was tanned, and there was a butterfly tattoo on his neck. I was starting to feel a little nervous.

"It didn't sound like a pencil to me," the man said. "It sounded like you were stepping on something—kind of like this," he said, beginning to tap his hands on his knees.

Ton, Ta-tan, Ton
Ton, Ta-tan, Ton

He moved his feet in time with his hands.

Ton, Ta-tan, Ton

That was when I dropped my sandwich. "That's the sound?" I said. "That's the sound you heard?"

"That's the sound. I've never heard anything like it before at the library. I've never heard anything like it anywhere! What was it?"

I was at a loss for words. How could I explain? I couldn't tell him that it was the sound I heard in my head all the time. I couldn't say, "It's just Kutze, wheat-stepp'n." Or, "Sorry, that's just a sound that leaks from my head sometimes. I'll try to patch over the cracks in my skull with plaster." So I just said, "I don't know. I have no idea what that sound is."

"But you're making it."

For a moment, I fell silent again. "I really don't know," I mumbled.

The man appeared to be deep in thought. Then he said, "It's my ears. They pick up sounds I'm not supposed to hear sometimes. A dog's fart. A nun's burp. That sort of thing. It's not that I'm trying to eavesdrop. I just hear them. I wish I didn't have to hear so much. But then sometimes I come across some of the most interesting sounds. Some very rare sounds. It would be a shame to miss out on those."

He placed a big hand on my shoulder, and I immediately felt its heat.

"The sound I heard coming from you. It was truly fascinating. It seemed simple, but it had a deep quality to it, too. And just when I thought it was over, it continued. I didn't know what was making the sound, but seemed like there was a lot of…care going into it. I don't know about you, but to my ears it was music."

I looked up slowly.

"I was on the train the other day," he continued, "when I heard a funny sound coming from the seat in front of me. This skinny old woman was cracking her neck over and over again. Maybe it was a habit of hers. I could hear her muscles scraping against bone, it was very disturbing. *Crack! Crackle! Crack!* Her neck must have been so stiff. But since it was an express train, I couldn't get off or change seats even if I'd wanted to. Soon enough, her neck cracking started to spread to the other passengers until the train car was filled with the sounds of *Crack! Crack Crackle! Crack! Crackle!* I wanted to scream for everybody to stop, but then the train came to an abrupt, screeching halt. When it started up again and we eventually got to our destination, it sounded like I was surrounded by snapping branches. Everyone was cracking their necks like crazy as if they'd never had a good night's sleep. Everyone except for one person, of course."

"One person?"

"The old woman herself," the man laughed, raising both hands in the air. "The moment she got up from her seat and stood up straight, her entire body went *snap-snap-snap-snap!* Her spine must have just snapped into place! Very impressive. Like an avalanche of back muscles. I felt like she deserved a round of applause for such a performance. So you see, it's not always a bad thing to have such good hearing."

The story made me smile. Despite the man's intimidating appearance, he seemed a decent person. He seemed gentle. And as he was telling his story, a little white butterfly had landed on his purple sweat pants. He didn't shoo it off, he just let it rest there.

I noted the little black dot on its wings. "That's a pretty butterfly," I said.

"Huh? Oh, the tattoo! Don't ever get one," he said, covering his neck with his hand. "I got it back in the old days when I was up to no good. Now people call me Butterfly Man, which at my age sounds ridiculous."

"I was talking about the butterfly on your pant leg," I said.

The man raised his sunglasses and glanced downward. "A butterfly on me?" he said shyly, then laughed. "I should have told you earlier. The Butterfly Man can't see."

Later that day, I wrote the postmaster about the Butterfly Man. Six days later I received a reply:

> I'm very glad that you've made a friend. But it worries me that you aren't making any friends your own age. Are you going to school? By the way, your grandpa has recruited the vice-principal into the brass band, and he's teaching him percussion. He's a good student and he's about the same age as your grandpa. Why don't you find some friends your own age too, then you can invite them back here for Christmas break and we can all perform together.

After our first meeting, I saw the Butterfly Man almost every day. There was a gym just behind the library where he worked out in the morning. He came over to the library at lunchtime because it was quiet and a good place for him to relax. I guess the town was full of more unpleasant sounds than my ears ever noticed.

"Sometimes I get this terrible itch deep down in my ears," he said one day, "and no matter how far I stick my finger in, I can't reach it."

As I got to know him better, I learned that he hadn't always been blind. As a young man, he'd been a promising professional boxer. He even made it to the finals of a major tournament for newcomers, where he landed a beautiful right hook on the chin of his opponent in the first round, sending him to the floor. Then he knocked him down again before the first round was over. The Butterfly Man went on to knock his opponent down in the second and third rounds, too—leaving his opponent's face swollen and bloodied, like a Brussels sprout splattered with ketchup. Then, in the fourth round, his opponent drove a thumb into the Butterfly Man's left eye as he was crouching down.

"He didn't mean to do it. I'm sure of that," the Butterfly Man said. "Thumbing is rare, not like head butting or hitting with the elbows. People don't do it intentionally. I was in the ring with him. I was there. I know that it was an accident. No question about it."

Despite the injury to his eye, the Butterfly Man refused to leave the ring. He kept throwing jabs and leading forward on his left foot, which is when he felt something soft underfoot. He looked down and saw it was his mouthpiece, and at that moment his opponent launched a wild swing that hit him square in the face and sent the Butterfly Man flying sideways until he hit his head on the corner post. That's when the lights went out for the Butterfly Man. From that moment. Forever.

"I wasn't strong enough," he said, laughing again. "That's all there is to it. If you're a world-class boxer, you never say you lost a fight because you were unlucky. Every punch, every step is calculated. There's always a logic, always a method. And though I still don't know for sure if it was the thumb in my eye, the impact of the punch, or the concussion against the post that damaged my optic nerves, I know for sure that I was not a world-class boxer."

Amazingly, the Butterfly Man didn't quit boxing even after he lost his sight. Of course, he couldn't fight anymore; they wouldn't let him in the ring. So instead he boxed in the corner of the gym, raining down punches on the punching bag hanging there.

"I was afraid to quit," he said. "I knew that if I was boxing I wouldn't have to worry about getting hit by a bike or falling down a manhole."

No matter how randomly the punching bag swung, the Butterfly Man's gloves caught it squarely. His punches became more accurate since he lost his sight, and even his movement seemed more refined. He got featured in a magazine for beginner boxers.

A boxing coach, speaking to a group of young amateurs, said this: "This guy might seem like the perfect role model, but don't try to be like him. It's impossible. If any boxer came across fancy footwork like his in the ring, he'd have to stop to admire it. The fight would be over, right then and there. You young guys are just starting out in boxing. For now, you need to focus on landing punches on your opponents."

So it seems the Butterfly Man was no longer a boxer. He had become boxing itself.

Eventually, the coach who ran the gym got into some sort of scuffle and the gym was forced to close down. So the Butterfly Man started working out at the local training center instead. At first, he made his way around there with cautious steps as he relied on only his memory. Then, after going there for a couple of years, his stride became smooth and confident. As he walked along, his ears captured all the sounds on the street. The blare of car horns, the hustle and bustle of people, the voices of store clerks, the clutter of construction. In time, he built up a mental map of sounds, and whenever he came across a new one, he'd add it to the corresponding location.

As the Butterfly Man cruised through town guided by his sonic map, there was nothing he couldn't sidestep—bicycles, pedestrians, even luggage left on the ground.

"Everything," he said, "makes a sound. All you have to do is listen. Listen to the bicycle tires, doors opening and closing, footsteps. All these sounds mark places on the map. And they make your ears itch like crazy!

"Clocks always come in handy," he went on. "Among the clocks in town, no two are the same. Each one makes a completely different sound. I listen to the first chime, and I know exactly which street I'm on."

"All right then," I said, "where are we now?"

"We're on the corner diagonally across from the bank," he answered without skipping a beat. "We're standing in front of a store and underneath my feet is a manhole—the cover was just replaced last month. If you look five meters behind us, you'll see the baker has set up a stall to serve his late afternoon customers. He's just put some bread out. Five loaves to be exact."

As I stood there wide-eyed, he reached into his pocket and said, "It's not just my ears that work well. My nose works really well, too. Can you smell that? It's gorgeous! Can you go get me one of those walnut breads, please?"

The Butterfly Man invited me along to boxing practice. He said that he sensed something boxer-like in me, and though I was interested, I had to decline.

"I'm not allowed to engage in any strenuous exercise. It isn't good for my heart."

"Strenuous exercise?" he said in a loud voice muffled by walnut bread. "Are you telling me that boxing is strenuous? Don't be silly. Boxing is like walking down a street, unconsciously moving your feet forward at just the right tempo. The important thing is to feel the flow of your own body. That's all there is to it."

"Your own body." That phrase alone was enough to bring me down. After all, it was my body that had split my mother in two. My body that couldn't move in time with the *choo-choo*s. As I stood silently, the Butterfly Man stared at me with his unseeing eyes.

"Here comes the tone!" he announced, turning to his right and letting the afternoon sun illuminate the butterfly on his neck.

On the top of the bank building was a large golden clock, surrounded by statues. Its design somehow reminded me of the banister on the stairs where my father always sat. Then, exactly as the Butterfly Man predicted, the carved wooden lid opened up and a couple of soldiers shuffled out on either side of the clock.

Bong! Bong!

It was five o'clock.

Bong!

As we stood there, several passersby stopped to watch the clock. It was as if they'd noticed the clock for the first time.

Bong!

The tone of the bell seemed perfectly suited to the sunset. And if it were a color, it would have been orange. A large, translucent tangerine that you'd never reach, no matter how far you stretched out your arms.

Bong!

After the final chime came and went, we remained standing. We listened as the bell's resonance faded and as the hustle and bustle of the streets came back to the fore. But for some reason, everything sounded different than it had before.

"See," said the Butterfly Man, "the clocks in this town aren't so bad, are they?"

"No," I said, "they're not bad at all."

We walked for a while, side by side, through the orange town washed clean by the chimes of the clock tower as we savored the sweet flavor of the freshly baked walnut bread.

I said goodbye to the Butterfly Man and headed back to my apartment, where two envelopes were waiting for me.

One envelope was a familiar small one that contained a letter from the postmaster. He gave me the latest news on the band—mainly focusing on the lessons Grandpa was giving the vice-principal. He also mentioned that a salesman had suddenly showed up in town.

> *It seems he's been staying at the inn for about a week now. He's a delightful man, a shoe salesman, and he's so good at his job that once you give him your attention, if you're not careful, you end up buying three pairs from him!*

There was also a large brown envelope from Dad. I tore it open. On the back side of the letter was scribbled all sorts of complex equations and formulas. On the front side, Dad had written:

> *Finally, I'm going to be able to finish my proof. I'm making great progress and the mice are acting as I predicted—moving around in sets of prime numbers. I have my new buddy, the salesman, to thank for it.*

What he was talking about? And what did he mean by "my new buddy"? It wasn't like Dad at all to call anyone his "buddy." How could a smooth-talking shoe salesman possibly help him?

Ton, Ta-tan, Ton
I was caught by surprise.
Ton
It was Kutze's familiar steps.
Ton, Ta-tan, Ton

Then the steps faded away, and a different, more harsh sound came from the living room. With a hammer in her hand, the postmaster's sister appeared in the doorway. She looked surprised to see me.

"Oh, sorry," she said. "I was putting up a new painting. Hope I didn't bother you. Well, dinner's ready! We're having chicken stew with cabbage."

The new painting was a landscape—a lake reflecting the mountain foliage, a boat in the lake with two figures sitting across from each other. It was the same with all the other paintings on the wall: each had a man and woman in a hat—facing each other. On a narrow countryside path. On the beach. Among the crowd at the racetrack. The two figures were everywhere. And they were always about the same distance apart, always looking into each other's face.

"Let's eat," she called out.

The two of us ate our chicken and cabbage stew, sitting side by side.

In a room covered in paintings. A room without a single clock in it. The stew was delicious. I ate in silence. As I licked my spoon clean, I began to wonder, why is there not a single clock in this house of a woman born in this city of clocks?

The Waltz of the Red Dog and the Blind Boxer

The Butterfly Man didn't just have good ears, he was a great listener, too. I talked to him nonstop. About Grandpa's timpani. About Dad's mathematical proof. About the day it rained mice in town. About the dark mice and my meowing. And the caretaker's last march. Every so often he would stop me to ask a question.

"What shape was the fishing boat?"
"Did the dark mice have a smell?"

After I'd answered his question, he'd look down and nod, like he was drawing a picture of my hometown in his mind. Of all the stories I told him, the Butterfly Man seemed most interested in the tales about Kutze.

"Tell me again," he said, scratching his neck. "Tell me about this Kutze guy. You know, when I first heard his footsteps, I thought they were all the same. But now that I think about it, they're all very different."

"But Kutze himself said they were all the same," I replied. "But I don't really know what he meant by that."

The Butterfly Man brought a hand to his chin and sat in thought for a moment. "Wheat stepp'n, you say? I don't really know what that is. I've never even seen a wheat field. But I guess each bushel of wheat is different from the last, right? If he says they're all the same, then this Kutze guy is either hopelessly dumb or pathetically earnest."

I wasn't sure what he meant by "pathetically earnest." I guess he meant being earnest to such an extent that you started to seem like an idiot. If so, those words didn't just apply to Kutze. They applied to me, too.

I never talked about school. After all, I was ditching class to hang out at the library. So my heart skipped a beat when the Butterfly Man one day suddenly said, "So school's dull for you?"

Immediately, I felt blood rising to my face. Just then, the librarian walked past us toward the fountain. His chin was raised so that his eyes wouldn't meet ours.

"You know, young boxers experience similar frustrations," he said. "Jab, jab, hook. Jab, jab, uppercut. Jab, hook, jab, uppercut. It's not so difficult to learn how to punch. But the first time you go through a round of shadow boxing, everything goes to pieces."

"But music and boxing are hardly the same."

"D'you think so? Well, I suppose they are very different. But they're also very similar," the Butterfly Man said, raising his muscular right arm. "Young kids often make the mistake of thinking that you're supposed to punch with your arms. But you've got to punch with your whole body. That's what boxing is all about. Moving your body in time. That's what music is about too, no? Think about it—you swing the baton, pull the bow across the violin strings. But that's not music. For music, you need every movement to be connected from start to finish, no matter if it's a solo performance or an entire orchestra."

The brass band performance at the cemetery suddenly came to mind.

"But musicians have it hard," said the Butterfly Man, putting a hand on my shoulder. "I mean, this world is already filled with such horrible sounds. It's like shadow boxing in the middle of some terrible racket. But what you need to do is to look straight at that world. Listen carefully to just how bad all those sounds are. The mark of a world-class musician is the ability to mine the smallest gems from that great awful landscape of noise, then let it resonate—I mean *really* resonate—in our ears."

"That's impossible," I said, on the verge of tears. "I can only hear normal sounds."

The Butterfly Man took off his glasses and turned his cloudy white eyes toward me.

"That's not true," he said firmly. "You can hear Kutze's wheat stepp'n."

I bit my lip and stared into his eyes. At first they looked scary. But you couldn't help admire them. They were like magical mirrors that didn't reflect anything, but were able to turn any passing sound into vision. I wondered what kind of images my mumbling and clumsy steps were conjuring up for him.

"How come you have such great ears?" I asked, feeling slightly ashamed.

The Butterfly Man put on his sunglasses and grinned. Then he faced forward and began talking about the school for the blind he had gone to:

Not long after he lost his sight, he started going to that special school. It was a boarding school at the edge of a lake—exactly on the opposite side of the lake from the castanet-shaped town we were living in. There were three seeing-eye dogs on the school grounds, and whenever a student waded waist-deep into the lake, one of the dogs would come paddling alongside to make sure the student was okay. The dogs were named after colors—Red, Yellow, and Green. And they wore collars the same color as their names. Not that the Butterfly Man saw this for himself, of course.

According to the Butterfly Man, it was quite an unusual school for the blind because most of the teachers were blind, too. But other than that, the school looked just like any other, with no Braille signboards or handrails along the walls. There were even some staircases with no handrails. As training for the students, there were desks, wooden boxes, and other obstacles left intentionally in the hallways here and there. The classrooms were divided by boards that were regularly rearranged to keep the students alert to uncertainties. It was the school's aim to prepare the students to live full and normal lives in the world outside.

At first, the students meandered through the halls in slow, timid steps, feeling the floor beneath their feet. Every now and then, someone would kick a chair or bash a kneecap on an object that wasn't there the day before. Teachers could also occasionally be heard bumping their heads, falling down a step, or tripping in the hallway. The two most important things a blind person could learn were how to bump into things and how to fall. But the school made sure that the students were never hurt too badly. And their insurance against that were the three dogs: Red, Yellow, and Green.

The Butterfly Man got along best with Red. Red was the color of the trunks he wore when he was a boxer. Red was his preferred corner of the ring. So despite his inability to see color, the Butterfly Man felt an affinity with it. The other students had similar feelings, with different sentiments touched the "color" of the dogs. Red brought back memories of a cozy evening in front of a roaring fire or of a brand-new pleated skirt. Yellow conjured up images of the summer sun or leaves falling in the autumn. Green was reminiscent of freshly picked cabbage or an invigorating springtime walk.

Every morning the Butterfly Man trained by the lake. As he shadow-boxed, he heard a steady, rhythmic breathing around him. It was Red, prancing around, never staying in the same spot for more than a second. He'd jump around, but never get too excited. And he'd always keep the right distance from the Butterfly Man; he was the perfect sparring partner.

"I felt like I was boxing against myself," the Butterfly Man said. "A self that could see."

After his training, the Butterfly Man took a quick swim in the lake, then headed back into school. He'd negotiate his way through the maze of hallways, following a trail of familiar voices to the right classroom. Interestingly, there weren't any schedules for class. They just started as soon as ten students were present. The end of a class was decided in a similar way, which meant that sometimes class could go on in one room for an entire afternoon.

"Everyone loved music," said the Butterfly Man.

"Music?" I asked, leaning forward. "What kind of class was that? Did you play instruments? Did you sing?"

The Butterfly Man shook his head, his expression gentle as usual. Apparently music class took place everywhere in the school—both indoors and out. It was a very simple lesson in which everyone sat in a circle and remained silent for about ten minutes. Then the teacher would ask the students what they could hear, and one by one the students would share the sounds they heard.

"I hear waves."

"A car braking."

"A passenger boat's whistle."

"Somebody burping."

"The guy next to me chewing on a cracker."

"A thrush, singing."

"Yellow and Red. They're playing with each other."

"I heard the phone ringing."

"A sound like adhesive tape being peeled off something."

"The principal swearing after hitting his knee in the hallway."

The students were of different ages and from very different backgrounds. Sometimes during music class, they'd laugh. Sometimes they'd let out sighs of admiration when the more subtle sounds were mentioned. Then they'd listen even more intently in the hope that they could hear the same sounds. It seemed that each student could hear at least one sound that nobody else could. This was natural. After all, the world was overflowing with sounds; it was impossible to hear every single one of them.

Within ten minutes of his first class, he'd recognized a sound that nobody else had and the game began again.

"The sound of a lathe turning."

"I heard a bird dive into the lake, then fly back up into the air."

"There's a plane. A propeller plane."

"There's somebody practicing the trumpet."

"I can hear visitors; they're whispering to each other."

"Somebody's dropped a pan in the kitchen."

"That's an owl, hooting."

The list went on and on.

Music class taught students how to listen. So much so that some of the students went on to become famous musicians now performing with large, renowned orchestras. As for the other students, they went back to their own towns, where they succeeded in living full and normal lives. It was just a matter of knowing how to listen and how to fall. There's nothing wrong with living a normal life, after all. A normal life is no worse than that for many people who can see, said the Butterfly Man.

About ten years ago, the school closed. A new student had tripped and fallen down the stairs, breaking his nose, and his parents sued. A school where the only safety measures were three sprightly dogs didn't stand a chance.

"I've always been prepared to be taken to court one day," said the founder of the school in court. "For forty years, since the day we opened, we've had not a single accident, not a single lawsuit. Each of our students has graduated with happiness and health—and that includes students from ten years old to almost sixty years old. All of them got along so well, surprisingly well. It's easy for those of us who cannot see to feel timid. Maybe that's why the school is our refuge, because we live in constant fear that at any moment we will find ourselves confronting a ferocious monster. For a long time we've been prepared ourselves. Now that attack has come in the form of a lawsuit, we will close the school."

Red, Yellow, and Green were adopted by different students. The Butterfly Man wished he could have kept Red, but someone else claimed him first. For some time after, he could still sense the presence of the dogs around him. But he knew they would never bark or approach him in public, since they were so highly trained.

"That was twenty years ago," sighed the Butterfly Man, "and sometimes I swear I can feel Red's warm breath on my legs. Like he's sitting right behind me, watching me, making sure I won't fall over."

When I got home, a thick letter from the postmaster was waiting for me. I hoped it had the answer to the question I'd asked in my last letter to him: Why were there no clocks in his sister's house?

My sister's husband was a skilled clockmaker. I myself own one of the clocks he made. And to this day it remains true down to the second. When he was around, the walls of my sister's apartment were covered in clocks. They were very happy together, and I often thought of them as being like the long hand and the short hand of a clock. Even when they were far apart, they seemed to be a part of each other. Sometimes they'd ask me to go fishing with them. But lake fishing isn't really my kind of thing. I prefer to go fishing in the ocean. Anyway, her husband was a very precise, punctual man, just like the clocks he made. If we promised to meet in a café at seven, he would arrive at precisely ten seconds to seven. By the time he'd stepped in the door and walked over to greet me, it was seven on the dot! My sister noticed it, too. She'd joke that he would come home from work every night at eight and ring the doorbell on his arrival, so her doorbell became like a clock that only chimed at eight o'clock.

One morning, as always, my sister saw her husband out of the door at precisely six o'clock. But then, just several minutes later, she heard the doorbell ring. She was shocked to see her husband standing there, his face streaming with a feverish sweat.

"I feel dizzy," he said. "I think I'm going to lie down for a bit before going to work."

He settled in on the sofa, fell asleep, and began to snore. By lunchtime he was still asleep, and still snoring. My sister decided to call an ambulance.

Tests were done. A radiologist was called in. He told my sister that a potentially fatal brain tumor had been discovered.

For two days and two nights, my sister stayed by her husband's bedside, listening to his snoring, hoping he would wake up. She noticed that his snores were punctual, occurring every two seconds. She told me that it was the same exact pattern of snoring she'd always known, that maybe there was a chance he would wake up soon. I tried my best to reassure her. What else could I do? On the third night my sister noticed that her husband's snoring pattern was different. She immediately turned on the light, and her husband opened his eyes very slightly and said, "Hi there."

"Good morning, my love," she replied, fighting back tears, "you've really overslept."

"Overslept, have I? That's not good. But I would like to sleep just a little longer."

"You mustn't!" my sister exclaimed, panicking. "If you don't get up now, you'll be late for work."

"Please, just three more minutes. Even one minute would be nice," he pleaded, then he closed his eyes. Precisely sixty seconds later, he passed quietly away.

The next day, my sister removed all the clocks in the house and sold them and the store to another clockmaker in town. She refused to leave the house since the town had so many clocks. But I think she's doing much better now. When I saw her last year she'd put on a bit of weight. She told me she'd started to feel better after enrolling in a cooking school. Good food is such an important thing. Cat, you'd better watch out that you don't put on weight while you stay there. Watch what you eat. And thanks for the stamp with the picture of the autumn festival.

I slid the letter back into its envelope and looked at the paintings lining the walls. I stood up and looked at each one more carefully than I had before, seeing scenes of fishing on the lake, of afternoon horse races, and of festival crowds. The paintings were like a scrapbook of the times life she and her husband had spent together, and within the four corners of each frame I could see time flowing differently than in the world we live in. There were two shadows in every single scene, one for the postmaster's sister and one for her husband—like a long hand and a short hand facing each other, bound together, moving together, always close.

As I peered into the scenes before me, I could begin to hear their sounds—the ripples in the lake, the galloping of horses, the ticking of the second hand. I wondered if this was how such paintings would appear to those who couldn't see. Was this how they would look in their minds?

"Oh, you're home. What are you doing there?" It was the postmaster's sister.

Slightly startled, I turned around to see her with arms full of grocery bags and scallions spilling out of the top. Wiping my eyes quickly, I pointed to one of the paintings. "I was adjusting the frame here. It was a bit crooked," I said.

Over dinner that evening, I told the postmaster's sister about Kutze. And though she didn't really seem to understand what I was telling her, she laughed and said that Kutze was an amusing name.

When I went to my room, I didn't feel like listening to music. I lay in the dark, closed my eyes, and listened to the sounds around me. A bit after midnight, I heard a noise on the other side of the door. It was the sound of a broom gently caressing the floor, and the floorboards responding with soft gives and takes. It was the sound of the postmaster's sister walking around the room, then stopping, perhaps in front of a painting, and moving on to the next, and the next. She walked around the room, from painting to painting, from floorboard to floorboard. And each time she came to a stop, I saw the things as she did. Her husband's back as he walked down the staircase of the apartment building. His delicate fingers around a glistening trout he'd just reeled in. A horse crossing the finish line as the clock maker turned to his wife and said, "That's a record for this course! Two minutes, fifteen point three seconds. Two minutes, fifteen point three seconds!"

I began to picture the lake at the school for the blind the Butterfly Man attended. Not as I might see it, but as it appeared to the Butterfly Man. And as I did, I ran my pen along my notebook in the dark. Slowly, through the night, my notebook became populated with musical notes. I'd written *The Waltz of the Red Dog and the Blind Boxer*. It was the first piece I'd ever composed.

From my scrapbook, October 12th

★

Don't worry if your grades aren't so good. It's just because you're too kindhearted compared to the other students. Unlike them, you don't feel the need to push people aside so you can get where you want to go. Just keep doing what you're doing, and eventually things will fall into place. By the way, good luck with your end-of-the-year performance. My sister tells me she'll be there, but unfortunately it looks like I won't be able to make it. I'll have to make do with a tape recording.

The whole band is really looking forward to playing with you again. I know you're busy with everything, but if you're able to take some time off you should come home. Though I suppose it's not such a bad thing for there to be a period in your life when you focus your energy on something to the extent that you don't even have time to think about your hometown for a while.

★

The mice move in packs of primes, with the density of the pack being directly related to that prime. But which prime number makes for the most stable group? I need to continue experimenting for a while. Need a bigger cage. I'm sure my buddy will help me find something.

★

The Genius Horse with the Foolish Owner
  The secret of the Genius Horse has finally come to light. As many remember, the Genius Horse became renowned for its ability to answer questions involving multiplication and division, the ages of visitors, and even the population of towns. The owner would simply ask the horse questions like "What's five times four?" or "How old is this person?" and the horse would raise its fore leg and tap out the numeric answer. It has since come to light that the horse was not actually making any calculations but was reacting to the people around it. After each question, the horse would begin tapping while carefully watching the owner and the audience. When it reached the right number of taps, the horse was able to sense a slight increase

in the heart rate of the crowd, smell a change in the sweat on people's foreheads and armpits, and stop tapping. This all came to light because a student intern at the newspaper conducted an experiment in which he put the horse in one room and asked it questions from another. No matter what the horse was asked, it just stood still and smiled. Nevertheless, the horse did display an exceptional level of sensitivity in its trick, which is nothing to be scoffed at. After all, animals interact with this world using an array of senses unavailable to us, so if anything it's the horse owner and journalists who built up the story who are the real fools. They genuinely believed that the horse could calculate. Perhaps the horse was smarter than humans after all!

From my scrapbook, November 3rd

★

I was surprised to learn that you've decided on an original string quartet piece for your end-of-the-year recital. Your grandpa didn't seem at all surprised, though. He says that the cello, the viola, and other instruments with strings that are plucked or have bows drawn across them are just an extension of percussion, and that the list we sent you includes not only string quartets but piano and harp sonatas, too. Do you think you'll ever compose something for the harp? I always think of the harp as an instrument played by women in frilly dresses and an unwavering grin on their faces. It's hard to imagine you composing for anything like that.

By the way, Cat, I wanted to recommend that you don't come back to town for a little while. Something has happened here recently. It just smells wrong. It's a smell that is nothing like the one that dogged us last year, although it has spread throughout the town in the same way. I'm afraid of the damage it might do to our noses and ears, and I wouldn't want any harm to come to yours.

★

The experiments all support my theory. I am both scared and excited that I may be on the brink of entering into an entirely new mathematical frontier. I'm going to write up my findings, and by next year's symposium I'll finally be accepted into the Academy of Mathematics.

★

Blind Boxer Lands Pickpocket a Right Hook!

Last night something strange happened on a train heading out to the suburbs. A powerfully built sports trainer caught a pickpocket red-handed. To catch a thief is not so unusual, but what is extraordinary is that the hero was a blind man, who later said:

"I heard the sound of a razor cutting the fabric of the suit of the person standing next to me. Normally, I would have let something like that go. But in this case, the poor guy had just given up his seat in politeness to an elderly lady. So the moment I heard the thief's hands touch the guy's wallet, I whipped around and grabbed the thief and my right hand found his chin. I went easy, though. I didn't break any bones or anything."

The hero of our story was once a professional heavyweight boxer who had been ranked third in the nation. His boxing career came to an abrupt end when he lost his eyesight in an accident in the ring. But after bravely and successfully undergoing a rehabilitation program, he stays fighting fit in his current role as a sports trainer.

"I don't know if it was a good thing or bad thing, losing my sight," he said. "But I have no intention of trying to regain what I lost. I also just want to say that it was very unlike me to do what I did."

Following his heroic actions, the railway's security department offered the sports trainer a job as a special security guard. But the heroic blind boxer just laughed as if he'd heard the funniest joke in the word. Then he skipped away from the scene.

From my scrapbook, December 21st

★

The Letter I Never Sent

Dear Postmaster, Grandpa, and everyone in the band,

I hope you are all doing well. Because I am not. I had a recital yesterday in which I was to play my new composition, The Waltz of the Red Dog and the Blind Boxer. *As I may have mentioned to you, this was intended to be a percussion ensemble, but the teacher decided to change it into a piece for a string quartet and I'm afraid I didn't manage to get to the end.*

As soon as I got up on stage, I could hear people in the audience giggling. Then, from a section where the older students were sitting, one of the kids shouted out, "Look! It's a circus act! There's a clown on stilts!"

Soon, everyone was applauding. Not at me and my music. But at that stupid joke. I started to feel a little giddy, but I made it over to the podium. Then a woman in the audience shouted, "Can you get out of the way? I can't see my child!" Of course, that was followed by another round of immature laughter.

I decided to go on anyway and swung the baton into action. But by the time I'd reached the thirty-second bar, the first violin stopped playing. Then the second viola. Then the cello. I stood there dumbfounded. The kid on the first violin said, "I'm sorry," in a voice that reverberated throughout the auditorium, "but I can't go on. My neck is hurting too much from straining to look up at you."

Of course, another dreadful wave of laughter made its way through the auditorium. I immediately stepped off the podium and walked off the stage.

Afterward, the teacher said to me, "You simply aren't cut out for conducting. That waltz wasn't music. It was noise! Perhaps you should concentrate on learning to play the piano." Then he gave me a piece of gum. I guess even he felt bad for me.

From my scrapbook, March 23rd

★

Long time no see! How are you doing? Drop me a line when you get a chance! Things are going well here. The band has been doing very well since last year's fireworks festival, and the vice-principal has become quite proficient on the snare drum. I look forward to his parts when I stand on the podium conducting. Your grandpa really is a talented man, although I have to say he hasn't talked to me much recently.

By the way, I have some news! Me and four other band members are buying a boat together! It's a foreign-made, seven-seat schooner with a cabin, and it should be ready by this coming summer. What's more, the band is going to make a record! Isn't that amazing?

★

Not much longer until my mathematical theory is complete. My buddy and the mice in the cages are all watching and awaiting my final steps. I'm so close now. Pray for me.

★

The Reincarnating Man Remembers
Welcome to the column in which, every week, we interview the Miraculous Reincarnating Man with three thousand years of memories. This week, we have asked him to go back seventy-five years to when he was a demolition expert. By the way, we are receiving lots of inquiries about his photograph, and we want to be clear that the picture you see of him in the newspaper is in his current incarnation. He does look very young since he has been in his present incarnation for only nineteen years, but if you were to meet him you would sense immediately that you are in the presence of a very, very old soul.

"Back when I worked in demolition, I always knew immediately where the explosives were best placed in a building. I didn't need to see the blueprints. I'd just picture the building exploding in my mind, with its flash of light, the dust, flying debris, and smoke. If I could picture that scene, then I could trace the best place to set the charges. As in my other incarnations, I wasn't just an engineer, but someone with special abilities. The moment I stepped into a vacated building, all the mice, roaches, flies, mosquitoes, and even dragonflies would emerge from their hiding places and escape through the nearest exit. But the day I remember most clearly was seventy-five years and thirty-three days ago—a day on which I knew in advance I would lose my life. But, as is always the case with me, I wasn't sure how it would happen. On that fateful day, I went around the building carefully installing the charges. I remember it was an ideal building, and what I mean by that is that I could envision it exploding in my mind in a very clean manner, with those flashes of light followed by that mass of brick and stone collapsing to the ground like a huge pillar of salt.

"After I finished setting charges on each of the twenty floors, I went down to the basement. You see, to make sure that a building collapses vertically in a controlled manner, you have to pay particular attention to the way you set the charges in the basement. As I toiled away down there, I noticed how incredibly humid it was. And as I wiped a bead of sweat from my forehead, I heard an unfamiliar sound in the dark. I pointed my lamp to where the sound had come from, only to find a mouse blinking at me. It was an unusually large mouse. Perhaps it was too big to run away like the others. But it looked aggravated and it was nibbling at the wiring! At that moment, I knew what lay in store for me. I quickly blew out my candle. I saw sparks dancing in the dark and the faint sound of the mouse scampering away. Then, before I could take another step, the tip of one of the wires contacted the gunpowder and I was enveloped in a thunderous roar!

"Even today, the body I inhabited for that incarnation remains buried deep in the ground underneath what is now a district of government buildings."

Join us next week, when the reincarnating man will be sharing his memories from five hundred and forty years ago, when he was appointed royal bard!

The School for the Blind in Summer

The Butterfly Man was leaning against the handrail on the deck of the passenger boat with the downy hairs on the back of his head swaying in the breeze. As I walked up from behind, he turned to me, chuckled, and said, "Ice cream!"

He took the cup I'd brought for him, cracked its frozen surface with a spoon, and carefully slipped the first spoonful into his mouth. His was raspberry, light pink in color. Mine was vanilla.

The passenger boat made three trips around the lake a day. That particular day was a holiday, and we were there early, with only a scattering of people on deck. We watched in peace as the soft June light bounced off the crests of the waves and listened as three maritime whistles echoed lakeside.

"This is delicious," said the Butterfly Man, pointing with his spoon. "The ice cream on this boat is way better than it was ten, twenty years ago. Nothing else has changed, though. There's still that funny-sounding whistle and the engine that sounds like it has a bad case of asthma. The guy even says the same exact thing when he takes your ticket: 'If there is anyone who cannot see, please wait until everyone else has boarded and use the sounds of the people in front as your guide.' I don't know why he still says that. Surely there can't be many blind people who need to cross to the other side anymore."

I thought back on the six months since I'd composed the *The Waltz of the Red Dog and Blind Boxer.* I'd actually written another twenty pieces since then. And each time I'd completed one and take it to school, my classmates and teachers responded with disdain.

"Another percussion piece?" my head teacher would say. "Who wants to listen to a whole hour of drums?"

Once he questioned an unusual part I'd incorporated into a piece. "What is this—'glass falling on a carpet'?"

"Well that's basically what it is," I explained. "You lay a carpet out on stage and drop a dozen glasses on it at once."

"That's ridiculous," he sneered.

In conducting class, all the other students had progressed to practicing in concert with the senior students—not me. The headmaster would sit in on their performances, occasionally calling to the teacher and saying: "Get that big one standing at the corner of the stage. Get him up onto the podium." Then the headmaster and his friends would watch me drag myself onto stage, laughing out loud and clapping their hands above their heads.

None of my performances lasted longer than three minutes. The violinists, the oboists…everyone would start to make mistakes and soon enough would stop playing altogether.

"Sorry," they'd say. "We're not used to a conductor so tall."

When I walked into town I always got a terrible ringing in my ears that wouldn't go away—not even when I was back in my room listening to the records Grandpa had gotten me. But eventually the ringing would subside and I'd hear the sounds that would let me sigh and relax.

Ton, Ta-tan

Kutze's steps in the distance.

Ta-tan, Ton

Those soothing steps.

Ton, Ta-tan, Ton

Another thing that kept me from giving up on music forever was the file of sheet music left me by the caretaker. One day, I took one of the compositions from the file and traced my finger along its complex notations, trying to make sense of them. As my throat grew parched, I suddenly realized I had a masterpiece in my hands.

At a first glance, the piece appeared to have no order to it. It had been inspired by the caretaker's gossip magazines and the sounds of the school playground, and it brought back, through sounds, vivid memories of the many scrapbooks he kept. It was like a map that guided me the way through this crazy world, reminding me of the sonic maps drawn in the minds of blind people. The more I studied the piece, the more I came to recognize its hidden order, with distant notes working together and connections appearing where there had been only disconnection before. As I learned its secrets, I begun to swing my baton in time, and I didn't put it down until dawn.

I thought back to that day I'd arrived at school late as usual and immediately sent to the teacher's room where I was abruptly told that I had failed. "All the teachers and the other students will be busy preparing for the concert from now," said the teacher, popping a piece of gum into his mouth. "We won't be needing you to come in until next semester. That is, if you still have plans to continue."

So here I was, standing on the deck of a boat with the Butterfly Man, who was excited to be visiting his old school.

"A couple of former staff members still live in the caretaker's office." He said. "I'm sure they'd be happy to let us walk around the grounds if I ask."

As we approached lakeside, I could see parasols dotting an empty lakeside stretch. The Butterfly Man was leaning against the railing, appearing to be enjoying the breezes on his face.

"Quiet, isn't it," he said. "It's like things just stopped here."

A gravel path stretched up a gentle hill from where the boat moored. The Butterfly Man set off, stepping as if savoring the feel of the familiar gravel under his feet. Along the sides of the path were summer plants swaying in the breeze, and I watched as the Butterfly Man stopped occasionally to drink in their gentle sounds.

At the caretaker's office, an elderly couple was taking a nap.

"Oh, it's the boxer!" exclaimed the woman, getting up. She was missing a front tooth. "It's so nice to see you! It's been such a while. I can see your tattoo has faded."

"I know. It's good to see you, too. Would you mind if we took a stroll around the grounds?" asked the Butterfly Man.

"Sure, sure. Go ahead." The woman smiled as she handed him a ring of keys, adding, "If you happen to come across any soda cans or other trash, pick them up and throw them away for us, will you?"

As we neared the reddish brown brick walls of the school building, there were yellow-flowering weeds everywhere. The Butterfly Man felt for the doorknob and slowly inserted one of the keys. The building was cool. Both sides of the hallway were lined with tall boards—each of which had the scribblings of rude words. These must have been the boards that served as obstacles to train the students for dealing with the ever-changing street life outside.

I followed the Butterfly Man through the dim hallway. Every so often, he'd stick his hands out in front of himself in search for some long since removed obstacle.

"This is where I jammed my toe," he said with a whisper that travelled along the hallway. "And who would have expected to find a chair sitting on top of a desk here?"

The Butterfly Man continued to navigate his way past memories of other obstacles until he came to a classroom. The room was empty but you could tell where the blackboard used to hang on the wall. He told me that they had used a blackboard in class even though nobody could see what was written on it. The students who had been born blind seemed to be able to write with nice smooth strokes. The Butterfly Man told me that he could tell that those students were writing on the board using, not just their hands, but their entire bodies.

"I always sat here. At this desk," said the Butterfly Man, turning to face me. "I was a big guy, so the headmaster had a chair and desk made specially for me. It was a very simple thing. Just four legs nailed to a piece of wood," he said, his hands demonstrating. I loved sitting up at the front. I could hear everything the teacher said. My big old makeshift desk was always right at the very front."

"It was the exact opposite for me," I said. "I always had to sit in the back because I was so big. Even when I went up a grade, or when the class changed seats in the middle of the year, my seat was in the back. I didn't think much about it at first, but later I thought it wasn't right. Why was I the only one stuck in the same seat all the time? I never got used to it, looking at everyone's back all the time. The view never changed."

"What did it feel like?" the Butterfly Man asked.

"Like I was a spy from somewhere else."

"Funny. You know, even when I was sitting at the very front," said the Butterfly Man, "I still felt like I was sitting at the very back. In that way, I guess it didn't matter where I sat. There was such a pitch-black gap between the teacher and me. Gaping jaws with sharp teeth in front of me, with the teacher far on the other side."

The Butterfly Man paused briefly before continuing.

"But if you stretched out your arm far enough, you could reach the teacher. Maybe every kid at the school felt like he was sitting in the very back. I can't explain it, but that's kind of what being blind feels like."

When we returned to the caretaker's office, the elderly man served us tea in paper cups.

"We get four, five graduates like you stopping by every month," he said. "It's interesting, they always bring a seeing friend along. This was an unusual place, so it shouldn't be surprising to think that seeing people might want to come here to look at the place, too."

"No wonder then the announcement on the boat hasn't changed," said the Butterfly Man as he sipped his tea. Then frowning, he sniffed at his paper cup, and the caretaker responded by passing him the sugar bowl. As I watched the Butterfly Man plop four cubes into his tea and the caretaker return the bowl to his desk, it would have been easy to forget that both men were blind. When I tasted the tea and noted its peculiar color, I realized how having sight had handicapped me from enjoying that same beverage.

The caretaker's wife had sight. She'd been responsible for the school's accounts, and it was at the school that she met her husband, who'd lost his sight in an accident involving a gas leak. After the school was closed, they'd stayed behind and lived in the caretaker's quarters. They'd been living there for some thirty years now. Apparently, at their wedding, the caretaker—who was still a novice at being blind—accidentally set fire to the bride's veil. The Butterfly Man also told the story of when a lady in town hit the caretaker with a shopping basket when she caught him walking hand in hand with a young woman. The young woman was actually a nun who had lent him a guiding hand.

One of the jobs of the caretaker and his wife was to manage the trust fund that had been set up by the school's alumni. The wife would read out the numbers, the caretaker would do the calculations—in his head—and the wife would write them down in the ledger. "When I do calculations," he said proudly, "I can picture about twenty gas meters in my mind, and all of them are moving. Not once have I ever gotten a calculation wrong!"

"By the way," the caretaker suddenly added, "were you ever close to the dogs? One of the graduates who visited about six months ago told me that Green, the dog he'd adopted for his daughter, had given birth to seven puppies."

"Is that right?" said the Butterfly Man, looking up. "Who was this guy?"

The caretaker gave the name of a famous cellist, one whose records I'd listened to, as if it was no big deal.

"Oh, him!" said the Butterfly Man. "He came to the school the same year I did. He'd lost most of his sight after a botched cataract operation. He was pig-headed, but for some reason the two of us got along well."

"He lives abroad now," said the caretaker. "He came back to the city looking for a new cello and stopped by."

"So he took Green, eh?" said the Butterfly Man, nodding to himself. Green, he later explained, was the alpha dog, often reining in Red whenever he got out of hand and encouraging the timid Yellow.

"How about the other dogs? Where'd they go?"

"Are you there?" called the caretaker to his wife in the direction. "He's asking about the dogs. Tell him what happened to them."

"All right, all right," said the caretaker's wife as she came out from the back, wiping her hands on her apron. She was covered in chicken feathers and had a large chopping knife in one hand.

"It's always the dogs, dogs, dogs. Why does everybody who comes back want to know about the dogs? When the school shut down, I was busy taking care of accounts. It's been ten years since then. As I'm sure he knows very well, they're not here anymore."

"But he just wants to know who took them and what happened."

"Well then, why don't you open that stinking mouth of yours and tell him yourself?" the caretaker's wife grumbled. "Oh, all right. Yellow was adopted by some old man who worked in City Hall. I'm afraid one night his owner was attacked by a gang of thugs and Yellow jumped in to save him. Unfortunately, poor old Yellow took a nasty kick to the stomach, and he died soon after."

"That's terrible," said the Butterfly Man.

"The other dog was adopted by the headmaster's nephew, who was the last graduate of this school. A good kid, though a bit absent-minded. Anyway, there was a reunion that summer after the trial, and the headmaster visited for the first time. His nephew was coming over on the last boat of the day, along with the dog. The day was very windy—windy enough to take my husband's overalls off the clothes line and blow them away! The nephew was all excited about the reunion, walking all over the deck, when a sudden gust of wind took off with his straw hat. He tried to catch it and fell over the railing and into the lake! Instinctively, the dog jumped in after him. Within a few minutes, a rescue boat managed to pull the poor nephew out of the water. But his hat was gone. And so was the dog."

Ruefully, the caretaker's wife stood, then turned away. Before she got to the back of the office, she turned to face us again. "They were such admirable dogs," she said. "Why don't you guys follow their example? Wear a collar and grow a tail if you have to. You might be the better for it."

The caretaker stirred the thick tea in his mug and said, "She may have a foul mouth on her, but she loved the dogs more than anyone."

"Yes, I remember that," said the Butterfly Man. "She was the one who bought them different colored bowls."

"When she came back to the office and saw that the dogs were gone, she was so upset. But they were so highly trained, I thought that rather than live out their days here doing nothing, they should fulfill the roles they were trained for. That's why I talked to the headmaster and asked visiting students if they'd like to adopt them."

"I see," said the Butterfly Man, putting out his right hand. "I don't think you made the wrong choice."

"Thanks," said the caretaker with a smile as he touched the back of the Butterfly Man's hand. "All the visitors say that. But I know I could never bring myself to get another dog."

The Butterfly Man and I spent the rest of the afternoon walking around the school grounds. We walked along the path that snaked through the woods like a maze, past the workshop overrun with weeds, until we came to the dormitory. The walls of the two story red brick building were covered in names—names former students had carved on their visits, some way down low near the ground and some so high even I couldn't reach them.

"Where's yours?" I asked.

The Butterfly man smiled shyly and pointed to a picture carved above my head.

"You should carve your name as well," he said, handing me a piece of broken brick. "I know you're not blind, but you're one of the visitors here. I think you have just as much right to leave your mark."

I took the piece of brick from him and stood in front of the wall for a few moments, listening to the sounds of pine trees swaying in the breeze and chickens flapping their wings. Then I closed my eyes and started to draw. Even with my eyes wide open, I'd never been much good at drawing, so I saw no harm in doing it blind.

"It's a cat, isn't it?" said the Butterfly Man from behind me.

"That's what it was meant to be anyway," I said, embarrassed by the crude drawing. "I should have kept my eyes closed! I don't even want to admit to drawing that."

"Well, it looks like a proper cat to me," he said. "I see its ears, its whiskers, four legs, and a tail."

"I totally forgot to draw in the whiskers and tail!"

"Oh! I didn't notice that," he said. "I guess that must be one of the disadvantages of being able to see."

Onward we walked, through the pine forest until we reached an opening onto the lakeside beach, where the sun was setting in the western sky, the evening breeze blowing fine ripples across the glassy surface, and the sails of the boats were tinged a brilliant red.

The Butterfly Man took off his windbreaker and stood with his bulging chest straining at his tank top. Then nodding in my direction, he started running along the deserted beach—going at a leisurely pace before sprinting, then slowing, then sprinting again, until you could see his sweat glistening in the fading light and hear his breathing, like a steam engine, against the gentle sounds of lapping water.

When he eventually came to a stop, he did several star jumps, crouched down, and sprang up again. Then he launched into a bout of shadow boxing. I'd already learned a little bit about boxing from him, so I knew that t the quick snap with his left was a jab, the long straight punch with his right was a cross, and the quick turn in his left arm was a hook. He kept his left foot in front of his right and shifted his weight by using your left foot like a spring whenever he threw a punch.

The Butterfly Man looked as if he was dancing with an invisible partner to music nobody could hear, surrounded by students no longer there. I watched him swing his big arms in the direction of Red's breath, and I found myself humming that waltz, the first piece I'd ever composed. It was a piece that seemed perfectly matched to his movements, and the mood even captured Red's bounding around his ankles.

I listened to the Butterfly Man's steady breathing, each intake of breath linked to a specific movement. This made me remember the caretaker back home saying how Grandpa was "music itself"—which I didn't understand then at all. But now as I witnessed the Butterfly Man with his fluttering agility dancing by the edge of the lake, I saw that *he* was music embodied. I found myself unconsciously tapping out a beat with my fingers on the rocks. It wasn't anything like *Fanfare for the Fighting Kids* or *The Waltz of the Red Dog and the Blind Boxer*. It was like an entirely different kind of music that seemed to seep in from another world, welling up through the beach, washing over the grounds of the school, sending echoes through the dark hallways, and bouncing off the names and pictures etched into the walls of the dormitory. Then, off it went across the serene sunset surface of the lake beyond and deep down to the bottom where Red lay in peace.

As the Butterfly Man continued throwing jabs in the setting sun, small waves flowed over the tops of his sneakers. It was the wake of the boat making its final trip of the day. The Butterfly Man bent down to feel his sneakers, and the sight of his shadow, with his head bowed, stretching across the sand was like a prayer to the sunset. A prayer that would never be answered. At least, not in this world.

"I didn't hear the boat at all!" exclaimed the Butterfly Man. "All I heard was the sound of the waves and the beat you were tapping out on the rocks. That's what really got me going. You know I haven't moved like this in a while. But we missed the boat and have to stay the night. It's no big deal. I guess it was just meant to be."

A little while later, the caretaker's wife came out to meet us and give us some of her chicken soup. The Butterfly Man quietly sat there sipping on it, occasionally blowing on his wrists and arms to shoo the mosquitoes away, which then came and settled on me!

After the sun had set, the sky remained quite bright, and the surface of the lake glowed in the rising moonlight.

"This place hasn't changed at all," said the Butterfly Man. "But one important thing has. And there's no way of changing it back."

"What's that?" I asked.

"The obvious. You don't hear people's voices. The night breeze is still a western wind. The sounds of fishing boats still come from the same direction as before. But the whispering of students in the dormitories, the late-night radio shows the teachers used to listen to—those sounds have disappeared. You'd think you'd be able to hear the sound of the wind and the waves better now, but for some reason those sounds seem more foggy, harder to hear."

"Perhaps you're just getting old," I said.

"Perhaps you're right."

The Butterfly Man lay down on the sand, and I did the same.

I looked up and gasped.

"What is it?" asked my friend.

"The sky," I said, seeing the carpet of stars above. "It's breathtaking." Beyond the blurry brightness that ringed the moon and the lights of the town in the distance, the sky was simply covered in specks of light. Oddly enough, not one twinkled. They just emitted a constant glow that was reflected in the water below.

"The air around here is so clean. And this is the highest point on the island," said the Butterfly Man, yawning. "The temperature stays constant, too. That's why the stars don't twinkle. At least that's what I've been told. Is it that different from in your town or in the city?"

"It's different," I said. "Completely different."

"You know, I just remembered something. Something from twenty years ago," he said, rolling over to face me. "One night, right around this time of year, we had a music lesson out here on this very beach. We sat listening to the sounds all around us until the teacher asked us to describe the things we'd heard. One boy had heard something skipping across the surface of the lake. Another heard a pair of owls. Yet another heard cicadas, and on and on. But eventually, one of the students shouted, 'A shooting star!'"

I sat up immediately. "Do you mean he was actually able to hear the sound of a shooting star?"

"That's what he said. We all turned to him, sure he was pulling our leg. But he was a stubborn kid and he insisted. 'How come you don't hear the stars?' he said, 'especially when they're raining down on us all the time.' The teacher suggested that we all try to listen. We lay down on the sand, facing the sky we couldn't even see. We couldn't tell if there were any shooting stars or not. We could hear the sound of waves lapping up against the shore. We could hear each other's breathing. I thought the whole exercise was silly and was just about to sit up when somebody shouted, 'I heard it!'

"'A shooting star?' asked our teacher.

"'I don't know exactly what it was,' said the boy, 'but something was whizzing across the sky.'

"At that moment, several other students called out that they could hear it, too. The teacher asked them to calm down. 'Some of us haven't been able to hear it yet. Let's keep listening. That's the only rule we have in this class.'

"Everyone immediately fell silent. After a while, I began to think that I was actually hearing the sound of motion. I held my breath and strained my ears. No question about it. And not my imagination. I could hear a sound in the night sky! What's more, I could also sense it was emitting heat. *Had* to be a shooting star. In the end, we stayed out on the beach listening all night long. And every time I heard another shooting star, I felt as if these eyes of mine could see again."

After letting out a deep sigh, the Butterfly Man turned to me again. "We all fell asleep like that on the beach. Then, the next morning, I apologized to the kid who first heard the shooting star. He just laughed and said, 'Grains of sand.'"

"What?!"

"That's what he said. He said he really had heard a shooting star. But since everyone made fun of him for saying so, he took things in his own hands. He took a couple grains of sand between his fingers and flipped them into the air. 'You can make them fly far if you snap your wrists right,' he explained. 'I really did hear a shooting star. I just thought I'd let you guys experience something similar, that's all.'"

I couldn't help but laugh. The Butterfly Man smiled as well.

"Made me like the kid a lot," he said. "He'd make unusual sounds during class, and I started looking forward to listening for them. But then he graduated a year ahead of me and went back to his home country, where he became a famous cellist. He's the guy who adopted Green."

I looked back up at those infinite specks of light that peppered the sky and wondered what kind of music they made. I couldn't hear anything with my eyes open, and shutting them didn't help. All I could hear was the sounds of waves at the shore. The whispering breezes that meandered through the pine forest. A pine cone as it rolled along the beach. The merry-go-round in the amusement park at the other side of the lake. The Butterfly Man rubbing his shoulders. And the footsteps, so very far away. Further than the stars in the heavens above.

It was Kutze, stepp'n on wheat.

Ton, Ta-tan, Ton

I closed my eyes.

Ton

Ta-tan, Ta-tan

I opened my eyes.

The Butterfly Man was gazing into the night sky he could not see, coughing to the rhythm of Kutze's steps.

"I've been thinking," he said. "Why don't you go visit him?"

"Visit who?"

"The cellist. You can learn about music from him. I'm sure he'll like you. You know, the city isn't a bad place. But I think we both know it's not really for you. I think you should venture out to a different world—one farther way. Go to where the cellist lives. It's a town filled with music and everything else, too. With the most unpleasant things you can imagine. And the most delightful things, too!"

It sounded as if the Butterfly Man was speaking about the town where Grandpa and Dad were supposed to have had such a horrible life that they left. I asked the Butterfly Man if that was really the place he was talking about.

"That's right," he said. "That's the town."

"And you have heard this guy play the cello?"

"I heard him give a solo concert about five years ago. He was making music with his cello and bow that was out of this world."

Ah! At that moment, I remembered the comment written by Grandpa on the list of records he'd made for me: *This is a performance that makes you think of the very first person to have ever laid hands on a cello.*

This made me think of Grandpa and me walking home after rehearsal and how he'd often say, "You know what, Cat? I've always wanted to play the way the monkeys did with the first-ever percussion instruments."

For a moment, I fantasized about the Butterfly Man's suggestion. Then the real world came back to me. "Thanks, but there's really no way I could go," I sighed.

"Why not?"

"I couldn't afford it," I said with a laugh. "There's the travel, the room and board, the study…Even if I found some work there, I'd probably still just scrape by. And I wouldn't have any time to practice my music. I like to read quite a lot of papers, too, you see. And I know that times are tough there."

"But you won't have to worry about living costs," replied the Butterfly Man. "He'll pay for it all. If you do odd chores around the house, like polishing his instruments, he'll even give you lessons. Whenever he's not traveling to perform, he has plenty of time on his hands. He can be a bit stubborn guy, but I know the right way to ask him for a favor."

"It's not just the living costs," I insisted. "If I quit school now, I'll have to pay back my scholarship. I've only been there a year, but even that would add up to a lot of money. I don't want to be the kind of person that runs away from a debt. My grandpa never was. My dad isn't. And I'm not."

The Butterfly Man took a deep breath, as if readying to say something grand. Then he let out his breath again, put his sunglasses down on the sand, and turned on his side, letting grains of sand trickle down his back.

After a while, I could tell that he'd fallen asleep. I looked up at the sky again and thought of the cellist, of the puppies born of a dog named Green, and of the unpleasant town where Grandpa, Dad, and Mom, too, had lived before I was born. Such unpleasant things. Such delightful things. Such a horrible life.

I gazed deeper into space. I started to feel as if the stars were shining even brighter than before and that the darkness that lay between them was darker than I'd ever taken the time to notice. It was a darkness that connected the stars across infinity. A collective without end. And I wondered how those same stars might look from the deck of a ship bound for a foreign land.

The Butterfly Man rolled over in his sleep again. Above us, the infinite sky above moved, slowly, soundlessly.

The next day, we boarded the boat to make our way back to the city, and despite the early morning hour, the boat was crowded. It appeared that people used the boat to go to work. And unlike the clear night before, the sky was now filled with dark clouds.

Once we got to the other side of the lake and disembarked, the Butterfly Man waved at me and said, "I'm going straight to the gym." It was eight o'clock in the morning.

As for me, I needed to run home for my books and my baton before heading off to school. I dashed up the stairs to the apartment and found the postmaster's sister dozing on the couch with her kitchen apron on. I did my best not to wake her, tiptoeing to my room. But as soon as I placed my hand on the doorknob, she sat bolt upright.

"Cat, oh, Cat!" she cried, running over and placing her arms around me. "I got a telegraph from my brother last night. You need to go home right away. Something's happened to your father!"

Let Shiny New Black Wings Carry You to a New World

When I arrived back in my town for the first time since the summer of the year before, the postmaster met me at the station. It was raining. Not mice, though. Just regular old rain. Several staff members were sweeping away water that had flooded the waiting room.

I'd heard on the train that the town had been experiencing record rainfall, but I knew it wasn't the rain that was responsible for the depression engulfing the town.

"The firemen have been searching the canal since last night," said the postmaster from under his umbrella. I noted his sunken cheeks and his hair that seemed to emit a stench that stung my eyes. Later I learned the smell was from a new hair-growth tonic he'd bought from the travelling salesman. It was a smell that got worse by day, one you couldn't get rid of, no matter how many times you washed your hair.

"The canal is flowing too fast," continued the postmaster as we walked along, "so that's really held us back in searching for your dad."

When I arrived home, two police officers were waiting for me. They asked if Dad had written me any letters. I took the scrapbook I'd brought with me and showed them what I had.

"Where's Grandpa?" I asked.

"He's resting upstairs," said elder officer. "The postmaster went to register him at the hospital this morning. He should be able to admit himself by noon tomorrow."

"This doesn't really help," mumbled the younger officer as he snapped the scrapbook shut. Then he turned to the postmaster and asked, "Are you sure the salesman didn't say where he was going next?"

"Yes, I'm sure. If I had any idea," replied the postmaster, his voice so full of distaste he sounded like he just gulped down a glass of mud, "I'd go there right now and punch him in the face!"

"That would be letting him off easy," the younger officer snorted. "I'd nail him by his tongue to the bottom of the river!"

"That's enough," said the elder officer, gesturing for me to sit down.

"What happened?" I asked, aware that everyone was staring at my huge frame.

The elder policeman let out a sigh. Then he began to tell what turned out to be a very long story, with the younger policeman—whose mother, I learned later, had been hospitalized the night before—piping up from time to time.

Dad, or "the Mouse Man" as some people referred to him, had found his fit in the town where I grew up. He'd made a name for himself through his many odd experiments and his habit of bringing baskets of mice with him to the schoolyard—before classes or after classes, that is. You wouldn't say that he was a particularly popular man. But his experiments at least provided comic relief for the local drunks when they got tired of their idle chitchat or for the local children, who would find a seat in the corner of the school grounds and cheer as Dad let loose a herd of mice.

One morning, a stranger walked through the school gates and out onto the field. His hair was heavily greased and neatly parted down the middle, and he was carrying a leather briefcase. He wore an iridescent suit—one of those expensive items that changed color depending on the angle you were viewing it from—and there were neat creases in his trousers and a deep shine to his shoes.

"Good morning!" he called out as he approached the crowd of people sitting in the corner of the field. "I've just arrived in town. Can any of you tell me what on earth that man bending down in the middle of the yard is doing?"

"He's doing an experiment with mice," said a sailor's son.

"An experiment? What kind of experiment?"

Nobody knew the answer.

Without wasting another moment, the man strode over to my dad. "Good morning," he said.

Dad didn't turn around.

"I hear you're doing an experiment with mice," said the man.

Still, Dad didn't move.

"Is the experiment going well?" asked the man.

"Please, can you be quiet?" said the Mouse Man, without taking his eyes from what he was doing. "You're scaring the mice."

The man folded his arms and observed the mice in the basket for a while. Then he said, "I don't think a school yard is the best place for conducting pharmaceutical experiments on mice."

"Who said anything about pharmaceutical experiments?"

"Well, an ecological experiment, then. Or is it a medical experiment, perhaps? You know, I used to work in the field of science before I got into the business of selling shoes."

"Then you should be able to tell," said my father, "that I'm conducting a mathematical experiment."

"A mathematical experiment, you say?" The salesman sounded genuinely surprised.

"Can I take it from your tone of voice that mathematics is something you're familiar with?"

"Somewhat familiar, yes. But, to be honest, this is the first time I've ever come across a mathematician so interested in conducting experiments."

"Listen here…" said Dad, stopping to glare at the salesman, "it may interest you to know that mathematics is the source of all phenomena in this world. Everyone knows that mathematics comes into play in astronomy, river currents, the weather, and population change. But what I'm trying to do is apply mathematics to the seemingly random actions of humans and animals. And the two key concepts involved are 'prime numbers' and 'sets.'"

"I see." The salesman nodded, emphatically. "Prime numbers, eh? So I imagine you're trying to find the largest prime number of mice that will form a set. Is that right?"

"That's exactly right."

Immediately, Dad stood up, gratified to discover the stranger's hidden intelligence. Then he immediately reverted to his usual grumpy self. He wanted to explain more about his mathematical findings, but he had yet to identify any kind of order in the sets of mice. In fact, all the mice he'd released in the schoolyard the past couple of months had simply scrambled in different directions in small prime groups of three or five. But the salesman didn't give up. He was like a hunting dog with his jaws locked onto his catch, keeping on asking questions of my dad in a cheery tone. Soon enough, the salesman succeeded in getting Dad to share all his findings.

"I was surprised to hear the Mouse Man talk so much," said the barber, who had been listening to their conversation. "That salesman certainly had a talent for getting people to talk. In my forty years running this business, I've never come across a smoother listener."

When the salesman appeared in the schoolyard the very next day, he sat down next to Dad, opened his leather briefcase, and removed a pair of surgeon gloves. The nosy crowd took a step closer.

"I hope you don't mind," began the salesman. "Your idea is truly visionary. But there is one fatal flaw. I was giving it some consideration last night, and I came to the conclusion that an animal's instincts for prime numbers may be dormant. Perhaps you need to begin by awakening those instincts."

As the salesman babbled on about numbers and sets, he pulled sheets of metal mesh from his case and slowly pieced them together to form a cage in the shape of a pyramid. Each of the sheets had been fashioned from a number of ordinary mousetraps.

"What's that you've got there?" asked the Mouse Man.

"A cage," said the salesman, with characteristic cheerfulness. "You see, the shape is very important. It helps the mice to sharpen their instincts toward prime numbers. This one here is still a very rough prototype that needs work, but if my calculations are correct, then this should do the job for single-digit sets."

All of a sudden, Dad's face took on a fierce expression.

"D'you think I'm stupid!" he growled, pointing his finger at the salesman. "D'you think I'm soft in the head? I'm doing mathematics here! Not stupid magic tricks!"

But the salesman smiled and said, "Why don't we just give it a try?"

There were more than two hundred mice in the cage on Dad's cart and the salesman asked Dad if he could let a prime number of them out into the yard. "Three would be fine," he said. Dad took a breath, opened the lid of the cage, and picked out three mice at random. Then he placed them gently on the field. Unsurprisingly, all three scurried away in different directions.

"Now," said the salesman, rolling up his sleeves. "Let's try it again with my cage."

The salesman picked three mice out of Dad's cage with his gloved hands and placed them in the pyramid cage. He watched them for a while, then he said, "I think they're ready." The salesman picked one mouse at a time from the cage and placed it on the dirt. For a moment, all three mice stood together in one black clump. Then everyone watched in amazement as the mice scrunched even tighter together and scurried away as one into the corner of the schoolyard—like a ball of black yarn being blown along.

The same thing happened again when he tried it with five mice, then again with seven. Once they'd been put into the pyramid cage together, they'd stick together when they ran through the schoolyard. When the school bell rang, marking the start of the school day, the salesman walked up to Dad and said, "I'm just a salesman. I'm not trying to interfere with any of your experiments. I give people what they need. So, what do you think? Do you think you might need a bigger pyramid cage?"

"Yes, I suppose I do," mumbled the Mouse Man. "For starters, can you get me one that fits at least fifty-nine mice?"

With that, the salesman took off his rubber gloves, fixed his tie, and stuck his right hand out to shake my dad's. And according to the townspeople who were watching all the while, their two hands were so equally pale they might as well have been attached to the same body.

Obviously, the salesman was a fraud. I guessed that his trickery had something to do with the rubber gloves, the ones he'd used to pick the mice up out of the pyramid cage. Perhaps he'd sprayed them with some sort of chemical that attracted mice. Then, when each of the mice had received a good coating of the chemical, the salesman donned another pair of gloves—this time with no added chemicals—and picked the mice out of the cage and placed them down on the schoolyard. So it didn't really matter if they were in groups of prime numbers or not, they still would have stuck together like tangled balls of yarn. But, as the policeman pointed out, the pyramid cage served as the perfect diversion, drawing everyone's attention away from those tainted rubber gloves.

I wasn't there to see how smoothly he operated. Or how his confident manner might have won everyone over. Who was I to say that Dad had been a fool to trust him? After all, Dad wasn't the only person in town to fall for the salesman's tactics. Almost everyone in town had been taken in by one of his scams. He seemed to be able to find out what each person wanted in remarkably short time—even if that person hadn't yet recognized such a need for themselves! It was as if he had the power to make people feel that he could grant access to whatever it was people had been waiting for.

I turned to the older officer who picked up the story where he had left off. By the time the end of autumn had arrived, the salesman's van could be seen all over town. By the town hall. At the docks in front of the warehouses. In front of the bar. On the side of his van was printed Shoe Sales & Repairs, etc. And because of its shape and color, the van actually looked like a boot from a distance, running around town on its own. But the salesman's business interests extended far beyond footwear. There seemed to be no worldly product he wasn't able to procure.

One day, the salesman was talking to an 82-year-old woman who had lost her son at sea thirty years earlier. Within days, the salesman made his way over to the octogenarian home with the sailor's diary in hand. When the old lady opened it, she found a photograph of her rather fuller, thirty-years-younger self, and on the inside of the cover she could see her son's signature. As she gratefully served tea in the living room, the salesman told her how he'd checked all the auction houses specializing in seafaring accidents and found the diary that way. Then he whipped out a contract, flashed her a smile that reminded her of her late son, and said, "Please sign here." Which she happily did, before offering him another cup of tea. And off he went with the rights to her heirloom cabinet that had been in her family for three generations.

The 72-year-old owner of the fishing supplies store near the sailors' lodgings was well known around town for the tortoises he kept. His prize specimen was a huge tortoise he'd had in the shop since his father's time, which sat so still at the entrance to the store that many customers mistook it for an ornament.

"That's an impressive statue you have there," they'd say. "It must be very old."

Whenever he heard such remarks, the shop owner would smile. He didn't know how old that tortoise actually was. But over the past few years, he'd realized it might be coming toward the end of its life. The poor animal's rear legs seemed to be permanently stuck inside its shell, and as for its front legs, they seemed to have dried up completely and were as hard as stone. One day a regular customer was surprised to find the shop owner in the back, clapping his hands like a child. In front of him was the huge tortoise, moving along the pier with a gusto he'd never seen before. But every time the tortoise took a step forward, it seemed to be accompanied by an unusual clanking noise. On further inspection, the customer could see that small wheels had been attached to the underside of the tortoise—the same kind you find on shopping carts and cheap suitcases.

"The springs work well, and he never slides sideways," said the shop owner with a laugh. "You know, the salesman's quite a guy. He says these things are specially made for tortoises these days. He had this one specially delivered from an institution that specializes in the protection of exotic animals."

Soon enough, the salesman had everyone looking forward to whatever he might bring to town next. From long-life light bulbs to ice trays and detergents. From collectibles to antique books and maps. And even new pharmaceutical products to cure anything from hair loss to freckles. Then there were the shoes, of course. For some reason, there had never been a single shoe shop in the town. So the men, women, children, and even the elderly of the town had always relied on the same old sailors' boots. In fact, the only people in the whole town who owned a pair of proper lace-up leather shoes were the bartender and the members of the band, who kept them carefully stowed away for musical performances.

"Let Shiny New Black Wings Carry You to a New World!" That was the headline that appeared on a range of ads in the local paper all the way through autumn and winter. And even better, the salesman was offering them at a special rate because he'd sold the ink to the newspaper company that made printing much easier and produced more legible results. But those shoes did seem to be very good value. You could buy a pair of those shiny black wings for as little as it would cost to buy three adult meals. So soon enough, all the young women in the town were tottering along on the heels of their brand new footwear.

Without anyone noticing, the salesman had become vital to the town. People thought he was one of the few good things that had happened to it since the band won first prize in the competition. But while he'd been mesmerizing the people of the town with his lessons for walking in high heels and his magic tricks for children, he was preparing to rob our town of everything it had. He had no morality whatsoever. He'd go from shop to house to shop, striking deals that tightened his grip of the town, not caring whether it was good or evil. Onward he marched, stomping his feet with a *thump, thump, thump* that drowned out everything save his ambition.

Chapter 3

A Peg on the Nose

According to the postmaster, Grandpa's cane struck the salesman with a spine-quaking crack. Fortunately for the salesman, the members of the band intervened right away. If they hadn't, he'd never be able to stoop to tie his shoelaces again.

"Damn those trumpet players," the police officer said to me later. "And those horn players, too! They should have accompanied the old man's attack with fanfare rather than stepping in to stop it!"

Everyone is welcome at Warehouse #2. This golden rule was still adhered to even after the caretaker and I were long gone. When the salesman showed up there one day wearing his loud suit, nobody so much as batted an eye. He exchanged friendly greetings with audience members sitting on the floor, sat down, and listened to the performance while gazing at the trophies in the glass case. From time to time he raised his eyebrows, put a finger to his lips, and mumbled to himself. When the band stopped for a break, he clapped and cheered louder than anyone.

"Fantastic! Absolutely fantastic!"

Upon hearing the salesman's booming voice, the postmaster lowered his baton and exchanged a chuckle with the pipefitter on trombone. Although the salesman's cheers were arguably over the top, they seemed undeniably sincere. A few moments later, the salesman approached the stage—squinting in the direction of the band as the light played off the brass instruments, while taking three pieces of red cloth from his pocket.

"Please give these a try," he said. "They're made of a new kind of material. Just one quick rub with this cloth will take off more than just dust and sweat. It will clear any kind of stain like it's taking off a layer of skin!"

The leader of the clarinet section was the first to grab the cloth. He gave his instrument a casual wipe and was taken aback at the results. Then he passed the cloth onto the next band member, who gave it a try before passing it on to the next, and the next, and so on, until nearly all fifty band members had given it a go. Finally the cloth reached the postmaster, who gave the handle of his baton a quick wipe—revealing the beautiful patterns of its wood from beneath the grime. (The pieces of red cloth had probably been soaked in the latest type of detergent that dissolved any grime that was on the instruments.)

"You must be the salesman," a band member called out on. "My daughter was talking about you. You know, I don't know the first thing about vacuum cleaners, air fresheners, or that sort of thing, but I do know a good thing when I see it. So how much is the red handkerchief?"

"Consider it a gift," said the salesman with a smile. "A thank you from me for a great performance."

Then, one by one, the band members stepped off the stage to go for a cup of coffee or to shave their reeds in readiness for the next number.

That winter, the town's band was invited to play at a different concert nearly every week. They were to perform outdoors at the New Year's Eve festival where the town was planning a spectacular fireworks exhibition in an attempt to paint over the memory of the fire. Flyers were sent to neighboring towns, and permit after permit was issued to foreign ships wanting to dock on New Year's Eve. The greatest attraction leading up to the fireworks was to be the concert on water by the band that had taken first place in the competition for two years running and was now the pride of the town.

While the band members were taking their break, they continued to study their music furiously. The salesman walked around trying to exchange pleasantries with them, but the postmaster intervened. With a polite cough, he said, "I'm sorry but please can you wait until after practice? We have a rule, you see. We don't talk of anything but music when we're in the warehouse."

"Oh, I see. I'm very sorry about that," said the salesman, slapping his forehead. "I couldn't help myself. Whenever I see people working so hard, the passion rubs off on me. I get involved, wondering if there's anything I can do to help. But I thought everyone was taking a break. Can a little chitchat really do any harm?"

The salesman wasted no time opening his leather briefcase and taking out some papers. The postmaster, with a quick glance, saw the salesman was holding a catalog of collectible postage stamps—it was a catalog he'd never seen before. The stamp on the cover featured a chimpanzee with his tongue hanging out. This left the postmaster feeling weak; he was dying to pore through the catalog. But keeping to his word, he said to the salesman, whispering, "It's against the rules. I'll give you all the time in the world after practice. But please sit quietly now. You'll find a chair in the corner of the room."

On stage, two elderly men stood focusing on their snare drums. The one with the straight back occasionally tossing a ping-pong ball onto the drum was, of course, Grandpa. And the one with a red face and tears in his eyes, tapping out a quick rhythm with his drumsticks, was the vice-principal, who'd been Grandpa's student for three months now. Grandpa was teaching him a little trick for practice—the art of holding a rhythm so that a ping-pong ball would keep its bounce on the drum's surface.

"They're so diligent!" the salesman exclaimed, jumping onto the stage before the postmaster could stop him and heading in the direction of the percussionists, clicking the heels of his tiny shoes. This caused the vice-principal to glance upward, causing the ping-pong ball to fall from the drum's surface and end up bouncing on the stage floor.

Grandpa's expression remained unchanged as he tossed another ball onto the drum. "Continue," he said.

"I see now!" the salesman declared loudly, holding on to his leather briefcase.

The entire band was pretending to be studying the music on their stands, but everyone was keeping a close eye on what was going to happen next.

"I've heard that percussion is the very foundation of a band," the salesman went on for everyone's ears. "To be that foundation, the percussion must really work itself to the bone. Look at that ball rising steadily on the skin of the drum. Look at it go! It's twenty centimeters above it, maybe twenty-five! Go go go!"

At that moment, the ping-pong ball bounced away from the drum surface and landed on the floor. Grandpa produced another ball from his pocket and tossed it onto the drum.

"Continue," he said to the vice-principal. "And this time don't stop."

For a moment, the salesman stood silent. But his silence couldn't last. After several seconds, he ambled over to the side of the percussionists and began to speak over the drumbeat.

"You know, my younger brother played the larger snare drum in his school band, and he said you shouldn't be *banging* the drum. You use force of the leather drumhead bouncing back to form circles with your drumstick. The only time you apply force is if you stop the drumbeat while the drumhead is still responding. *Don't say it looks easy, big brother,* he used to say to me. *Another word like that from you and I'll shove you into the drum and roll you down a dirt road.* Oh my goodness! What a bad mouth he had! But, you know, he's actually a great brother. You know, he bought a present for our parents out of his first paycheck last year. What do you think it was? A dehumidifier! My parents live in a dark apartment and moisture seeps in from the ceiling. Of course, my mother was delighted. Why wouldn't she be? There's no reason not to be happy. So she hugged my brother and kissed him all over his face. I thought she was going to swallow him whole!"

By now, the ping-pong ball was reaching an altitude of nearly a meter. When it dropped to the floor it made the most modest of sounds. The vice-principal tried to wipe the sweat from his brow with his sleeve, but he couldn't muster the strength to raise his arms above his chest and his hands were shaking.

Grandpa gestured to the vice-principal that he should move on to the xylophone, and turned his back to the salesman. "Be quiet, will you," he called out without turning to make eye contact. "You're making it difficult to hear. If you're not here to enjoy the music, then please leave the warehouse immediately."

"Ha!" laughed the salesman. "I finally got you to say something to me!" Addressing the vice-principal, the salesman said, "You were very good." Then turning back to Grandpa, he said loudly, "Not here to enjoy the music? Don't be ridiculous! I was literally moved by that performance. If only you could give my brother a lesson like that!"

"Listen to me!" Grandpa said, his expression blank as he gathered the ping-pong balls from the floor. "I don't care what your brother did or didn't do. But I do know this much—you stink! You smell so bad it makes me sick! Do you understand me? So please, get out of my warehouse this instant!"

The postmaster gulped, as did the other band members. The salesman stood still with shock written on his face, as if he'd just dropped a crate of eggs. Grandpa had a point, though. The salesman did smell—like a mixture of fig juice and soapy water. But nobody found it nauseating like Grandpa did. It was the salesman's cologne, which was actually quite nice.

This was the first time Grandpa had spoken so harshly to someone who wasn't a member of the band. Tapping his cane on the floor, Grandpa stepped away from the vice-principal, who was now standing before the xylophone with the mallet in his hand. Grandpa stopped when he reached the other end of the stage. "Go ahead," he called out.

The vice-principal struck a D, then followed it with a second and a third strike.

"No, no!" shouted Grandpa. "You're way off. You don't hit the instrument. You touch it. Don't you understand? You touch it and pull away. Acknowledge that your fingers are there for support. Sneak in a strike as if you shouldn't be touching the instrument, but you just can't help it!"

"Hmmph! So I stink!" the salesman blurted out in voice louder than the strikes on the xylophone. "What a nasty thing to say." Quickly enough, though, the salesman recovered his smile.

But on the other side of the stage, the vice-principal was starting to look increasingly pale as he continued to tap his mallets.

Diiiing, diiiing, diiiing.

Now, suddenly, the salesman turned toward Grandpa. "I probably should have mentioned," he said, a little smugly. "I know a little bit about you. You're the father of that genius mathematician who's been working day in day out on that brilliant experiment of his."

Grandpa slowly turned toward the salesman as the xylophone notes continued to ring out.

Diiing, diiing, diiing.

"You may know that I am, to a very minor degree, assisting him with this undertaking. According to the professor, he will most definitely be presented the International Award for Mathematics next year. And yes, I agree. His experiment is fascinating."

Diiiing, diiing, diiing.

"You, on the other hand, are the head of this fantastic band. There must be something in your genes! Mathematics and music. In medieval times they were the same subject, you know. Tell you what. I've been lending equipment to your son for some time now. I'll bring something for you next week. I think you'll like it very much."

Diiing, diiing, diiing.

By now, the salesman was standing right next to Grandpa, and he took a deep breath as if relishing the sound of the xylophone. Then he whispered something in Grandpa's ear. Every member of the band watched as Grandpa's eyes open wide. Then the salesman smiled broadly, laughed, whispered something again to him, and winked, as if it were all a game.

Suddenly, Grandpa lifted his silver cane high above his head and brought it down hard on the salesman's behind with a sickening crack. The pipefitter told me later that he'd always thought that if a person was hit that hard on his behind then he would reflexively leap forward. But in fact, it seems that's not always what happens. In the case here, the salesman actually jumped straight up and higher than you'd think a man could jump! It was like he had springs in his shoes. And then he let out a mechanical screech. That really surprised me.

He seemed to feel a lot of pain on landing again as well.

Ayyyyyyee! Ayyyyye, ayyyyye!

By now, the salesman was on all fours, with his body shaking, in shock. Already, Grandpa was taking aim to deliver another crushing blow with his cane, but the members of the band rushed in and held him back. The vice-principal, who was dumbfounded, standing before the xylophone, took note of Grandpa's icy glare and began striking the xylophone again.

Diiing, diiing, diiing.

And with this as the background music, the salesman and his loud suit were rolled out of Warehouse #2 on an old trolley.

Three days later, the postmaster visited the salesman in hospital. He was surprised to see the door to the ward crowded with women of all ages lining up. When he tried to squeeze in, an elderly lady with a flower in her hair bared her silver teeth as she warned him not to cut in line. The postmaster quietly took his place next to a junior high school student with acne who was flipping through a set of vocabulary cards.

After a tedious wait of more than two hours, the postmaster was finally allowed to enter. The scene that met his eyes shocked him. All sixteen beds were occupied. There was a young man lying with his leg suspended in the air and an old man with a bandage on his head. All the patients were munching on fresh, appetizing fruit.

"The conductor is here!" cried the salesman, who was lying on his stomach in bed and waving from the other end of the ward. "Or should I say the postmaster is here?"

Around the bed the floor was piled with wicker baskets adorned with pink ribbons—all these women, the postmaster realized, had come bearing gifts for the salesman. What an incredibly popular person he'd made himself in such a short time!

The salesman was wearing yellow and black striped pajamas, which made him look like a bumblebee.

"How are you doing?" the postmaster asked.

"My tail bone is fractured," said the salesman with a wry grin. "But there's nothing to worry about. I've been told that I can start making sales calls tomorrow as long as I wear a corset."

"I really don't know what to say," said the postmaster, taking a chair. "The old man is usually quiet and gentle—except when it comes to matters of music.... All I can say is I've known him for many years and that's the first time I've ever seen him hit anyone. I have no idea what came over him."

"It was my fault," said the salesman, shaking his head. "You have to forgive me. You warned me, but I kept on blabbering away. I was very rude. To you and to that man." From his position on his stomach in bed the salesman managed an apologetic bow.

Moments later, two nurses arrived to take the salesman's temperature. They chatted and laughed with him and whispered that they were going to buy the electric shaver from his catalog after all. The salesman twisted his body around, looked up at them, and proceeded to tell them about a complementary blade that came with the shaver, skincare techniques for after shaving, a way to bathe patients that minimized swelling in the legs, and an investment their parents should not be without.

"What does a sick man who can't stand up and a pile of savings have in common?" he said to the two nurses.

They didn't know.

"Neither can go for a walk!" joked he salesman, laughing gleefully. "Please tell your parents that as soon as I am back on my feet I'll be coming to visit them. I'll take their housebound money for a healthy walk. I have an investment opportunity that is perfect for them."

Even after the nurses had left, the salesman kept on smiling as if replaying the conversation in his mind.

The postmaster had to cough to bring him back to the moment. "About that stamp catalog you showed me the other day…"

"Ah yes."

"I do get a little tired of looking at stamps all day in my profession. Still, I was wondering if there might be anything unusual in that catalog."

The salesman reached under his bed and clicked opened the latches on his leather briefcase. Then he presented to the postmaster with the catalog of the official Stamp Collectors' Club, a club so exclusive that even renowned collectors had trouble getting in.

Breathing loudly through his nose, the postmaster began turning the pages slowly in silence. He was fascinated. In fact, he later admitted that he would have been willing to kiss the salesman's behind at that moment. Though he was reluctant to admit to the salesman, the postmaster had actually gone into his profession purely because of his love for stamp collecting. He'd been crazy about stamps ever since he was a little boy, he'd never taken as much as a single day off work in more than fifty years of service, and he always kept an eye out for any unusual stamps. And when he came across a letter with a rare stamp on it, he would take the initiative of delivering it himself, then return to the office with the stamp in hand.

"What do you think?" asked the salesman. "Personally, I don't know much about stamps, so I'd love to hear your estimation of the unusual stamps available there."

"*Unusual stamps?*" the postmaster repeated, struggling to conceal his excitement. "Take a look at this one. This is a stamp commemorating the fourth anniversary of the railway company. I saw a black-and-white picture of it when I was a child! And, oh I can't believe my eyes, the perforation is crooked!"

"The perforation?"

"Yes. The little holes at the edge of the stamp. You see, crooked stamps like these are almost always immediately discarded. For a stamp like this to be kept in this condition...I'd be willing to wager that there isn't another one of these in the world!"

The salesman in the bumblebee pajamas craned his neck to get a better look at the stamp. "I see what you mean. You're right. It is indeed crooked. Well, I think stamp collectors are very lucky for being able to find pleasure in such a fine point as the punch line around a stamp."

"Actually, more often than not, the feeling isn't one of pleasure but frustration at not being able to get your hands on stamps like these," the postmaster said. "But still, just looking at this makes my heart dance. It's not so different from the way I feel when we blast out the final notes of a fanfare!" The postmaster shrugged lightly, closed the catalog, and handed it to the salesman.

"No, you keep it," the salesman said with a smile.

"You must be kidding."

"Not at all. I told you I love watching people who are passionate about something. If that catalog can take you to another world, then there is nothing that can make me happier. Besides, I have connections. I get the latest catalog every month. But I'm not a romantic man, so a crooked line doesn't bring tears to my eyes. I might as well pass the catalog on to you every month."

The postmaster stared at the salesman's cool brown eyes, which at that moment filled his heart with warmth as if a cup of cocoa had just been poured down his throat. (At the inn where the salesman had been staying, ten pairs of brown contact lenses were later found.) The postmaster touched the salesman's pale hand as it rested by the pillow. Then he stood up and said his goodbye.

But before he left the room, a question came to his mind. "By the way, if I may ask, what did you say that drove the gentle old man into a rage?"

The salesman looked more pained than ever. "It was about a sound reflector," he said, squeezing out the words. "I can get a hold of a high-grade foreign-manufactured one cheaply. I told him I could bring him one."

"That was it?" the postmaster said, amazed. "You got such a beating for that?"

The salesman signed and shook his head. "A sound reflector with microphone. I'm not sure if that's in his heart the thing he wants more than anything else. Part of me feels like it is. But another part of me feels that's wrong. All I can say for sure is that he has a truly unique way of going about things."

The postmaster stepped out of the room with his catalog in hand, only to find the elderly lady with a flower in her hair sitting on the bench.

"You tell that pompous old fart," she yelled at the postmaster, "who does he think he is, assaulting such a nice, hardworking young man! The next time he comes to my shop I'm going to shave off all his hair and tell my grandchildren to draw on his head!"

The postmaster hadn't realized who the lady was under all that hair and makeup, but he now recognized her as the hairdresser. He continued walking down the hall, clutching the catalog to his chest. "A reflector—of all things!" he chuckled to himself.

After the incident between Grandpa and the salesman, all band members found themselves under attack from their wives and daughters for being selfish and not spending enough time with their families. The typical next line went something like this: "I'm not letting you go any place where a kind soul like the salesman could get hurt. If you want to continue practicing your instrument, you must guarantee that he's free to conduct his business whether or not it's in the warehouse!"

Some band members reported a car horn beeping them as they walked in town. It was the salesman, fresh out of the hospital, waving and smiling as if he was genuinely pleased to see them.

"Hello there!" he'd call out. "I was just about to visit your home with some skin moisturizing lotion."

"Hey there! How are those shoes working out for you?"

"Can I offer you a ride to the dock? I'm heading over to collect a shipment."

The salesman was back to wearing that same shiny suit, and he seemed to have each and every band member's name, occupation, and family history logged in his memory. What's more, he listened carefully and responded enthusiastically to any request, puffing out his chest and saying, "Leave it to me. I'll take care of it!" After which, band members would a few days later receive a package containing the exact items desired—a shawl for an elderly mother, an electric drill with an unusually powerful motor, or bananas from a southern island that a son was partial to. And in every instance, the sale came with a complementary twenty percent discount.

On the day the Fireworks Committee was gathering for its first meeting at Warehouse #2, the salesman appeared again. It was almost as if he'd timed it for maximum drama (which, in retrospect, he had). The band was taking a break when he pushed the big warehouse door open. In his hand was a large leather case. Everyone fell silent, glancing toward the stage where Grandpa was intently adjusting the tension on his timpani.

Slowly, the salesman approached the stage, his shoes clicking with each step. Then he came to a stop.

"Hello!" he called to Grandpa. "Please forgive my rudeness the other day."

Grandpa didn't reply.

"I've brought a small gift as an apology. I wonder if everyone might like to take a look. It has something to do with music, of course. Why would I bring anything else to this warehouse?"

No one could imagine what was in the leather case, its sides and its silver handle polished to a sheen. Suddenly, the town treasurer, who was also the band manager, gasped.

"What's the matter?" asked the concertmaster and trombone player who was also the pipefitter.

"It's the missing percussion case!" exclaimed the treasurer, "The case that got lost before last year's contest! How did you find it?"

"Well," said the salesman, "when you're in this business as long as I've been, you find yourself connected to many roads that take you to different places. Do you know what happens to stolen instruments? They end up being turned into cups—brass cups for outdoor use, to be precise. So when thieves get ahold of a set of instruments, they immediately go to a cup factory. There the instruments are pounded and stretched, again and again, then a brass line is added, a handle is attached and you get a beautiful cup. Some are even treated like collector's items if they still bear the production number of the instrument, you know. But as you can guess, the person who got ahold of this particular case was disappointed to find that it only contained percussion instruments, castanets, and temple blocks. By chance, I happened to hear about this, so finding the case was pretty easy."

The band members gathered round—the older members whispering in low voices, while the others whistled *Fanfare for the Fighting Kids*. The pipefitter and other brass instrument players, however, were outraged at what had happened to their instruments. And the woodwind section, wanted to know what became of clarinets and oboes. All of this chatter was going on at once, when suddenly the timpani sounded an overpowering G.

Boiiiinnggg!

Silence was immediate.

"You can talk to this guy," Grandpa boomed from behind the timpani, "but only under the condition that you do so *after* practice. And as for you, Mr. Salesman, you are *never* to come up on this stage. I don't want your stink polluting my band's air."

The young music teacher who was the clarinet player seemed slightly displeased. Perhaps it was because the salesman had given him a great price on a wide-angle camera lens and projector.

Or perhaps it was because the salesman had just sold his wife three pairs of high heels in different colors including a course in how to walk in high heels. (The same with the wives of all the other band members.)

Grandpa said nothing more. He turned his attention back to adjusting the knobs on his timpani, pounded another thunderous G, and then commanded, "Music! Everyone, it is time to make some music."

The band members climbed onto the stage with their instruments. And from the back pocket of each band member was hanging a distinctive piece of red cloth.

"Well, that worked out well, didn't it?" whispered the postmaster to Grandpa. "I mean, we got the case of percussion instruments back. Even you must be happy about that!"

"Don't be ridiculous," Grandpa spat. "I don't like any of this. Not one bit. But there's nothing we can do about it. That man has latched on to everyone in town. The only thing to do is carry on with our music. And as long as our notes fill the air, there'll be none left to carry his putrid breath."

"You know, I wouldn't say he stinks," the postmaster said, trying to be conciliatory. "It's cologne. It's not as bad as you say it is."

That night practice dragged on until midnight. Although the band members were exhausted, they seemed to draw strength from the boom of Grandpa's timpani. Meanwhile, the salesman, a smile on his face, waited quietly. When the practice ended, he stood and applauded enthusiastically before going around and inserting catalogs into each band member's instrument case.

"It's too late in the night now," he spoke loud enough for everyone to hear, "so I'll come tomorrow to explain the products. You guys sounded great, by the way."

"Wait a minute," called out the treasurer, as the salesman whipped around with a smile ready on his face. "How much do you know about the music business? We have quite a collection of recordings and all they're doing is gathering dust in storage at Town Hall. If we could sell them, the income would help the band's finances."

"How much do I know about the music business..." the salesman pondered out loud. "Well, interestingly enough, I do have a little experience in that area."

Soon after, the salesman's involvement in the band took a different turn. He wasn't merely appointed as the producer of their records. According to articles in my scrapbook, he'd become the overall advisor for the entire fireworks festival by the very next week and was placed in charge of the concert on the water. Here's what the article said:

> *What our town's brass band has been lacking until now is proper business management. The salesman told us in an interview that he was genuinely shocked when he first heard the details of the band's finances. He said that the band has been bleeding red now for far too long but that in the near future a major record company executive was arriving in town to hear them perform. This comes at a time when Warehouse #2 is in dire need of renovation; however, the fireworks festival must take priority because the outcome of this year's fireworks festival will determine the future not only of the band but also of the entire town.*

The fireworks festival turned out to be a great success. On New Year's Eve, the docks were packed with tourists from neighboring towns, accompanied by rows and rows of stands selling sandwiches, beer, and popcorn. There were bright neon signs everywhere, which were to be turned off right at the moment the fireworks began and the ocean that evening was calm and quiet. A pontoon stage was built across several small boats moored together.

As the band prepared to take the stage, the postmaster noticed something odd about Grandpa's appearance. "What are you doing?" asked the postmaster. "You don't normally like jokes."

"It's not a joke," said Grandpa, adjusting the clothes peg he'd clipped on his nose. "The place stinks so bad. Why are we even performing here? Let's get this over with so we can all go home and listen to music on the radio."

The salesman, wearing his signature shiny suit, was sitting in one of the seats reserved for the organizers. His arms were crossed firmly in front of his chest as he gazed out at the lights that filled the port. It was the first time the town had been filled with such colorful lights and their reflection in the water only added to the beauty of the scene. Everywhere people munching on sausages and roast chicken as they gazed out on the ocean of colors—feeling sweet sensations bubbling up in their hearts and washing them down with refreshing ice-cold beer. They seemed to merge into one large, black blob as they sat waiting for the fireworks to begin.

"Okay," said the postmaster, "this is our cue!" He lifted his baton and the sound of clarinets drifted out across the crowd. People whistled in response from the decks of the three ships floating out at sea. This had been the idea of the salesman, who'd sold special viewing seats on the decks of the ships and rented out their cabins to people wanting to spend the night. Inside each of the ships, there were dance parties with their own live music, as well as a bevy of scantily dressed dancers.

Behind the stalls, the power generators were buzzing away. A fat vendor called out, "Still time before the performance begins! Get your fresh popcorn while you can!"

The postmaster took his spot on what was really just a large piece of wood swaying on the sea as Grandpa stood at the very back with his mallet in hand and clothes peg on his nose, which the postmaster later complained was very distracting.

As soon as the performance came to an end, the neon lights were shut off and the fireworks were launched into the sky from a boat moored further out in the bay—with the smaller fireworks soon building into a crescendo of garish display that filled the night sky with red then purple then white.

In all, there were five barges for the fireworks, and ten people responsible for the fireworks, including the engineers and their assistants. It was an event so much bigger than Town Hall had imagined it would be, with the salesman having taken care of everything from sourcing the vendors to drawing up the schedule of events. In fact, it no longer seemed like just a small town fireworks festival. It was a large-scale circus that had somehow been painted on the sea.

A few moments later, a burst of yellow blossomed like a sunflower, covering half the sky and raining beads of light down on the crowd with an awe-inspiring boom. The people gazed up with mouths open, mesmerized, as if they were the last living animals on the planet witnessing the end of the world. Or witnessing the birth of a new one—the world of the salesman, in which everyone was nothing more than a tourist.

A flourish of red filled the heavens, followed by an especially large bang that shook not only the ships at sea but even the pier—causing at least one elderly lady to lose her footing and stumble to the ground. But as those flowers of fire filled the skies, Dad remained in the school grounds, wearing his thick, heavy coat and blowing steamy breaths onto the mice in his pyramid-shaped cages before setting them free to run together in the darkness of the school yard.

The End of the Mouse Man

As the weeks went by, the postmaster began to lose interest in his once-prized stamp collection. It may now have seemed pathetic compared to those rare finds that lined the pages of the members-only catalog. He asked the salesman if he wouldn't mind finding a buyer for his collection. In usual fashion, the salesman wasted no time at all in offloading the collection. And when the money arrived from the sale, the salesman promised, there would be enough for the postmaster to make a down payment on a yacht. One day, the postmaster approached four friends after band practice and proposed that they go in with him on the purchase of, in fact, a yacht: the postmaster would take ownership of fifty percent of the boat from the proceeds of his stamp collection, and the other fifty percent would be split by his four friends.

The consortium settled on a schooner with three masts, and the postmaster spent the next week going through a catalog to select the design for the flag to be hoisted at the stern.

At around the same time, an executive from a record company arrived in town to visit Warehouse #2. He was a fat man of middle age who looked grumpy as hell when he greeted the treasurer and the pipefitter. For the length of the performance that followed, the fat man simply sat without saying a word. Then he got back into his black van and drove off without a farewell. It was later learned that he'd been so quiet because the salesman had ordered him to keep his mouth shut. In fact, he wasn't a fat, grumpy record executive at all. He was the fat, grumpy popcorn vendor the salesman recruited from the fireworks festival!

"He had a really strong accent," said the police officer who interrogated him later. "I knew right away he wasn't from around here."

This all happened while all the young women in town were waiting with bated breath for their new summer dresses to arrive. The latest fashion was for sleeveless linen frocks that barely covered the knees. Until that time, no one in town had even heard of a dress without sleeves. Until that time, no one in town had even known that fashion was something that changed from season to season. Every day, you'd see them tucking in their cotton skirts so the hems just about covered their knees as they practiced walking elegantly in the markets in preparation for the coming summer.

Meanwhile, the savings of the elderly people were on the move, too—flowing through the salesman into a paradise resort investment opportunity. The paradise? A place where flowers were always in bloom and the scent of fresh fruit filled the air. Warm and dry during the day, cool in the evenings, with just the right amount of rain. It sounded just like one of the stories the caretaker used to make up and I remember thinking how people everywhere pictured paradise as the same kind of thing. They say the salesman always closed his investment pitch to the elderly, saying: "Even the wind is music. If you close your eyes you can feel its harmony flow through your body. That's the kind of life you can live there."

When I think of this silly pitch now, it almost makes me laugh. The wind isn't nature's music. The wind is just wind. And far from being in harmony with the soul, it lashes at the downtrodden, throws sand into your eyes, razes homes to the ground, flings dogs and rafts out of reach. That's what the wind does.

For the elderly, though, the salesman's pitch was on the money. These were people who'd spent a lifetime in a place where the salty ocean tore at the shore and where the fighting never stopped. The dream of spending the rest of their life in a place where the wind blew gentle music was just too good to pass up.

For six months the salesman plied his trade—like a demolition expert strategically placing sticks of dynamite, readying to bring a gigantic tower to the ground, while leaving the surroundings untouched.

The police suspected that the salesman had been after the fireworks budget from the start. The people at Town Hall figured he was after their entire budget, including funds allocated for the brass band. The elderly lost their life savings in one fell swoop. The postmaster never saw the schooner he'd sacrificed his stamp collection for. It was all so personal, with every person in town believing themselves to be the main target. Of course, what had really happened was that each person had allowed themselves to be blinded by their own individual vision of paradise—with each person hanging on the salesman's words as he painted the promise of some faraway fantasy. But as everyone soon found, there's no such thing as paradise in this world. It was something that only existed in the tall tales of the salesman.

One Saturday afternoon, during a period of record-breaking rainfall, the Mouse Man dashed madly into the inn where the salesman lived, his coat drenched and smelling like garbage.

"Where is he?" Dad demanded, out of breath.

The innkeeper was asleep in the back room, so his wife was at the reception desk. She immediately assumed Dad was referring to the salesman, since the two of them had been busy counting and releasing mice every morning for some time now.

"He's probably in his room," she said.

"What's his room number?"

"203. But you can't just go…"

It was too late. Dad had already flown up the stairs, alarming the innkeeper's wife, whose husband had instructed her never to let anyone enter the salesman's room—and had also informed her that the salesman's bill had already been taken care of.

Dad stomped over to the salesman's room and pounded on the door. There was no answer. Dad then started slamming his slim body against the door. Within seconds, other guests on the second floor peaked out their rooms to see what the commotion was about. Fortunately, the innkeeper's wife felt comfortable enough about Dad to let him in. She thought he was a rather glum man, but he struck her as honest.

"I wouldn't have unlocked the door if it was the grandfather," she told the police later that night. "That man is off his rocker. And when he has that silver stick in his hand, he's pretty scary."

The salesman's room was a mess. Carbon paper, loose pages, and scribbled notes were scattered everywhere, and the smell of medicine was overpowering. Without a moment's hesitation, Dad began to sort through the papers littering the floor.

"Stop this at once!" shouted the innkeeper's wife. "You can't touch a guest's property. I'll call the police!"

Dad ignored her. He yanked the closet open and pulled out a stack of boxes. A tangled pair of black laces fell on his head, and he whipped around. "It's not here!" he gasped.

"What's not here?"

"My research paper!" screamed Dad through gritted teeth. "He said he was going to make copies. That was a few days ago. That was the last time I saw him!"

"Maybe he's just gone to the next town to stock up on supplies. Why don't you calm down and wait until tomorrow? I mean, it is raining very hard right now."

"Tomorrow?!" The rage in Dad's eyes made everyone take a step back. "Don't be a fool! Today is the deadline! The paper must be postmarked today, or it will be rejected!"

Everyone watched in amazement as Dad turned, dashed out the door, and leaped down the stairs three steps at a time. Then they all ran to the window to watch him sprint out into the pouring rain. Off he ran toward the center of town, splashing through puddles and streams of rainwater on the pavement. Some of the guests at the inn swore that they'd seen a dark, semi-transparent blob moving along in his wake.

The bartender described what happened next:

"The Mouse Man burst through the door of the bar in tears, scanned the place for the salesman, and then ran out. The scene was repeated soon after, as one person after another came rushing into the bar also looking for the salesman. That's when I realized something terrible must have happened. Something more awful than when the mice came raining down. You learn a lot about people by working behind the bar. You learn a thing or two from the behavior of different drunks. You learn the difference between someone just venting and someone at their wit's end. Between someone who's angry and frustrated and someone who's ready to smash their head into a wall. Back when it was raining mice, it was a tough time for everyone. But it wasn't the end of the world. It was like a terrible disease, but one for which there exists a cure. But on this day, the people of the town had clearly hit a dead end. It was immediately clear from the looks on the faces of all who came rushing into the bar. Some of them were stubborn. They couldn't accept they were facing a dead end. They would smash their heads against the wall. They were in denial."

That night, Dad showed up at Warehouse #2. Despite the heavy rain, ten band members were there practicing—Grandpa, the vice-principal, and members of the brass section, including the pipefitter—in preparation for the studio recording the following week. They were performing an upbeat piece called *The Country Farmer's Dance*. The tuba played the main melody, which mimicked the cries of a pig, while Grandpa tapped away at a cowbell. "It's good to have a selection of serious pieces," said the treasurer, "but it's good to have a repertoire that includes humorous numbers, too."

The pipefitter had discussed the band's set list with Grandpa, and together they'd decided on *The Country Farmer's Dance*, *The Bat Fanfare*, and *The Twin Sailors' Whistling*. As they struck up again, the members of the band became distracted—not by the rain beating down so hard on the roof, but by a smell so foul they thought their noses would fall off. It was so rancid the tuba player started to choke. The band turned to see that the metal door to the warehouse was open and that standing there in the darkness was Dad, looking like the dregs that had been pulled out of the sea along with an anchor.

Seeing the bedraggled man in the doorway, the pipefitter almost shouted, Mouse Man! But he stopped himself, remembering that this was Grandpa's son. Instead he called out, "Hello, sir! You're in quite a state there." The pipefitter, with a smile on his face, added, "Why don't you go use our shower? While you do that, I can call my friend from the sanitation department. We should probably get that spot you're standing on disinfected."

Stepping off the stage, the pipefitter poured some corn soup from a canteen into a paper cup and held it out for Dad. But Dad remained motionless.

"Where is he?" said Dad. "Where did he go?"

I later heard from the vice-principal that it sounded like Dad was mumbling to himself instead of talking to the pipefitter. He was distant, in a world of his own—as if he was standing on the other side of a thick pane of glass.

"Do you mean the salesman?" asked Grandpa. "If you do, he isn't here. I'm happy to say we haven't seen him here for three days. Why don't you just give up this thing you two are doing? It's one thing to lose yourself in mathematics, but this is nonsense. . . ."

Dad stood there in silence, melting into the darkness of the warehouse.

"All right then," said Grandpa from the dimly lit stage. "We're in the middle of practice here, but you can stay and listen. We're not bad. But if that damned salesman had stayed away, we'd have a much nicer ensemble for you. The vice-principal is coming along well, but he's not in the same league as good old Cat yet."

"Don't call him that!" Dad's booming voice shook the warehouse, making the pipefitter glad he'd refrained from calling him the Mouse Man. "And I could say the same thing about you, you know! What good is all of this? Forcing your stupid little pastime on everyone while you swan around like a big shot. You're suffocating! That's why the boy left! And he was right to do it, too!"

The rain kept pounding on the roof.

"Don't you understand?" Dad kept going. "You're not doing anyone any favors. All they wanted to do was to play for fun. But for the past ten years, you've had them practicing, practicing, practicing, night after night. And what do they get for all their hard work, eh? A compliment? You don't see it, do you? You're just sitting atop a mountain of sacrifice built by the hard-working people of this town!"

"That's not true," said the pipefitter, his cup still in his hand. "You shouldn't say such things."

Dad shut his mouth. Then he quietly disappeared into the darkness. The warehouse door creaked shut, and the rain continued to pound on the roof. The pipefitter looked down into his cup of lukewarm soup and gulped it down in a single swig. Then he blew his nose and ambled back up on stage.

He was one of the few people in town who had not bought anything from the salesman and one of the few who didn't relish the salesman's visits to the warehouse. It was enough that as the salesman went from house to house peddling his "revolutionary" detergent and flexible brush and pole—now nobody needed the pipefitter to clean their pipes anymore. Business was suffering. But being a resilient man, the pipefitter didn't let that stop him from going around town and telling dirty jokes all day. He was also rather popular with the town's ladies. ("It's the trombone, Cat," he once whispered to me. "It puts the timpani to shame. It's a magical instrument. You'll understand one day.")

As the stink began to dissipate, the pipefitter hoisted the trombone onto his shoulder. "I hope he took me up on the offer of using the shower," he said to Grandpa. "And I hope he remembers to scrub behind his nut sack. I know you're related, but I just thought I'd mention it. I mean, really! What a stink!"

Grandpa waited patiently for the pipefitter to finish his rant, then he gave his cowbell a light tap. "Okay, let's get back to music," he said.

And with that, two tubas blasted out the introduction to *The Farmer's Dance* as if in a duel.

The postmaster was the last person to speak to Dad. He was still on duty that night, sorting letters, daydreaming about the name for the schooner he expected to take delivery of soon. He'd been set on the *Express Delivery* until just the day before. But he had to agree when the other four owners said that it might not be a good omen to have a boat with a name suggesting one-way travel.

"All right then," the postmaster said, "how about *Extremely Fast, Precise Postal Delivery* instead?"

"That's too long!" the four others had cried out in unison.

Hearing the sound of the rain getting heavier, the postmaster looked up to find the Mouse Man standing by the door, in the yellow hue of the electric bulb, dripping. For a moment, the postmaster swore he could see right through Dad's body; he rubbed his eyes in disbelief. Oddly, he didn't notice the stink that had assaulted everyone else's senses so violently. But it is worth noting that the postmaster had lost his umbrella during his morning rounds and his nasal passages were terribly congested.

"Well, this is a surprise," said the postmaster. "Come in. It may be summer but it's deathly cold out there. There's a towel over there on the counter—feel free to use it."

"I have a package to mail," said Dad, without moving from the spot.

"I'm sure you do," said the postmaster, blowing his nose. "This *is* the Post Office, after all. Not too many people come here for other purposes." And with that, he reached over and pushed the button to turn on his electric postal scale—the same scale the salesman had told him was rare among post offices even in big cities.

"About my package," said Dad in a voice that quivered, "I don't have it with me."

"I see. Is it too big?" asked the postmaster. "Normally, I wouldn't mind going to pick it up for you, but I'm the only one on duty right now. I can't leave my post now."

"It's not at home," replied Dad. "It's with a friend. But tomorrow, it will be with me for sure."

The postmaster remained silent as he toyed with the scale, placing his hand lightly on the weighing plate several times and watching the needle sway. "I have a suggestion," he then said, moving his gaze toward Dad's direction. "Why don't you come back here tomorrow once your friend returns your package? That seems like the best plan of action to me."

"That won't work, I'm afraid," said Dad. "You see, I'm going to need to send the package postmarked with today's date."

"I'm sorry. Can you say that again?"

Dad repeated his request.

"Let me see if I understand correctly. Are you asking me, the postmaster, to commit postal fraud on your behalf? Is that what you're asking? Because if you are, then what you're asking is deeply disrespectful not only to me, but to every single person who sends, delivers, and receives letters. Letters become mail the very moment they are postmarked. Do you understand? So if that very first step goes wrong, then every step after that will also be wrong. The postmark must be correct. There are no exceptions. We may look like we're applying the postmark mechanically, but all postal workers understand the significance of that postmark. It's much more important than you realize."

The postmaster loved to lecture people like that, no matter whether it was a band member who forgot to stamp a letter or an elderly lady who forgot to include the postal code. Sometimes he delivered his lectures gently. But at other times he could be rather officious. He told us later that he had never been so incensed as when Dad made his outrageous request.

The postmaster was all about precision when it came to the band, too. He'd swing his baton at the same pace from start to end—just like a postal officer methodically stamping one envelope after another. I imagine that was why Grandpa trusted him so much. Both demanded absolute precision from the band members. But they went about it in very different ways. Grandpa's timpani seemed to put pressure on the band from behind, while the postmaster's baton gently guided them toward the right tempo from the front.

In any case, from the postmaster's point of view, Dad's request must have been equivalent to being asked to turn his back on the band mid-performance and start dancing the twist instead.

"Look at the time," said the postmaster, pointing to the clock on the wall. "It's almost tomorrow. Why don't you and I just forget we ever had this conversation, and I'll be happy to postmark your package and send it on its way when I see you later."

The clock read 11:59. It was a clock given to the postmaster by his younger sister's husband in celebration of his promotion, and its hands moved along with a soft, pleasant ticking. One moment later, the minute hand made a juddering move forward, eclipsing the other hand.

"It's twelve," declared the postmaster as he got to his feet and started making his way to the back room. "I've already forgotten what happened yesterday. Now, why don't you use that towel over there to dry off, and I'll make you some coffee. We have really good coffee here, and we just purchased a new coffee machine last month. I often drink up to five cups a day! Tell me, do you take sugar?"

"Did you…" said Dad in a quiet voice, "happen to buy that machine from the salesman?"

"This machine? Yes, of course."

"And have you seen him today?"

"You mean yesterday," said the postmaster, returning to his seat with two steaming cups. "Yes I have. He came in just a little before lunch. He came to mail a brown envelope; a really thick one. I asked him if it was a financial report but he said it was something far more special than that. He was looking very pleased with himself."

"Did he mention whether he was sending it on behalf of someone else?" asked Dad, his eyes bulging as if he was choking on his own words.

"No, he didn't mention anything like that. He did say something about it bringing in money for him, though. Now hurry up and drink that coffee."

The postmaster gulped. It looked to him like the Mouse Man had suddenly visibly shrunk in stature. In fact, under the night light he now looked no taller than a trashcan. And he seemed fragile and helpless, like a mouse that'd just crawled out of a dark, dank sewer. Then, my miniature dad turned on his heels and ran. Immediately, the postmaster got up and ran after him, leaving the door swinging. By now the rains had subsided and he could just about make out a dark, semi-transparent blob spraying a trail of water into the air as it faded in the distance.

Around the same time at Warehouse #2, the tuba had sounded its last note of the night and the pipefitter stepped out into the wet night.

After practicing, he always felt numb in the ears. But the pounding of the rain penetrated the numbness easily.

"What do you say to a late-night drink?" the pipefitter said to Grandpa.

Grandpa shook his head. "I feel a cold coming on. I think I'll go straight home tonight." And off he went, tapping his cane in the puddles that lined the street.

The pipefitter headed off to the bar with three other band members. As soon as they opened the door, they were met with a huge commotion. There were people on the ground in tears. Others were engaged in heated arguments. And there was a buzz of hysteria that seemed to come from everywhere.

From deep in the crowd of people, the bartender poked out his head and yelled, "Hey, what can I get for you?"

"What on earth is going on?" the pipefitter yelled back, mindful to gesture for four beers at the same time.

"It looks like a wake," said the bartender. "Like we're mourning the town. You guys should drink up now. Because tomorrow, you might not be able to."

At that moment, their conversation was interrupted by the sound of a glass being shattered at the back of the bar. Then another. Then another. Tomorrow had already arrived.

The treasurer was taking a walk along the canal. He was deep in thought as he strode along, oblivious to the drops of rain that pitter-pattered onto the canopy of his umbrella. He'd been going through his books all evening. But no matter how many times, nor how carefully he redid his calculations, the numbers wouldn't add up. It was a difference of more than a few pennies. In fact, when he took into account the balance of the fireworks festival, the band's finances, the town's beautification project, and a whole range of other items, the ledger seemed to be as much as two whole digits off. This was no simple miscalculation. Could that nagging old woman in charge of the books have made such a blunder? Such an incredibly huge blunder? Wouldn't that be something, he thought.

Suddenly someone pointed a flashlight at him from a side street. The treasurer froze in his steps. He'd always been wary of sailors, especially drunken sailors. He subtly stooped to roll up the legs of his trousers in case he needed to make a run for it.

"Good evening," came a voice that belonged to neither a sailor nor a drunk.

"Oh, officer. It's you!"

A police officer stepped out of the shadows, followed then by another officer whose radio was buzzing on his belt.

"Is there a problem?" asked the treasurer.

"I wouldn't go that far for now," said the officer as he shone his light into the waters of the canal. "But we'd be very interested to know if you've seen the shoe salesman lately?"

"No. I haven't," said the treasurer. "But then, I've been glued to my desk all day."

"Well, right now," the officer began, "the police station is like a center for lost children. People are rushing in, one after the other, all asking where the salesman went. So we ask them what this is all about, but everyone says the same thing, *It's personal*. And that's all they'll tell us. Since noon today, we've had more than twenty people rushing in to ask us about the salesman. And we've had so many phone calls that we've lost count."

"Have you looked for the salesman's van? You know, the one that looks like a boot."

"We have. But it's not at the inn, and it's not at the school."

"Maybe it's at Warehouse #2."

"No, we checked there, too. We checked all the docks. We can't seem to find him anywhere."

The officer had no idea that at that exact moment his mother was being rushed to hospital in an ambulance. The treasurer was starting to feel hungry and cold. So much so that he temporarily forgot the problem with the books.

"Hey!" the other officer whispered suddenly. "There's somebody there!"

The treasurer followed the beam of light as it skimmed the surface of the canal. The water level had risen noticeably, carrying clumps of foam as it flowed toward the gates of the lock. A little further in the distance, all three could just about make out a thin shadow standing on top of the bridge, staring down at the water below, like a dead winter tree.

"It's the Mouse Man!" exclaimed the younger officer. "What's he doing? Don't tell me he's trying an experiment with swimming mice now."

"No," interrupted the older officer, very seriously, "there's something wrong."

Without another word, he took off in the direction of the bridge, with his flashlight bobbing in his hand and the younger officer in tow. Not knowing quite what else to do, the treasurer trailed along behind. As they got closer to the bridge, they watched helplessly as the Mouse Man lifted one leg, then the other, seeming to remove his shoes. Then he appeared to be cutting something with a pair of scissors.

"Don't do it!" yelled the older officer. But it was too late. Dad tumbled into the canal and was gone.

When the three reached the bridge moments later, all they found was a pair of shoes—one of the standard pairs peddled by the salesman all over town—and next to them were shoelaces cut to pieces. I can only imagine that Dad made a conscious decision to die without wearing a single thing bought from that despicable man.

The treasurer said that when Dad fell, he dropped like a hand that had come loose from a clock tower, tumbling end to end, breaking the water with the tip of his skull. There was hardly a splash. His body surfaced a surprising distance away, and was then carried by that black current toward the floodgates.

The policemen and the treasurer saw something else as well—small gray objects that seemed to jump off the bridge, one after another. For a moment, they formed a single dark blob on the surface of the water. Then in a flurry of bubbles they disappeared below, as if chasing after Dad.

"You say they weren't dark mice?"

"Definitely not," I replied to the young officer.

It was nearly dawn, but I kept talking despite my exhaustion. How could I not?

"Last year, I saw them with my own eyes," I told the officer. "Dark mice all over the place, scampering off in different directions. I think Dad's mice only huddled together because of the chemicals the salesman used. That's what Dad smelled of, and I think that's why the mice followed him."

The older officer remained silent as he sat on the sofa, arms crossed and eyes closed. He wasn't asleep, though, I could tell that much. Muffled voices came drifting out of the younger officer's radio.

We're at the sluice gate now. We've had the boats out for two hours now but nothing yet. I'll check in again later.

"Roger that," said the younger officer, resting the radio beside himself. "I wonder if your dad got out of the water somewhere and went off to conduct another experiment. It's nearly morning now. We'll find him in the daylight."

The older officer's eyes remained closed.

"I'm sure they weren't dark mice," I said again. "They couldn't be."

"Bring the kid a blanket," said the older officer. "He's shivering. Which is no surprise. He might not look it, but he's still sixteen."

The morning sun began to pour in through the window. The rain had stopped and rays of bright light threw glowing emphasis on the mathematical equations scribbled on the kitchen wall in chalk and ink. It reminded me of the dorm at the school for the blind with its walls bearing the signatures of its students, carefully written as lasting proof that they were once there—a roll call of students as plain as day for future students who'd never see them.

"I have no idea what this is. I can't even make out what it says," the young officer said. "Do kids learn stuff like this these days?"

Of course kids don't learn stuff like that these days. But there was one phrase even I recognized. One that seemed to appear again and again among the squiggles, formulas, and figures. It was a phrase that always made us groan whenever it came up in our school textbooks, and now here it was, scribbled in slanted letters on the kitchen tiles, across the stove, and even on the old cabinet.

Prove it. Prove it. Prove it.

Grandpa's health began to deteriorate, but since he refused to be hospitalized it was decided that the doctor would visit our house twice a day to give him his shots. Soon the doctor would have to fit him in among his visits all over town since bit by bit, the hospital beds were being filled with elderly people suffering from shock.

"Take care of your grandpa," the older officer said to me at the door. "I know why he didn't want to go into the hospital. It's because he's waiting for your father to return. Waiting like that can really take a toll. Keep an eye on him, will you?"

When I took a cup of tea up to Grandpa, I found him tapping the metal basin by his pillow to the music of panpipes and chorus of shepherds playing on the radio.

After the rain stopped, the town heated up almost immediately. And by as soon as lunchtime, the sheer scale of the damage to the town was becoming clear.

"There was a sightseeing tour of the resort planned for Saturday," said the father of the tuba player from his hospital bed. "There were thirty of us waiting at Town Hall. We waited for more than an hour, and still no salesman. He was never late before. Because it was pouring, we got worried something might have happened to him. That's when one fellow had the bright idea of calling the number at the bottom of the investment contract. I went into Town Hall to use a phone. I dialed the number. 'Hello, this is Petline,' came a voice from the other end, 'here to answer all your animal questions.'"

The tuba player's father was sure he'd gotten a wrong number, so he dialed again. It was the same animal helpline. It was the same animal helpline every time he dialed.

Of course, the elderly men and women of the town couldn't bring themselves to admit that their contracts were actually worthless pieces of paper. But in the end there was no denying it. The lion's share of their savings and retirement funds had been whisked away for the down payment. The funds had been sent to a private mailbox overseas, which had, the police later learned, been emptied on Monday morning.

The tragedy extended far beyond the promises of resorts, of course. There were the shares for the new shipping company, a new type of life insurance that accepted applications from customers over seventy, and there was a pile of other contracts stating ownership of assets that never had, and never will, exist.

Town Hall was also hit hard. All the money allocated for next year's budget had vanished from the safe, along with anything else of any monetary value such as deeds and bonds. Though the treasurer had been praying for nothing more sinister than a mistake in the books, no mistake was ever found. It wasn't just the postmaster who liked to be precise. All of the government employees in this town took great care in going about their work. But the numbers they'd been given to work with had never made sense from the start—not unlike a letter stamped with a fraudulent date.

Speaking of postage, I can't help but remember a line from the letter Dad had received from the mathematics competition the previous spring.

Detrimental gaps created by the fatal contradiction increase exponentially as the proof proceeds to its conclusion. This is only natural because the starting point is flawed.

For some reason, it made me think of a giant black snowball of sheep, rolling all over town and flattening finances wherever it went.

Back at the police station there were crowds of women waiting to question the salesman about the sleeveless dresses they'd ordered. They were supposed to arrive on Wednesday but nobody had received a thing. The dresses didn't arrive the following week either, even as summer gave way to autumn.

The innkeeper lost all of his assets, including the deeds to his land. I once heard someone say it was his own fault, but I think that's a bit harsh. You have to remember that the salesman was an excellent cheat when it came to playing poker, and the two of them had been playing almost every night. Bit by bit, the salesman had sent all his winnings to his private mailbox. Then a couple of months later, out of nowhere, an unfamiliar real estate company showed up with the deeds and razed the inn to the ground.

On Tuesday afternoon, Dad's body was found drifting out at sea.

A sailor had spotted a black blob floating amidst the waves, and it reminded him of the day when the ship covered with birds had found its way to port. The black blob was much smaller than the ship, however, and it was headed in the other direction, further out to sea.

As the sailor steered his ship closer, he saw that the black blob was actually a group of mice. They were clinging onto Dad's body, which was floating face down in the water, and they were huddled together and shivering.

"I'm sorry," said the sailor to me as he stepped onto the dock. "We couldn't pull the mice off, but we did get your father with a net."

The mice had to be pulled off of Dad's body one by one. The officer from Health Department that showed up at the scene counted one hundred and twenty-four mice in total. This wasn't a prime number. I'm sure Dad would have wanted to take into account the fact that some of the mice might have been lost at sea. By that weekend, the gossip rags had caught wind of the story and one of them ran the following article:

The End of the Mouse Man

The mad scientist renowned for his catch-and-release experiments on mice was seen jumping into the canal from the bridge two days ago. He was known around town as the Mouse Man and he'd been planning to submit the results of his experiments to a renowned mathematical competition. Unfortunately this never happened since his paper was stolen by a man he thought was a friend, but who actually turned out to be an infamous conman. According to the police, this man was well known for his tactic of posing as a harmless shoe salesman in order to win people's confidence.

The mathematician's body was discovered floating in the sea just beyond the harbor by a sailor on a ship. There were apparently hundreds, even thousands of mice clinging to the body. Sources inform us that the mathematician had been conducting research into mice herding and there was conjecture over whether this may have been a mishap during what came to be his final experiment, assessing the number of mice willing to follow him as he jumped off the bridge. If this information is accurate, then one must respect his outstanding dedication as a scientist. But I can't say I'm disappointed that I wasn't able to witness this incredibly, yet tragic event.

In the case of the postmaster, he received a different kind of nasty surprise. He'd been waiting several weeks to take delivery of his schooner. Then, ten days after the commotion in the town began to unfold, a small package arrived on his doorstep. Gingerly, he opened it. Inside was a scale model of a schooner with a triple mast (sails not included), which he left for display on top of the post office counter.

Perhaps the salesman had found it in his cold heart to take a minor liking to the postmaster. The police even found the postmaster's stamp collection in the salesman's room back at the inn (he may not have been able to find a buyer for it). The postmaster also got to keep his members-only catalog, which he placed on the shelf at the post office. And from that day on, people remarked upon the intricate level of detail on the boat perched atop the counter, with its new sails fashioned from used postage stamps and the side of its hull inscribed with the name, *All mail must be delivered precisely*.

The postmaster took his job very seriously and expected his employees to do the same. It didn't matter to him if they appeared silly in the eyes of others. It was their duty to postmark and deliver mail, day in and day out, even if it meant walking through wind and rain. The postmaster had been made to realize the inhumane nature of his profession by the salesman. As far as the postal service was concerned, there was no such thing as good mail or bad mail. Just like it said on the side of the schooner, all that mattered was that the mail was delivered accurately.

For all his expectations of a full-size schooner, all that the postmaster was left with was a piece of eye candy. But candy isn't always sweet. In fact sometimes it tastes like a rainstorm of mice.

At least the women of the town seemed to get something out of it all since the high heels bought from the salesman introduced the concept of fashion to the town. And though Town Hall had insufficient funds to hold a public event for quite some time, the fireworks event had been a big enough success to keep people talking for a while.

There was also the case of the tortoise on wheels and the diary of a sailor from thirty years ago. All of these were silly little constructions to help the salesman win the townspeople over. But while these were lies, they did at least grant the people a fleeting glimpse of paradise—a glimpse that lent a touch of glamour to the women's new clothes, the post office counter, and the memory of that unfortunate winter. People paid a hefty price, but you couldn't say that they were left with nothing.

That summer several older people in town could be heard mumbling similar sentiments. "I feel like the salesman might come to visit at any moment," said one elderly gentleman as he sat looking up at me. "You never met him, did you? He wasn't a bad guy. He must have been in a lot of trouble to do the things he did. If he had told me, maybe I could have helped."

Clutching at a Straw

I pushed Grandpa along in his wheelchair to Warehouse #2. Neither of us said a word. Grandpa kept a firm grip on his silver cane and kept his eyes fixed on the distant ocean. We'd heard that the warehouse had been plastered with legal signs following the court order forbidding entry without permission.

The insurance company had sequestered the warehouse—and all its contents—as collateral. Those instruments may have been nothing more than collateral to a dry old insurance company, but we knew them as the town's pride and joy! They were all in there, including instruments the insurance company had legally demanded that band members bring in—locked up behind the rusted but solid metal door.

Of course, the treasurer did his best to fight the insurance company on this, but in the end the debt held by the band was simply too great. Even the money for putting on the fireworks festival, which everyone assumed had been properly disbursed, ended up lining the salesman's pockets. Dealers in secondhand goods could be heard at the bar arguing loudly about how to split up the instruments among themselves.

When we arrived at the warehouse, Grandpa struck the door twice with his cane.

Dooong dooong.

We listened as the muffled sound echoed across the docks. Then he started to strike the door again—slowly at first, then with ever-increasing urgency. It was like he was trying to awaken the music that had been played in the warehouse over the last decade. He kept banging away until the coating on his cane chipped and the signs on the door were tattered. He was doing his best to hide it from me, but tears were quietly rolling down his face. It was the first time I'd since my grandpa cry.

Although he was in agony, he kept banging on the door—the same door he had banged on sixteen years earlier.

Suddenly, behind us, someone said, "Hey."

We turned around to find the pipefitter and the majority of the band members standing behind us. I was amazed. In their hands were things like an old washboard, a gray pipe, an accordion with holes in the bellows, a child's tambourine, a recorder, and even a bicycle horn. It was a symphony of instruments scavenged from the trash.

"We've just had a practice session in the grain warehouse," said the pipefitter, hoisting a water pipe on his shoulder. "Of course the acoustics aren't so good and it stinks of wheat, but the manager said he wouldn't mind us using it to practice. But without you, it doesn't come together. Would you join us, please?"

Light in the grain warehouse was dim, with millions of dust particles dancing in the sunbeams that shined in through the windows above. And there were narrow aisles, so narrow the handles of Grandpa's wheelchair kept getting caught on the bags of corn piled high.

"Wow!" I said, stepping into a clearing no bigger than the school's sandbox. "Where did these come from?"

It was four timpani, which the pipefitter showed us very proudly. "This is the work of the treasurer. He managed to get these deleted from the official list of band property. He told his boss there'd been a miscount. His boss fell for it—scolded him for being careless!" The pipefitter imitated the treasurer's boss: "You're always making mistakes like this. You need to pay attention!"

This made everyone laugh.

"And we still have the case of percussion instruments!" someone exclaimed. "This one he actually did forget to report. Really lucky carelessness!"

Without a word, Grandpa got up out of his wheelchair and wobbled forward with the aid of his silver cane. Then leaning over one timpani, he sounded the other with his outstretched hand.

Biiing.

"This thing is completely out of tune," Grandpa grumbled.

But the pipefitter wasn't listening. He was telling the story about how the vice-principal was running around town, frantic at getting caught in the salesman's life insurance scam. "He made his son the beneficiary, but the money he paid for the policy went up in smoke. What a joke! I warned him—never trust anyone promising a good deal!"

Grandpa wasn't listening to the pipefitter, either. He was concentrating, his eyes shut, as he adjusted the tension of the timpani with a focus that seemed like he thought everything be rectified if he could only succeed at tuning it. Of course, he knew that wasn't the case. Just like he knew that fallen rain can't rise back up into the sky. When things are gone, they're gone. You just have to deal with it.

As the group watched Grandpa go about his ministrations, the pipefitter spoke: "We're real sorry about your son. And I'm real sorry about saying he stank. But you know, we've just been saying how, in a way, we're all your sons. We may not have sprung from the inside your nut sack, but we're all your sons. Is that not true? Every member of this band is a son to you and a father to Cat. A father is always the rock to hold onto in a storm. You've held us together for more than a decade. And I hope you'll keep doing that. Please stay with us, please keep playing that big timpani of yours!"

"All right," said Grandpa, standing up and nodding. "All four drums are tuned." Then he wobbled into position behind the timpani, looked at the band members, and said, "Let's start. Cat, you conduct."

"What?!" I said, astonished at the sudden turn of events. "Right now?"

"Cat, a real musician is ready to perform 24/7," said the pipefitter, imitating Grandpa's voice.

"But how can I? I don't even have a baton."

"Use that." The clarinet player pointed to a long stalk of wheat. "It'll do."

I picked up the stalk of wheat. He was right. It was thick enough, firm and straight. It would do.

Since the space was too small for the band to take their places in any conventional arrangement, members sat where they could—on top of grain bags, looking down at Grandpa, the timpani, and me.

"Good thing you're tall, Cat," the pipefitter laughed from atop a bag of corn. "You don't need a platform for us to see you."

Grandpa's cane rapped on the floor. Everyone settled down. I looked at Grandpa, and he looked back at me. We were the only ones standing on the floor, and when Grandpa gave me the nod, I raised my hand.

When I brought my arm down, an ensemble of children's recorders let loose. From one of the grain bags came the low note of a water pipe, and in the place of a tuba came a low moan from the tuba player that sounded like he was being strangled. I kept my composure, waving my stalk of wheat conducting our makeshift junk instrument band.

We weren't in paradise. We were right here, in this world and in the moment, making the air vibrate around us. We were all over the place, but I will never, ever forget that moment. Our grain warehouse performance ranked as high in my opinion as our performance at the caretaker's funeral. It is one of the most memorable of my life.

"Again," demanded Grandpa. "The third recorder sounds funny."

"There's a crack," the clarinet player yelled from somewhere in the warehouse. "It's under my thumb hole. My kid pushed a screwdriver through the hole."

"Then fill it quickly!" Grandpa yelled. "Use your snot, mud, or whatever. Just fill the hole!"

A moment later, the ensemble started up again, with the timpani supporting the junk instruments with a low, soft beat. At first the piece seemed like a breeze, then an awkward wind that became stronger and stronger until it mustered enough power to blow out over the docks.

The Ball Connection

Two weeks after the salesman disappeared, his black van was found on the other side of the island. A lone hitchhiker described how it had come careening down a straight mountain road, swerving from side to side, out of control. The van slammed into a guardrail, went into a spin, skidding before smashing through a roadside grape stand and coming to an immediate cracking halt against a several-hundred-year-old pine tree.

"I was looking at the grapes," said the hitchhiker, "and if I hadn't been so quick in jumping out of the way, I'd have been crushed like they were."

The impact sent the salesman flying through the windshield and into the trunk of the tree, landing onto the shoulder of the road with a thud. His head was nearly severed. It was a surreal scene, with freshly picked grapes surrounding a lifeless body that looked like a worn-out shoe.

"The trunk of the van caught my eye," the hitchhiker went on, as a journalist from a local rag scribbled notes. "There was this sticky black liquid seeping out. At first, I thought it was gasoline. Then I realized it wasn't even liquid! You're not going to believe this, but it was a herd of mice! There were too many to count, and they all scampered off into the forest. Maybe they gnawed their way through the brake cables or maybe some got stuck in the engine."

When the police later examined the vehicle, no damage was found to the engine or to the brake cables. But there were three squashed mice just beneath the driver's seat.

"Perhaps one of the mice jumped out while he was driving and surprised him," the older policeman said to me later. "Maybe it made him lose control of the vehicle, the way he was stepping frantically on mice instead of the brakes. Like a little dance, a dance all the way to his grave."

To this day, I don't know if those mice were dark mice.

Following the salesman's death, the search for his evil takings continued, but nothing was found in his private mailbox, no cash was recovered, and all they found in the back of the van were piles of shoeboxes and bundles of shoelaces.

I'll never know if Dad knew a new member had been named to the judges' panel for the mathematics competition that year. Perhaps he didn't. But I bet the salesman did. That's why he stole Dad's thesis. Well, I say he stole it. But when I think about it, it was actually the salesman who took the paper and organized its information into something intelligible, something publishable. Although I hate to admit it, perhaps the salesman was more of a co-author than a thief. Anyway, as I was saying, there was a new judge who was better known for his odd behavior than for any contribution to mathematics. I mean, he was the kind of guy who would hear the phone ring somewhere in a restaurant, lift a bread roll to his ear, and say, "Hello?" He had actually won a medal in mathematics, so I guess he knew enough.

"There's something very interesting in this paper!" he stood up and declared during a meeting of the judges. "The language is crude, and the method of proof far from elegant. But there's something here. It's like a manic climber who keeps climbing despite one foot that's always dragging behind. And some parts are laugh-out-loud funny, too!"

On the strength of this single endorsement, Dad's thesis was awarded a special prize. And some time later, a student of one of the judges actually managed to put Dad's theorem of prime numbers and group dynamics to work in a more logical manner, which allowed him to solve a problem that, until then, had had mathematicians around the world stumped.

Interestingly, the rules of the international mathematics competition stated that in the event of a winner's death, the prize money was to go to the winner's assistant (which the salesman had claimed to be). In the event of the assistant's death, the prize money was to go to surviving family members. Nobody, however, knew the salesman's surname, let alone whether or not he had a family. All we knew about him was the whereabouts of an empty mailbox. In the end, the prize money was sent to me.

On the day I received the funds, I walked over to the stonemason's shop and asked for an epitaph to be added to Dad's tombstone. The stonemason got it done the same day. If you were to visit Dad's grave today, you'll see these words on the tombstone:

> PROVE IT.
> PROVE IT.
> PROVE IT.

I didn't know what to do with the rest of the prize money.

I went to visit Grandpa, who was practicing with the band at the grain warehouse. In the wake of the legal seizure of instruments, the band was left with small and large percussion instruments, but no woodwind or brass instruments. I asked the band which should be a priority or whether they might want replacements for certain instruments critical for performance.

Grandpa shook his head from behind the timpani. "No," he said. "You use the money."

The postmaster, who was sitting on a bag of grain nearby, leaned to me and whispered, "Yes, use it for yourself. Go study with the cellist. Do what the boxer said."

I turned in surprise, then glanced back at Grandpa, who was occupied showing the vice-principal how to shake a tambourine.

I'd stayed in contact with the Butterfly Man and in his "letters" he often talked about to the cellist. "I spoke to him on the phone the day before yesterday. I mentioned you, and he was very interested. He says he's got time to spare and wouldn't mind you coming and staying with him. I could hear dogs barking in the background."

These letters from the Butterfly Man were actually in the form of cassette tapes. In many ways they were better than written letters because they often contained additional effects like a clock ringing on the hour, or voices echoing in the gym, or the bustle of a concert hall.

I'd place my tape player on the counter of the post office and tell the postmaster what each of the sounds was and where it was coming from. I told him about the streets I'd walked with his sister and about the lake in her landscape painting. It had been a full two months since I was called home from school, and already the sounds of that castanet-shaped city felt far away.

One day after rehearsal, the pipefitter winked at me while wiping down his instrument. "Cat," he said, "you know we all think of ourselves as your fathers. But your real dad can't be replaced. You're connected by your balls, you know. You've got a ball connection. And that's something you must remember to be grateful for."

That night I lay in the bed I'd completely outgrown, unable to fall asleep, and I kept thinking of the last night I spent at the school for the blind. The sky full of stars. The gentle waves washing ashore. The Butterfly Man's shadow boxing. The talk of Red, Yellow, and Green. The blind students listening to the sound of the stars. I found myself thinking about maps. About how they're filled with roads and routes, but how they're useless in telling you which way to go. It didn't matter if you were blind or sighted; nobody ever really knew the right way to read a map. And since everything changes all the time, and the landscape of sound is continually redrawn, maps are immediately obsolete. Obstacles can appear out of nowhere, and the sand beneath you can suddenly shift. But however much the scenery changes, people have to keep on walking. Playing music is the same. You don't make music by staring at sheets of music.

My thoughts were interrupted by a tapping of a cane on the stairs, announcing Grandpa's imminent arrival. When he entered our room, I could smell alcohol.

"Grandpa," I said as he took off his tie in the darkness.

"What is it?"

"I'm going to move to where the cellist is."

"Oh," he said, then quietly lay down on the bed next to mine.

The cellist was living in the same town where Grandpa had had such a tough upbringing, and where he'd lived with my mom and dad, and it was a place that held few happy memories for him. And now, here I was—his only family member—drawn to that distant place like a butterfly attracted by the scent of flowers.

"I'm sorry to leave, Grandpa," I said after a while, "but I think I've made up my mind."

Grandpa didn't say anything. I could tell from his breathing that he wasn't asleep. I turned onto my back and looked up at the dark ceiling.

On the other side of the ceiling was the space where I used to poke my head in and listen to the sound. I'd shut my eyes and stick my head into the dark, dusty attic, leaving my oversized body in the room below.

At that moment, I heard footsteps. But not from above. It was a quiet sound coming from the stairs where Dad used to sit.

Ton, Ta-tan
Ton

It was faint, but it held my attention.

Ta-tan, ton

It was Kutze's wheat-stepp'n! His tapping echoed through my oversized body, though I could neither see him nor hear his voice.

"Watch what you eat, Cat." Grandpa said from my side. "The food there is dreadful."

"Okay," I said, my eyes still fixed on the ceiling. "I'll cook for myself—as much as I can. You know, I can make a pretty good omelet."

Ta-tan, ton

Stepping Forward for the Boat Ride

The day I was to leave, many of my "dads" came to see me off at the port, in a procession, each with a piece of musical junk in hand. Who would have thought these men were our band, the pride and joy of the town!

Grandpa handed me a bundle of papers. Having spent my formative years surrounded by sailors from around the world and leafing through gossip magazines from everywhere, I was familiar with different foreign languages. When I opened the bundle I was surprised to find a list of slang you'd never expect to receive from someone as serious as Grandpa.

"Grandpa," I said. "A guy like a skinned penguin? What does that mean?"

"Oh," Grandpa said calmly. "It means the guy is a chatterbox."

"Why would it mean that?"

"I don't know."

As the ship's whistle blew, I hurried along the gangplank, and the band members who had lined up along the dock played the famous farewell tune they'd been practicing for this day. It was a spectacular. Since they couldn't carry the timpani to the docks, Grandpa drummed away on a set of steel drums. And when the song was over, the deck erupted in a huge round of applause. Shouts for *encore!* were joined by another blow of the whistle, and as the ship moved ponderously out to sea, the band members held up their junk instruments and waved.

This was the first time I'd seen my hometown from the sea. I stood on the deck of the ship and kept my eyes on the silhouette of the island until it became nothing more than a pointy rock on the horizon, and then nothing at all.

I spent a week on that ship, and there was never a dull moment. I read through Grandpa's slang book and cut out interesting articles from the gossip magazines I piled up in the cabin. And as I walked around the ship I discovered that I knew a lot of the sailors, if only by sight, so there was always someone for me to nod to in acknowledgement. My oversized body had made me an easy person to remember. Among the passengers, there were several music-loving people, many of them elderly, who spoke to me like we'd known each other for years. I did have to be careful when around young children, though. If I happened to yawn, the child would immediately spin around and start wailing.

I ran into the short, music-loving ship's engineer who, grinning, took me down to the sailor's deck. When we got there, he proceeded to introduce me to a parrot sitting on a perch, with its tiny white feathers all puffed up and a squawk that said, *Gimme candy. Candy. Gimme candy!*

A sailor tossed a piece of fruit to it. The parrot craned its neck and clicked its beak as it skillfully caught the treat—its eyes like shiny black pearls and its gray beak that seemed to be smiling.

"I found him in a public bathroom on the docks," said the ships' engineer. "He looked really nervous and he was poking around the feathers on his belly with his beak. When he saw me he screeched, *Candy! Gimme candy!* And then he jumped on my shoulder."

The short engineer had no choice but to go back to ship with the parrot perched on his shoulder. Then, as soon as they were onboard, the parrot flew straight to the captain's quarters, where he tapped on the door with his beak and demanded, *Candy! Gimme candy!* for a long time. Of course, the captain wasn't there.

"I don't know whether the bird wanted to claw the captain's head," said the engineer, "or if it still liked the captain even if he was cruel. Who knows what it's thinking. It only says, *Gimme candy!*

"The only thing for sure is that it was the captain who taught the parrot to say that," the engineer went on, patting the bird on the back. "Seems a shame it can only say one thing. But then, if you could only learn one phrase, it's not a bad phrase to know."

The parrot looked at us and tilted its head. Then it began calling out that one phrase over and over and over again while rolling its black eyes—eyes that made me wonder what they really saw.

"The captain must have taken good care of the parrot," I said. "At least maybe in the beginning."

"I hope so," the short engineer mumbled, as he tickled the bird's white throat.

Gimme candy! Candy. Gimme Candy! the parrot kept repeating.

Every night, I fell asleep on a deck chair as I was gazing out at the calm sea. Then, one morning, I awoke to find the ship surrounded by a thick fog. Even through the fog, I could see dim lights shaped like balls of yarn scattered all around the deck.

"Cat, that's you there, isn't it?" It was the short ship's engineer appearing with a flashlight in hand and the parrot perched on his shoulder. "Terrible fog, eh?"

"Yeah." I said, lifting myself from the chair. "My whole body's soaked."

The ship moved forward slowly in the foggy sea, waves lapping against the bow. I wandered around on the deck, hardly seeing the fingers on my own outstretched arms. Occasionally, I was startled by voices that seemed to come from unexpected places, but like an illusion they seemed to fade away almost immediately. As the voices went on and on, I began to think I was in a crowd of people bustling along the deck, but I couldn't see a soul. The fog was so thick that it was like walking around the bottom of a bottle of milk.

Just before lunchtime, a sudden, high-pitched siren-like sound seemed to come from the waves, and the ship whistle responded with several low bursts of a whistle.

Somewhere on deck a small child cried, "Mommy, a dinosaur is coming!"

Then another short siren vibrated through the mist. I clung to the rail, trying to brush the white fog from in front of my eyes, straining to see into the distance.

"Calm down now. It's nothing like that," a mother said warmly. "The ships are just greeting one another. The sailors are just blowing whistles. It's not a dinosaur."

For the briefest of moments, the fog appeared to clear. And in that moment I saw—or at least I thought I saw—a huge black ship, so big it made our vessel seem like a row boat. Its chimney rose high into the sky. I wondered where it had come from, where it was going, and whether any port was big enough for it to dock in. At that moment, the siren sounded again, and our ship gave another blast of the whistle in response. Then that behemoth of the waves passed us, slowly and steadily.

"The dinosaur is crying!" the child yelled. "It's calling to another dinosaur!"

I strained to see through the fog, as the huge chimney appeared to bend before rising back into the sky and letting out a sound that resonated across the ocean—a sound so sad it seemed to come from an eternity of sorrow. Then, as quickly as the fog had opened up, it enveloped us once more and the sound faded further and further away. For several minutes, our ship continued to sound a whistle. But that was it. There were no more sad responses.

According to the cabin clock, the fog cleared on the strike of noon. But across the blue waves that stretched out in front, there was no sign of that huge thing that had passed us. Later that afternoon, I asked some sailors about it, but all of them said they'd seen nothing and they continued eating their shrimp without so much as raising their eyes.

One hour before the ship was to dock, an announcement was made in a foreign language asking everyone to prepare to disembark. It was simple for me: I only had a trunk with some clothes, sheet music, a baton, the reading material from Grandpa, and my scrapbook.

According to the Butterfly Man's audio letter, on arriving I was to:

Take bus no. 2 to the Botanical Garden gate. It should get there in around twenty minutes. Walk on the road the bus runs along, turn at the third corner. It's the fifth house on that street. The house is painted a bright color, and there are a number of dogs running around the lawn, so you should have no trouble finding it.

I held my new passport tightly and left the cabin for the deck, which was packed with people.

"Look!" someone yelled. "What an unbelievable building!"

Thanks to my unusual height, I had a great view despite being at the back of the crowd. It was an orange-colored building shaped like a castle, right in front of the dock. And it was the most unbelievable building I'd ever seen. All around, people were singing the building's praises. Then, from somewhere in front, the man in charge of crowd control called out in a bored voice, "That's just a warehouse. It's used to store empty containers."

Everyone fell silent.

As the ship made its way closer to the pier, I kept seeing larger and larger buildings. Each one looked like a small city to me. I realized I'd arrived at a true metropolis.

As soon as the ship docked, the gangplank came down. Passengers from other ships were lining up in the large building that housed immigration control and a plethora of different languages echoed throughout the room and bounced back off its cavernous ceiling. We proceeded quietly along the path marked by a metal fence. A security guard glared in my direction. I slouched as much as I could. A man behind me poked my butt with his umbrella. I was standing in the farthest right line for arrivals, beyond which were the lines for passengers departing—people wearing happy faces, gloomy faces, and every other kind of expression imaginable.

As I approached the front of my line, a very tired-looking woman stepped up to the departure desk holding a baby in one arm and the hand of a young girl in the other. She was wearing a thick purple shawl with an unusual pattern that made me wonder if she was from the countryside, and the girl was holding a stuffed bear with eyes and nose badly worn. Unlike her mother, the girl seemed cheery and unburdened, singing to herself in a strongly accented dialect.

Step, step, step, wheat-stepp'n Kutze, the girl sang as she swung her bear back and forth. *To a faraway sky, lifting those heavy shoes.*

"What are you waiting for?" someone yelled from behind me. "Move along already!"

White, black, and brown. Step them and crush them.

"I'm talking to you, you moron!" The same voice from behind me, followed by a sharp nudge to my back. Stumbling forward, coming to my senses, I grabbed the fence separating the arrivals from the departures. The mother and daughter were walking away, with the melody fading gently into the seaport sounds. I wanted to call out to them, try to get their attention. But I had no idea how to catch their attention in their language, and before I could think what else to do I received another shove in the back that propelled me into the immigration desk.

"Your passport. Hurry, please," the official said sternly, staring straight at me.

"It's…" I mumbled to myself in the foreign language. "I should have said, 'Wait a minute, young lady with the bear…'"

"What?" The officer lifted himself up off his chair and peered toward my trunk. "You don't have a bear cub in there, do you?"

Chapter 4

Seeing Green

There were four dogs out on the lawn. And when I rang the bell, the largest of them wandered over and sniffed my knees. A thin woman stuck her head through the door, and I told her why I was there.

"He's resting at the moment, but he did mention you were coming," she said. "Come on in."

She introduced herself as the housekeeper, and I followed her into a large circular room with black sofas and white sofas against the walls. A spiral staircase wound its way to the second floor, the steps covered in gray carpet. I sat down on a white sofa and looked around the room. The housekeeper brought me a glass of iced tea.

"I'm afraid he has absolutely no interest in interior design," she said, "so he lets his daughter choose everything."

"Did she choose that painting too?" I asked.

"She actually painted that when she was a little girl."

The painting had immediately caught my eye. It was of an open-air cello performance, and it seemed, even at a distance to suggest an incredible degree of detail—the expression on the cellist's face, the way he gripped his bow, and the faces of people in the audience. But shockingly, the painter had chosen very loud colors that seemed to ruin the atmosphere of the scene—as well as the room where the painting was hanging! Does growing up in a family of artists have an effect on your aesthetics?

"How old is the cellist's daughter?" I asked.

"She turned nineteen this spring," the housekeeper replied, then glanced up at the stairs as a small man, covered from head to toe in fluffy brown fur, made his way down. Leaning against the railing, he took one careful step at a time. He was about as tall as a bear cub on its hind legs, and his chest only came up to the railing of the staircase.

The furry man stepped onto the carpet with his short legs, then he let out a deep breath. The face sticking out through the hole of the outfit was as round as a ball. The eyes were foggy.

"Who's that? Who is it?" he asked in a high-pitched voice.

"It's our guest from abroad. The one who came by way of your friend's introduction," said the housekeeper, maintaining her courteous tone. "He just arrived. But if you're busy, I could show him to his room first."

"Either way is fine," said the man, his shoulders heaving as he breathed.

"Why don't I take the young gentleman's luggage to his room while you show him your studio?" the housekeeper said.

"Okay, I'll do that then," said the man. Then he turned to me, raised a finger slightly and said, "Follow me!"

The cellist walked across the living room in the direction of that horrible painting. He walked very fast for someone who couldn't see, and I had to hurry after him.

To say that his workplace was a tip would be a gross understatement. There were cello strings everywhere, coiled up like hedgehogs, and there were six cellos that lay on the floor like coffins. It was clear the room hadn't been aired out in a long time— it smelled like pickled sardines. There were also several fluffy brown outfits that lay under the cellos on the floor, as if the man had simply left them there after undressing.

On reaching the round chair in the middle of the room, the man sat down and stretched out.

"Go on then," he said.

"What do you mean?" I asked.

"Go on, start cleaning my room," he said matter-of-factly.

Despite my annoyance, I rolled up my sleeves without a word. I hung the cellos on the wall and collected the strings from the floor.

All the while, the man moaned in a low voice while swaying in his chair.

"Wipe the floor too, will ya?" he said.

I asked the housekeeper for a rag, then picked the brown outfits off the floor, which had the effect of filling the air with a pungent vinegar smell.

"Sir, you play the cello, right?" I asked, speaking in the foreign language as I wrung out the rag.

"I guess," he replied, dangling his feet. "Maybe I do."

"Well, I think your cello playing is the best in this world. My grandfather thinks so, too."

"That's an amazing thing to say," he said, fiddling with his earlobe. "That's really quite something."

The housekeeper brought me a bucket of water. I thanked her and turned back to the cellist.

"I've come here to learn how to conduct."

"That's nice."

"But I haven't come to be your cleaner."

"That's quite something."

"Excuse me," I said, dropping the rag to the floor.

The cellist absentmindedly stretched his hand behind his back and into his overalls. "Ah, I can't reach it. Can you scratch it for me?" he asked absently.

I let out a sigh that was loud enough for him to hear. Then I walked to him and started scratching his back through his outfit.

"Directly! Directly!" the man snapped. "Scratch it directly."

Doing what I was told, I pulled the zipper down in back. I was immediately caught by surprise. The man's backbone was visible through his skin. It was coiled and curved along his back, not unlike the cello strings on the floor. I scratched his back.

"There, there," he said. "You're a good backscratcher. You're called Cat, right? Well, Cat, I've decided I'm letting you into our group. You're part of our gang now, okay?"

According to the housekeeper this unusual man in his forties was indeed a world-renowned cellist. Until she confirmed the fact, I couldn't be sure since there were no pictures of him on the sleeves of his records, which instead featured photographs of women in lacy white dresses.

The housekeeper told me that the cellist had grown up in this town and that when he was a boy, he'd fallen off the back of a donkey. The trauma of the accident stunted his growth. When he was fifteen, he developed cataracts and underwent surgery at the national hospital. Unfortunately, the surgery was a failure, and he lost his eyesight. It was right after this surgery that he'd met the Butterfly Man at the school for the blind.

"He has no interest in anything other than music," said the housekeeper, crinkling her long nose while laying out black-and-white patterned sheets for me. That was the way she smiled, I grew to understand. "Deep down, he's a very kind man. When he says 'whatever,' he means we should do whatever we please."

"Oh," I said, as I stacked my scrapbooks and sheet music on the bookcase. I happened to look at the fingers on my right hand—the one I'd used to scratch his back. My fingernails were black with grime.

My room was on the second floor on the west side. A large greenhouse stood not far from the window, and the western sun reflected off the glass, sparkling like grains of sand.

"When does he practice?" I asked, narrowing my eyes.

"Practice?" The housekeeper turned around, surprised. "He almost never practices, at least not in this house."

"He doesn't play his cello?"

"No." She crinkled her nose again. "Especially not at night. It gets the dogs too excited."

"Ah," I nodded, "I noticed there were several of them in front."

"Yes, his daughter is really fond of them."

When the school for the blind was shut down ten years ago, the cellist came to our town to give his testimony. He brought his daughter with him to make a vacation out of the trip. That was when the principal of the school asked if he wanted one of the seeing-eye dogs.

"He had no preference as to which dog, as usual," the housekeeper said, "but his daughter took one of them in her arms and was definite about it being the one."

The seeing-eye dog named Green produced seven puppies before falling asleep one day and never waking up. Apparently there were three more dogs in addition to the ones I had seen.

"She took a liking to that particular dog because they had the same name as she did," said the housekeeper.

"The same name?"

"Yes, her name is Green, too." The housekeeper pummeled the pillows into shape. "She named the puppies different shades of green: Light Green, Yellow-Green, Viridian, Grass, Purple-Green, Blue-Green, and Deep Green."

"Well, that's something." I said.

"Oh, by the way, please be sure to close the window at dusk," the housekeeper said. "The wind from the Botanical Garden is extremely damp when it gets cold."

The dining room was in a small space just off the living room. All through dinner the cellist, who was still in his brown outfit, kept waving around a potato on the tip of his fork, causing it to fall onto the table from time to time.

"Cat, get that!" he'd say.

I'd grab the potato with my bare hands and stick it back on his fork.

"About your daughter, sir, there's nothing to worry about," said the housekeeper as she appeared with a bowl brimming with mashed potatoes and a garnish of parsley. "She called this afternoon. She said the lab was crowded so she'd be a little late."

"Whatever! Doesn't matter!" The cellist threw his fork with the potato into the salad bowl. It landed with a thud.

"Sir," I said. "Your daughter's name is Green?"

"Yeah?" He swayed in his chair. "That's my daughter's name."

"Why did you, um, ah, what is the origin of her name?"

"Hah, what a strange thing for a cat to wonder," the cellist said, a degree of irritation evident in his tone. "I don't know. Her mother named her. I couldn't give a damn if it was Green, Blue, Yellow, Brown, or Orange. Anything would have been fine. Hah! It's all the same, damn it!"

This line of conversation proceeded to drive the cellist crazy. He climbed onto his chair and bashed his head with a clenched fist. For a moment, I thought I should say something, but the housekeeper gave me a look that suggested I keep quiet.

"Names don't matter!" The cellist was on a tear. "Green is a good girl! She's my best friend in the whole wide world. Aha, I see what's piqued your interest! Cat, you're in heat, aren't you? Oh, I understand now."

He sat on the table and stared at me with his white eyes. Then he smirked and fluttered his tongue, in and out, in and out. He was really giving me the creeps.

"In heat, in heat, the cat monster's in heat!" the cellist sang, jumping up and down on this chair.

"Sir," the housekeeper said, "I understand you're happy to have a new friend, but we're in the middle of dinner and you're making him uncomfortable."

"Oh, okay," said the cellist, suddenly meek. Quietly he settled down in his seat and searched the tabletop for a utensil.

I picked up a fork and placed it in his hand. This brought a smile back to his face.

"Speaking of songs," I said, placing some salad on my plate, "have you heard of a song about wheat-stepping?"

"What's that?"

I cleared my throat and sang the song I'd heard while waiting in line at the port.

Step, step, step, wheat-stepp'n Kutze...

"What a terrible song!" the cellist immediately piped up, interrupting me.

"Sir!" the housekeeper said sharply, causing the cellist to look at the floor in shame.

"I'm sorry, I don't know that absurd tune," he said, fumbling with a potato.

"Wheat stepping?" the housekeeper picked up the conversation. "You mean what they do in the fields in the winter?"

"Do you know the song?" I asked, my mouth gaping open like an idiot.

"No, I don't know the song," the housekeeper said, "and it's too warm in this area for us to ever see people doing it, but

I heard wheat stepping is done a lot in the north during their winter. I heard the farmers line up in the snow and step from side to side…"

"Yes, from side to side!" Now it was my turn to stand up in excitement. "They go stepping sideways along the fields! But are you saying they do that in the snow?"

"Yes."

"Not on yellow dirt?"

"No, I don't think so."

I processed this bit of information, then asked if she knew why people do this. Setting her fork down, she said she'd only seen pictures of people doing it and she didn't really know. Then she straightened her back and walked off in the direction of the kitchen.

"Cat, Cat, Cat." The cellist now asked a little desperately, "Is it fun, this wheat stepping?"

I thought before answering. "I don't know."

"Why don't you do it for me." He stared at me with his blind eyes.

I didn't really want to, but I stood up, and slowly started stepping on the shiny wood floor—moving sideways and back.

Ton, Ta-Tan

Ta-Tan, Ton

"I remember now!" the cellist exclaimed. "He said on the phone. He said you hear weird sounds. You do, don't you?"

"I guess."

I figured that by "he" he meant the Butterfly Man, though I didn't think the Butterfly Man used the phrase "weird sounds." Meanwhile, the cellist was clapping his hands with delight.

"You're part of the gang, Cat! A true member!" the cellist squealed, scrambling down from his chair and performing cartwheels around me.

I continued my wheat-stepping, with the cellist managing to avoid my outsized shoes every time I stepped to the side. Then suddenly he stopped and shouted, "She's back!" and darted into the living room.

As the front door swung open, I could hear dogs barking. Then a skinny girl carrying a huge bag walked in. My heart skipped a beat. Never in my life had I seen anyone with such porcelain white skin!

She was wearing a light purple sleeveless dress like the one in the salesman's catalog, and her arms hung by her sides as if they were made of milk-flavored Jello. She had a small face, and she was wearing celluloid-rimmed green glasses. She was supposed to be just two years older than me, but she wore a calm smile that gave her an air of maturity.

"You're late!" the cellist proclaimed.

"I'm sorry," she said in a soft voice. "Everywhere was so crowded today. Anyway, here's your medicine, Dad. I already ate dinner, so I can take the dogs on a quick walk if you like."

"I'll come with you!" said the cellist, jumping up. "Give me a second, I'll get my cane!"

I listened to his footsteps as he shuffled off to his studio. Then I turned to the girl, who placed her bag on the floor, took off her glasses, and smiled.

"Um, nice to meet you. I'm Green."

"Yes," I said, "I know."

I quickly looked down at my feet. I wasn't moving anymore, but the sound of footsteps continued to ring in my ears, clearer than ever. It was as if the sound of wheat-stepping were echoing through my huge body.

Ton, Ta-Tan, Ton

Ta-Tan, Ton, Ta-Tan

"Thanks for waiting!" The cellist reappeared holding a white cane that was almost as tall as he was.

"Well, we're off for a walk," Green said, stretching. "You can tell me all about yourself later, Cat!"

She turned on her heels and left. And even as the cellist's voice and the barking dogs faded into the distance, the sound of wheat-stepping continued to reverberate through my head.

The housekeeper began clearing the dishes away from the table. It seemed this kind of thing might happen a lot, with the cellist losing all interest in food the moment his daughter showed up.

"I'll make some sandwiches from your leftovers," she said. "I'll bring them to you for a late-night snack."

I thanked her, and as I was returning to my room, I glanced at the large bag that Green had left open in the hallway. I could see a tripod, a diffuser, and a camera. Now that I thought about it, there were lots of photos displayed in the hallway upstairs. This girl was not like I'd imagined her at all—she didn't seem like the kind of person who'd choose such odd décor and paint pictures with such loud colors.

I climbed the stairs and looked closely at the photos. All of them were black and white. There was one of a friend smiling. One of the housekeeper cooking. There were plenty of dogs, dogs, and more dogs. And finally there was one of the cellist in a tuxedo. There was something about each of them that captivated me.

Ton, Ta-tan
Ta-tan, Ton

A single faded color photograph was hung at the end of the hall. I recognized the scene immediately—it was the caretaker's office at the school for the blind. The caretaker looked a good ten years younger than when I'd met him. He was crouching next to the cellist, who seemed angry, and Green, who was smiling with her arms around a dog's neck. She seemed about nine or ten years old, and while I couldn't be certain, I bet the dog was Red! This dog was the Butterfly Man's sparring partner who was supposed to have jumped into the lake to save his master, and here he was, in the middle of a photo with his tongue hanging out.

Ta-tan, Ton

"Is something the matter?"

The sound of Kutze's footsteps were replaced by the housekeeper's coming down the hall. In her hand was a plate with a potato sandwich that she placed on the table.

"Um, can I ask—was Green born with a defect in her eyes?"

"Yes," the housekeeper replied. "It's called congenital monochromasia One in 100,000 people has it. Green can't tell the difference between any colors at all."

"So was her father color blind, too?"

"No." The housekeeper shook her head. "To tell you the truth, the cellist is not her biological father. He adopted her when she was three. He probably couldn't bear to turn down taking her in once he'd learned of her eye condition."

The dogs started barking dogs again just then, and mixed in was a tune that the cellist was humming, accompanied by his daughter's soft laugh.

"You know, to him the only thing that truly matters is Green. Next to Green, even music is second," said the housekeeper on her way out. "You'll have to excuse me. I sometimes talk too much."

"I don't think so," I said to her. "Thanks for the sandwich. It looks delicious."

The housekeeper crinkled her nose slightly and carefully pulled the door closed. I listened as her footsteps moved out of earshot, only to be replaced by the familiar tap-tapping that still echoed through my mind and body.

Ton, Ta-tan

The Mirrorless Palace

It was soon after entering elementary school that Green realized there were colors in this world and that colors gave things a different character beyond their shape and brightness. That day, her homeroom teacher handed out a calendar indicating events for the upcoming month such as afterschool activities, parents' day, morning assemblies. Green glanced over at her friend sitting next to her and saw she was circling the Saturdays and Sundays. The circle around Saturday was light, the circle around Sunday was dark.

"Doing this really makes me like Sunday," her friend said.

"Why?" asked Green.

"Because red is kind of special, don't you think?" the girl replied. "My dad works on Saturdays, so I think blue is the right color for that. But it's still a lot better than the other days. I wish every day was a red circle day!"

Green looked at her calendar. Although there were slight variations in darkness, the days were all in black. She looked over at the girl's calendar again with its numbers that somehow stood out, as if special.

As the dogs dragged her along the path, Green said to me, "I finally understood. The red was making it special. The red made the day stand out. So I borrowed her colored pencil, went through my calendar and marked mine up, too. Then the girl frowned at me and said, 'I don't think green is the right color for Sunday.'"

"Is it just red and green?" I asked. "I mean, are those the only colors you can't tell apart?"

"All colors are more or less difficult, really," Green said. "Dark purple and green look the same to me, and I can't tell the difference between light blue and cream. I can tell if a color is deep or light. But when I stare at something a long time, my head starts hurting. That's when I think, *Ah, it's got color!* But this doesn't happen with black and white photos or books with just text."

Apparently, dark brown, the color of the cellist's outfits, was the easiest on her eyes. Since that day in elementary school, she began learning about color through trial and error. She'd heard that apples were red, and that grapes were purple. She knew that watermelons were green on the outside, but red on the inside. She knew that everyone loves the way the sky and sea are blue, but nowhere in this world would you be able to find food that is completely blue.

One thing that was always a problem was shopping for clothes. Everyone wore a uniform at her elementary school, and once she started junior high she stuck to wearing monochromatic clothes for a while. Then she heard that some boys had been calling her The Undertaker behind her back. Immediately, she went to the department store with the housekeeper and bought everything from skirts to sweaters in Green to match her name. Then she heard they were calling her The Frog.

"It probably didn't help that I wore green glasses," Green laughed. "You know, everyone croaked at me whenever they saw me."

Green studied hard. She didn't understand why she got teased, but she learned that certain combinations of colors could make a girl look silly. For example, wearing blue slacks and an orange shirt made you look like a clown, while dressing in a pink sweater and a red skirt made you look like candy cane. Green spent a half day choosing clothes while her head throbbed with pain. She eventually learned that there were colors that suited her face and build. Pale yellow and light purple looked good on her. She had no idea what these colors looked like, but they made her stand out, just like the red circle around Sunday. That spring at their school festival, Green received the Best Dressed award. And for the awards ceremony, she dressed in an outfit comprising slightly different shades of green from her hat to shoes. No one croaked at her anymore.

I stood outside the greengrocer's holding seven leashes, waiting for Green to purchase vegetables. She chose the freshest potatoes, onions, and carrots with hawk-like speed, and she could tell the freshness of a vegetable at a glance. And it wasn't just vegetables. No matter whether it was meat or bread, she could detect the slightest smell, touch, and even something like a voice that the food couldn't let out. She could sense everything with incredible accuracy. With the exception of color, of course.

Green hadn't realized that the dog she had adopted ten years earlier was wearing a red collar. Even the housekeeper didn't suspect that the color of the collar had anything to do with the dog's name. Red was supposed to be the calm alpha dog at the school for the blind. When they saw the dog digging up the lawn and playing in the mud, the housekeeper, the cellist, and his daughter Green had all assumed that the dog was just restless in her new surroundings.

If it had been a regular dog, the cellist may have realized their mistake on hearing its bark, but the three dogs at the school for the blind were extremely well trained and never barked, not even when they were very excited.

In the first audio letter I ever sent the Butterfly Man, I talked about my journey on the ship and about my impressions of the city before ending it like this:

> *As it turns out, your beloved Red lived quite a comfortable life after school. If it was Yellow who died from being kicked in the stomach, the very responsible dog that jumped from the boat into the lake to save his master was actually Green.*

Nearly every morning I walked the seven dogs around the Botanical Garden, and every afternoon I went into the vibrant city and took in the surroundings. Sometimes Green would show me around the market or the arcade on her way home from school. But I always remembered what the Butterfly Man advised me in his tapes: Be patient. Let your body discover what kind of place it is. "Besides," his voice continued, "the cellist may seem very temperamental, but I have no doubt he's thinking about what's best for you. That's the kind of person he is. Eventually he'll start teaching you music in his own way. Wait for that time to come."

I'd be lying if I said I wasn't feeling impatient. But I did understand, in a way, what the Butterfly Man was talking about. For example, at dinner the cellist would always request that I do the wheat-step. If I didn't do it right, he'd get mad and throw food all over the table. But it was clear that the cellist was carefully listening to the sounds I made. So I decided to try to wait patiently in the meantime and explore different parts of the city.

I took the bus to the train terminal, where you could catch the metro all the way into the city center. I felt dizzy counting the number of stations on the map. After all, even the largest city on our island didn't take long to walk around. But here, each station felt as big as an island. The metro was like a boat going round and round the city before I got off at some random station and mingled with the crowds.

I saw a library that looked like dozens of large plates stacked up on top of each other as well as a tower made purely from glass. I saw the palace at night, which seemed to be an endless line of buildings that stretched into the distance like cruise ships tethered along the docks. Snaking lines of cars filled the roads, and there was the sound of angry horns everywhere. It felt like all the world was gathered in one place, right here.

The newspapers were thick! When I first saw them piled up in a mailbox while walking the dogs, I thought that it was a whole week's worth. They were nothing like the ones back home that had a total of twelve pages. The sheer variety of stories in them was incredible, so I had new stories for my scrapbook pretty much every day. It was almost as if the city itself was a scrapbook! For example, on just one two-hour subway ride, I witnessed one incident involving someone jumping onto the train at the last second, three incidents of luggage theft, and three fist fights! But the fist fights were nothing compared to the ones I'd seen between sailors back home—they seemed to drag on and on without drama or interest. In two of the fights, people who weren't involved in the argument ended up getting badly beaten and had to be carried out of the station on a stretcher. But not one of these incidents made it into the paper—they were simply too mundane for this city to print.

I was happy to find a collection of music magazines in the library. None of them carried information about playing percussion instruments or about sheet music. Instead, the articles were about things like a famous guitarist who had killed himself, or how a harpist and a singer had had a shouting match on stage. Or how some poor violinist who hadn't performed in a concert in a while ended up putting on weight until he reached over 100 kilograms.

In one of the magazines, I found an article about the cellist. There was a letter from a reader in a column called "I-Witness!" where the author claimed that the world-renowned cellist was a regular in the red light district on the east side of the city:

> *His favorite place is the brothel called the Mirrorless Palace. He's been known to go with three prostitutes at a time in the middle of the day!*

It was a day in early September when I first visited the brothel myself, the third Saturday after I'd arrived at the cellist's house. I'd returned from walking the dogs after breakfast to find a luxury car that looked like a naval ship parked in front of the house. The dogs were scared by it and ran yelping toward the back, while the cellist remained sitting on his cello case by the front door, wearing an outfit of dark brown fur that seemed a little fluffier than usual.

"Come along, Cat," he said, standing up.

I had no idea where we were going, but I did I was told and got into the car.

We sat facing each other on the back seat and after an hour I could see a dust-covered town in the window. Two-story wooden houses lined the road, and at the entrance of each stood a somberly dressed woman with heavy makeup. She would call out to the men who passed by. Occasionally the doors to these houses would be open doors, and I could see women dressed like peacocks sitting with their legs crossed.

The car came to a stop in front of a fairly new house. Unlike the other on the street, this one was three stories high and had a wavy roof with fading red paint. A sign was nailed to the front door:

THE MIRRORLESS PALACE
NO MIRRORS ALLOWED

The driver slowly opened the car door, and I was hit by the strong smell of urine combined with alcohol and strange things I couldn't begin to guess at. A middle-aged woman strolled over from the dark entrance on the other side of the street.

"It's been a while since you've been here," she said, welcoming us. Her face heavily powdered, she turned in my direction. "I see you've found yourself a new partner. Come in. You're attracting too much attention with this car."

The cellist disappeared with her into the house. Then the driver got out of the car, the instrument case in his hands. "What are you waiting for?" he said to me. "Get going!"

"Um," I said sheepishly, "I have no idea what's going on."

"You'll find out soon enough."

It was cool in the house. The wooden walls were polished to a shine. It wouldn't have qualified as a high-end hotel, but it was clean and the atmosphere was relaxed, like a country hospital. It was certainly a lot better than the inns or the sailors' lodgings at the port.

In the waiting room, two girls in their negligees sat smoking cigarettes. The smell of sweet perfume mixed with smoke and disinfectant. The cellist was standing between the girls, who were stroking his head. Outside, the driver tooted the car horn before driving off.

One of the girls was in pink, the other in light yellow. The negligees were long, with edges that fluttered like the smiles on their faces.

"Let's see, who's next?" the middle-aged woman said, licking her finger as she flipped through the ledger. "It's Camellia on the third floor. A customer left just half an hour ago."

"No, no!" the cellist screeched. "We aren't following any order. Cat's going to choose today."

"Cat?" The woman looked at me. "Oh, I see. Your partner. He looks a bit naïve to me. Are you sure you want a boy this young doing the choosing?"

"I said it was okay!" The cellist jumped up and down on the spot. "Go on, Cat, choose whoever you like."

"But how?" I asked, bewildered. "Choose who?"

The woman burst out laughing and said, 'The girl you want, of course."

"Quick! Quick!" the cellist yelled from behind them.

The two girls looked my way, noticing me for the first time. The woman in charge, who must have been the mistress of the house, suggested it might be helpful if I looked through the photo book.

"We have about thirty girls in all," she said, "though half are sleeping right now."

I shook my head in a hurry. Then a familiar noise filled my ears.

Ton, Ta-tan, Ton

Kutze's footsteps were everywhere.

Ta-tan, Ton, Ta-tan!

"Quick, quick!"

"Are you all right?" asked the mistress. "You look terrible."

I took a deep breath. My head felt like it was about to explode. *Ton.* In the corner of my eye, one of the girls was smoking. *Ta-tan.* She tapped her cigarette into the ashtray several times.

Ton, Ta-tan, Ton

"I want the one in yellow," I said with my eyes closed. "The one in the yellow nightgown. The one with the cigarette!"

The girl in yellow smiled broadly. Then she put out her cigarette in the ashtray.

"He must really like you," the mistress whispered in my ear. "He doesn't like to choose for himself." She them nudged me in my butt. "Go on then, off you go."

I climbed the narrow stairs quietly, moving carefully through a tunnel of darkness, one cautious step at a time.

"Cat, over here, quickly!" It was the cellist.

I wiped the sweat from my forehead, turned the corner of the stairs and continued on my way to the third floor.

Ta-tan, Ton

Sunlight streamed into the room, bathing the girl in yellow as she sat by the window. She was wearing a different expression now, as if a haze had cleared to reveal the deeper core of who she was. When she smiled at me, there was something so beautiful and yet so raw about her that I was captivated and repelled at the same time.

The cellist was there, too. He tossed his outfit into the closet by the door and stood in his underwear, his twisted spine snaking its way along his back in plain sight. A large instrument case lay on the floor; the driver must have brought it up. The cellist took out an old cello that was almost as tall as he was.

"Okay, Cat. Do your thing."

I stood with my hand on the doorknob. I looked at the silver watch on my wrist, heard the quiet ticking away of time. The girl in yellow tilted her head, calmly gazing at the cellist and me.

"Do what thing?" I finally managed to ask. "What do you want me to do?"

The cellist turned his white eyes toward me, and I thought he might cry out in anger at any moment. Then the girl covered her mouth with her hand and laughed.

"You know, Cat," she said, "even though he can't see, he loves coming here. He's been coming for more than twenty years. He holds that cello and listens to stories."

"Stories?"

"Yeah. Stories about us girls sitting on our beds. About the kind of people we are."

The girl in yellow gathered her knees in her arms and glanced toward at the cellist.

"At first we told our own stories," she said, "but that got to be a little difficult. Eventually your friend started bringing a partner with him. Someone who could tell him what the girls look like. Today, Mr. Cat, you are that person."

I stared at her in amazement. She wore a smile on her face, but at the same time seemed to be entirely serious. I looked at the cellist again, and he must have felt me looking at him. He frowned, scrunching up his eyebrows, then mumbled some gibberish.

"Why don't you take that seat there and make yourself comfortable," said the girl as she took off her yellow negligee. "If you get thirsty, there's alcohol by the sink."

I tottered over to the chair, holding onto the back as I lowered myself into the seat. Then I took a deep breath, smelling the powerful perfume in the room. I had a duty to perform.

I cleared my throat and began, "There's a girl sitting on the bed, and she's very beautiful."

The girl opened her eyes dramatically.

"She's slim, and she has red hair. By her feet is a piece of lingerie, a nightgown, neatly folded. It's yellow. As the sun streams in through the window, her body glistens as if she's fresh from a bath."

The girl let out a giggle.

"Be quiet!" the cellist scolded her in a small voice. "Cat, continue."

So I did. I described her thin, long face and her well-defined collarbone. About the black cord that looped around her breasts and waist. About how the cord was decorated with tiny stones and how those stones clinked against each other whenever she shifted. I also found it fascinating for myself; I didn't know how varied and interesting underwear could be.

If I occasionally mixed in a flattering comment or something not quite believable, the cellist would swing his arms and scream at me to stop talking nonsense. But what was I to do? I'd never spent much time around girls, let alone a near-naked prostitute. So it wasn't long before I ran out of words to describe her with and my pauses between words became longer and longer. When I got stuck, the girl would help me out by doing something, like removing the string from around her waist or getting down on all fours. At one point, she lay down on her back in front of me and my eyes came to rest on her stomach. I don't know how I'd missed it before but she had a recent wound there; one with six little stitches and a tinge of red around the edges.

"There's a cut on her stomach," I mumbled. "But it's a small one, nothing serious. Like a razor cut."

"You guessed right," said the girl in a tired voice. "A man did this to me last Monday. A very jealous man. He went crazy with a razor, then he cried when he saw my blood."

Ton, Ta-tan

Kutze's footsteps were growing louder.

"I once knew a woman who had a cut on her stomach," I said. "But she wasn't so lucky. She died from it."

I then recited, word for word, the story of the Pigeon Lady that I'd read the summer I was seven. In rhythm with Kutze's footsteps, I related the tragedy of that circus performer when the stones she'd eaten tore open her stomach. As I was telling the story, the girl and the cellist did not say a word. All I could hear was my voice accompanied by Kutze's footsteps. Even after I'd stopped speaking, the two of them remained silent. Then I looked again at the cut on the prostitute's stomach and said, "Maybe a cut from the inside takes longer to heal."

At that moment, from the corner of my eye I saw the cellist lift the bow in his hand. Then a pure sound cut through the air, and the atmosphere in the room was transformed. As the cello breathed its magic, the room filled with music, with vibrations strong and delicate, from notes that were faint and that were vigorous. Having grown up in a port town, I was reminded of the great sea. The boundless ocean, with waves of a thousand heights, stretching far beyond the horizon. A single blue transparent stretch of water.

If a band played the music of the wind, then the cellist was playing the music of the sea—with each draw of his bow calling to mind a mirage over the water, before it faded away together with the waves. Meanwhile the cellist held the instrument tightly, as if he was in danger of falling back, his body all but hidden from view. Then, after several moments of bringing the tide to our minds, he brought the bow to a gentle stop. His shoulders relaxed with his breath, and invisible sparks bounced around the room.

At once, the cellist rose to his feet, walked over to the window, and collapsed on the prostitute who was now lying on the bed. He mumbled a few words, hugged her tightly around her waist, then promptly fell into a deep and peaceful sleep.

I stood up from my chair. I could no longer hear Kutze's footsteps. They'd been washed away by the tide of the cello. I gripped the doorknob, turned it, and slowly stepped out of the room.

"I was moved," said the girl lying naked on the bed as I left. "By your story as much as by his cello."

When I reached the parlor on the first floor, I found the mistress playing ring toss with two girls. They smiled at me and offered me a seat beside them. A girl with a fuller figure brought me lemonade. I lifted the glass it to my lips, then my head yanked back in surprise. It must have been half alcohol! That was when I noticed that the targets for the ring toss were bottles of booze, too. Soon after, I learned that on the first floor of the building next door was a bar equipped with a stage for performances.

"Your story must have really been something," said the mistress, wiping sweat from her brow. "I haven't heard the cellist perform so movingly in years."

"It wasn't a big deal," I said, pretending to sip the lemonade. "I told a story that actually had nothing to do with that girl."

"What kind of story?"

"It was a story about a circus performer who died when stones burst her stomach."

That left all three women puzzled.

I learned later from the mistress that the last partner of the cellist was a jockey who'd lost his job when he gained too much weight. The cellist had paid him nearly three times what he'd been making as a jockey. Then, after half a year, the jockey eloped with one of the girls from the brothel. But the cellist didn't say a thing. In fact, half his storytellers ended up eloping with a girl. The other half were killed in accidents, thrown in jail, or they escaped abroad where they couldn't be reached. Despite all this, no one had ever heard the cellist speak badly of any man.

The cellist had started frequenting the Mirrorless Palace soon after he left the school for the blind. The late madam who started the palace gave it that name because both the girls and the men who came there didn't want to see their own faces. The middle-aged mistress knew this because until three years ago she had been a prostitute herself. The madam, she said, was extremely fond of the blind cellist. It was she who started the cellist down this road; it was she who'd begun telling stories to the cellist about herself. It didn't matter that her stories were nothing more than white lies.

"I guess there were elements of the truth mixed in there, too," the mistress continued. "But I don't know how much. You know, for girls like us, it's not so easy to talk about yourself, whether it's the truth or a lie. We spend our days not wanting to see ourselves. Perhaps that's why we all feel safe around the cellist. Because of his eyes."

"His eyes?"

"Yes. Because he's blind," she said, as the girls began tossing rings at the targets again. "Being around a person who can't see you is reassuring. We can mix make-believe with the truth. And for a few moments, and for those moments alone, we can be the person we've always wanted to be. The same with the cellist. In a way, from the beginning, he's a mirror for our dreams, one that never needs to reflect who we really are."

"I'm not sure I understand."

"It's okay. I didn't expect you to!" The woman laughed out loud. "The madam who started this place came from a family that had eye problems. She understood. She had something in common with the cellist. She and several of her siblings were born without the ability to distinguish color. They had the same rare disease."

"She couldn't see color?" I asked, gulping down saliva. "Does that mean...Green is...?"

"Green, the cellist's daughter? Yes, the madam was her mother. On the day the baby was born, the cellist was playing his instrument in the basement. The madam named the child Green because green was the color the madam wished she could see most."

Behind us, the girls cheered and sighed. The game of ring toss over. A musician had walked in through the door, his head held low.

"Green's father was a customer," the mistress continued. "A sailor on a foreign cargo ship."

"Does Green know?" I asked.

"Of course she does. She lived here until she was three years old, when the cellist adopted her." The mistress smiled. "The cellist and everyone here are like a family. The cellist calls us his gang. After he listens to stories his partner tells about his gang members, he plays his cello. That's how it goes."

The mistress clapped her hands together and ordered the girls to get changed. Under the dim lights, the parlor floor looked as slimy as the bottom of a lake, while outside the neon lights slowly flickered into life as the shadows of people passed by.

"Could it be…" I said to the mistress who was now standing by the door looking up at the evening sky, "that the cellist is Green's father?"

"Are you stupid?" she turned to me. "Of course he isn't."

"But how do you know?"

"Haven't you heard? He had an accident when he was a child."

"Yes, I knew that," I said. "He fell off a donkey and hit his back, didn't he?"

"He didn't just fall on his back. There were other donkeys behind him, and when he fell he got trampled."

"Trampled?"

"Trampled. He got stepped on badly in an unfortunate place. There's no way he could be anybody's father," she said, taking a deep breath and shrugging her shoulders. "His testicles were crushed by the donkeys."

Proud to Be an Oddball

From that day on, the cellist and I visited the Mirrorless Palace from Monday to Friday. We'd go up to a room of one of the girls, and I'd start improvising a story, which the cellist followed with a performance on his cello.

One biting cold evening that winter, as I was replacing a light bulb out the front door—I was the only one tall enough to do it without a stepladder—the middle-aged mistress said, "Your stories are as popular as the cellist's performances these days."

The girls were giggling and throwing paper balls at me from the second floor window.

"What sort of story did you tell them today?" she asked nonchalantly.

"A story about dinosaurs," I said, screwing in the bulb.

The cellist and I had visited the room of the girl with the fullest figure in the establishment. Each of her breasts was the size of a truck tire. She gobbled down five sugar doughnuts in the time it took me to describe her impressive stature. When I spoke of the rolls of flesh that spilled from her armpits and hung from her thighs, she barked in delight like a circus seal. I stared at her in awe, but inside I couldn't help but feel sad. And before I knew it, I found myself telling the story of the massive black creature the caretaker had once told me about—the same one I was sure I'd seen with my own eyes from the bow of the ship. By the time I finished my story, the girl was in tears and the cellist was playing a piece of low notes with a solemn tempo. I swore that in this dark ocean piece, I could hear the cry of the gargantuan creature as its head rose above the surface.

"It's getting chilly, isn't it," said the mistress, shivering. "Cat, when you're done changing the bulbs, would you mind grating me some ginger, please. There's nothing like a hot ginger drink for a cold."

Once I was sure that all the red, yellow, and blue bulbs were functioning, I went to work on a piece of knobbed ginger root. I was careful. I didn't want to grate my fingertips, too, especially since I'd been picking up my baton and bringing it with us on these visits to the brothel.

It began when, while in the middle of a spectacular cello performance, I found my entire body swaying to the flow of the music. Suddenly the cellist shouted, "Too fast!"

"Huh?" I didn't understand what was he was talking about.

"You should be able to tell what's coming next. It's not just the cello. All music is connected."

From that day on, once the cellist began playing the cello, I closed my eyes and began to move my arms.

"Dance, Cat, dance!" the cellist cried out. "Music makes you want to dance. Feel it in your bones. Feel the urge to dance inside you!"

And so I danced. With my entire body I danced. I knew that the girls watching from their beds were trying hard not to laugh. But I didn't care. And not long after, by the time the northern wind had started to blow, I picked up my conductor's baton for the first time in a long while. It was not the one that Grandpa had given me, it was the long stalk of wheat that come from the grain warehouse.

I never ran out of stories to tell the girls. The carrier pigeons. The mouse paradise. The woman in the fur coat with the skunk-shaped lighter. The parrot who loved candy. After my stores, the cellist would play the cello, and I'd swing my baton and jump up and down. Both of us, so terribly serious, in these surroundings—we must have looked ridiculous.

When we finished, the girls would stand up on their beds and applaud and scream, "One more! Play one more song, please, just one more!"

And we always would. The girls would smile from ear to ear and clap their hands in time with the music. I was beginning to understand that music was always special when it was played for those who truly wanted to listen.

It was the new year before I'd learned to tell the seven dogs apart. By then, I'd turned eighteen, and Green was twenty. She'd started at a school for photography, so I usually didn't see her on weekdays. But when she was around, the three of us—Green, the cellist, and me—would go on morning and evening walks together. I guess the cellist had come to trust me. He never made an attempt to hide the fact that Green was not his biological daughter.

Green could do a fantastic impression of a dog whining, which was different, she said, from the distinct whine of the seeing-eye puppies (even though these puppies were eight years old).

The dogs had never learned how to bark properly from their mother, so they developed their own distinct sound. Green (the dog, who was really Red) never made a sound until later in life. But Purple-Green, Blue-Green, Viridian, and the other dogs had a kind of whistle that seemed to originate deep in their throats. And whenever they made that sound, the twenty-year-old human Green would join in, pointing her nose to the sky and vibrate her throat as she whistled.

"That's impressive!" I said the first time I saw her do it.

"Come on, do yours! Come on, Cat. Do it!" the cellist said, using his walking stick to jump up.

I don't know why, but I felt no embarrassment displaying that voice in front of them. Looking upward at the palm tree in the Botanical Garden, I tightened my throat in preparation and then let loose. When this cat's cry echoed through the garden, tropical birds flapped their wings. The dogs looked startled for a moment, but then they all joined in for one big chorus of whistles.

I squatted down to the level of the dogs and cried, *Meow! Meow!* With that, the cellist began to dance, and Green joined in with the chorus, too, our voices bouncing off the glass dome. The director of the Botanical Gardens could have complained, I suppose, but he didn't. Of course, many of the rare species there had been donated by the cellist. Oddly enough, there was not a single flowering plant—just plants with green leaves of all shapes and sizes. Leaves shaped like upside-down triangles, leaves that were jagged, leaves perfectly circular, leaves star-shaped. They were all in slightly different shades, too.

As Green, who said she could actually tell the difference between them with ease, stated matter-of-factly, "No two greens in this world are the same."

On weekends, Green would take me to interesting places around town. There was the black market, the painters' hangout, the underground beggars' village, the bonfire where undiscovered poets gathered. What struck me was that these people led such hard lives. But everywhere we went Green was welcomed with open arms. There was something about her—a gentleness—that seemed to put people at ease. Perhaps the women at the Mirrorless Palace had taken such good care of her when she was little. She accepted everyone—even those who'd been stomped on by life—for who they were. It can be so easy to bring someone down just by holding a mirror up to them. But there was never anything like that in the way she treated people.

"You're amazing," I told her one spring day as we were walking in the underground tunnel. It was a Saturday, and we were on our way back from a lunch the beggars had invited us to. The meal was like none I'd ever had—an assortment of strange dishes several of which I couldn't tell at all what the ingredients were. But Green ate every last morsel and looked happy and satisfied. I kept repeating, "You're incredible, you really are," as we walked through the dark tunnel.

"But you know," she said in a slightly tense tone, "there are things I'm afraid of."

"Really? Like what?"

She was quiet for a moment, then said, "Sirens."

"Sirens?"

"This happened when I was very small," she began, her feet splashing in a puddle. "I was playing at the Mirrorless Palace, and suddenly everyone was upset about something. I had no idea what was going on. I was in a daze. Then someone picked me up and threw me into the basement. You know, that dark, damp basement."

"Yes, I know the one you're talking about," I said. I was guessing it was the same room she was born in.

"I didn't know what to do. I could hear the footsteps of people rushing around on the floor above me. I was scared and tried to open the door, but somebody said, *Whatever you do, do not come out!* The sirens got louder and louder until they stopped—maybe in the front of the house. I stayed still. I heard whistles, voices, heavy footsteps. Then silence. Total silence. I told myself, *I must not go out, I must not go out.* I stayed in that dark basement until morning. Like a rock. Holding my breath."

I turned around slowly to face Green.

"Even now when I hear a siren, my heart beats faster, I have a hard time breathing, I have to squat. I can't move a muscle."

From where I stood, I could see her face quite clearly, even in the dark tunnel. Her lips were gray as stone. Unconsciously, I put my hand out and was surprised to find Green's grabbing hold of my thumb. I closed my hand around hers. It was smooth and cold, like a piece of frozen candy.

We continued down the path hand in hand until we got to the end of the tunnel, where we emerged into the gentle springtime sun dancing around us. Green put on a pair of sunglasses—her eyes were so weak in the light. She always carried a pair of green-framed glasses with her for her shortsightedness, a pair of sunglasses to shade her from brightness, and a pair of binoculars so she could look into the distance. Wherever she went, she always went with that pair of binocular swinging around her neck on a piece of bright green string.

"Are those cherry blossoms?" she asked, pointing to flowering branches hanging over the old railroad tracks.

"Looks like it," I replied. Perhaps they were late bloomers since their buds were still firmly closed, but for some reason, the sight of them put my mind at ease. Green, whose pale cheeks flushed pink from the sun, appeared to relax, too, as our eyes met. Swinging our interlinked hands, we continued along the rusty tracks.

Congenital achromatopsia, I learned from a book in the library, is found in one out of around thirty-three thousand people. Females will get the condition only if both parents have the genetic material for it. Sex-linked recessive inheritance—that's what they called it. My mind was spinning from all the x's and y's and puzzle-like symbols on the pages of the medical text in front of me. Everything was difficult to understand, but I took notes and copied faithfully the diagrams in my notebook.

According to the middle-aged mistress of the Mirrorless Palace, Green's father was a handsome sailor from a foreign country. When the madam, who was his lover, told him she was pregnant, he had very mixed emotions. Any pleasure he felt was tempered by his regret that he suffered from this rare form of color blindness. Surprised to hear this, the madam exclaimed, "What a coincidence! I can't tell the difference between colors either."

Laughing, she told the sailor that color blindness could never be a reason to end the pregnancy. They would simply raise the child to deal with a world without colors—just as they'd had to themselves. As time for the birth of the child neared, the sailor's ship went missing in the north seas. Once Green was born, the madam had no choice but to raise her on her own—at the brothel. In the summer of the child's second year, the madam got caught in a heavy rain and fell ill. She grew weaker and weaker and never recovered. The girls of the house observed three minutes of silence in her honor, then rushed back to their customers. As a sign of respect, they wore black undergarments for a month.

What are the chances of a man and woman—each with a disposition for this rare congenital disease—meeting, falling in love, and having a child? I bet my dad could have told you the answer in a second. But not me. I just knew the probability had to be even lower than mice raining down every year.

"It's not so surprising," the cellist said when I asked him about this later. He was changing the strings on his cello. "Strange people attract strange people. That was the case with Green's mother and father. The same with Green's mother and me too. And with you and me for that matter. You don't think so?"

"I guess, but still," I said. "We're talking about people who are one in thirty-three thousand, you know. And they meet at the Mirrorless Palace of all places!"

"Cat, you really are an idiot." The cellist's blind eyes stared at me. "What do you think are the chances of being trampled by donkeys and losing your eyesight? One in tens of thousands? One in less than that? One in more than that?"

I didn't say anything.

"How about the chances of someone being ridiculously tall, hearing footsteps all the time, and being able to meow better than a real cat? One in several hundred million? Don't be stupid, Cat. You can go around the world, and you'll never find anyone as strange as you!"

The cellist plucked one of the strings, then got up on the chair. Even then, he still only came up to my chest. "Odd people tend to find each other," the cellist started in again. "They go to school. To the whorehouse. To the local circus. To the theater. To orchestras populated entirely by gangsters. They come together somehow, and they couldn't go on living if they didn't."

"Couldn't go on living if they didn't?"

"Because they stand out. Because *you* stand out." The cellist sure wasn't mincing words. "Strange people stand out when they're alone. If they keep standing out, they suffer more difficulties than the average person who doesn't stand out. Imagine there are a lot of pigeons in the forest, but only one of them is pure white.

Which pigeon is going to be the target of a hawk? Or if there was one single apple on a tree that was much bigger than all the rest. Which one do you think the birds will go after into first? This is just the way it is, Cat. If you're the oddball, chances are you'll get hurt first."

I looked down at my own outsized body and then back at the cellist, who was concentrating on tuning his cello. He was right, of course. We were both oddballs, that was for sure, and we both stood out in this world. It was people like us who were the targets of hawks and donkeys, people like us who were rained on by mice. The Butterfly Man. The caretaker. Dad. Perhaps the salesman, too. We were all oddballs.

My little reverie was interrupted by the beep of a car horn.

"Come on," said the cellist. "Our ride is here."

As we got into the car, I could see five dogs watching us from the back garden. Little squeaks were coming from their throats. When I let out a *meow* in response, the driver turned around startled.

On our way to the brothel, the rain began. It began like a spring shower, then it came to resemble strings trailing from the sky. By the time we turned the corner near City Hall, the strings were a downpour. Although the windshield wipers kept wiping, we could barely see a thing. The pounding rain on the roof of the car drowned out all sound inside. But as I kept my eyes on those rhythmic wipers, I began to hear the stepping again.

Ton, Ta-tan

Ta-tan, Ton

Ta-tan, Ton

A car passed us, spraying murky water in its path.

Ta-tan, Ton

As we waited for the traffic signal to change at an intersection, the cellist piped up, "If you are an oddball who is weak, you'll end up alone. To go on living alone, on your own, it's imperative that you keep polishing your skills."

"Skills?"

Ton, Ta-tan

"That's right, your skills," said the cellist. He'd obviously been thinking about this. "If you develop a skill that draws attention, maybe unwanted attention, it could bring even more terrible things your way. But as an oddball, you must carry on regardless. Do you know why, Cat?"

"Because..." I began my reply, placing one clause carefully ahead of the other like steps on the ground, "because...it's the only way...I can ever be proud...of my oddness?"

The cellist pursed his lips. "Not bad for a Cat."

"Green isn't one in thirty-three thousand, is she?" I said after a bit. "She's one of a kind. That's what you mean by alone, right?"

The cellist didn't say anything. But in place of a response, he simply bounced up and down in his seat all the way to the Mirrorless Palace.

From my scrapbook, May 7th

★

Thank you for the sheet of stamps. It's so rare to find stamps depicting only leaves. Please buy as many as you can from the Botanical Garden where you found them. It doesn't matter if they've been franked or in mint condition.

By the way, I have good news. It looks like we might be able to enter the competition this year! We managed to get ahold of a couple of second-hand trumpets and clarinets. We'll look in much better shape with those four instruments, and I'm sure we'll at least get past the screening process.

I also want you not to worry about your grandpa. The town can't pay him a stipend anymore, but everyone knows the great things he's done for the town, so we've raised funds to help support him. When he heard about it, he got furious at us, as I'm sure you can imagine! Last Friday he started repairing ironware. He hammers away all day, knocking dented lids and broken bicycles back into shape. I watch him work and he's amazingly good at it. Everyone has been impressed. I guess a top-class timpanist can hit anything with skill.

★

The thudding the punching bag was taking came to a stop, and the voice of the trainer could be heard in the background, along with the rhythmic beat of a distant skipping rope.

I'm going to take a break for a minute, Cat. Thanks for sending me that great tape the other day. I listen to the dogs whistling every day before my morning run, and I think I can tell their voices apart. In fact, I think I can even get an idea of their faces and their personalities. I'm guessing Purple-Green is the one most like their mother. She's the one that got overexcited and bumped her nose on the microphone as soon as the recording began, I bet. She also responds the fastest when the girl mimics the dogs' whistles. I think if she was a boxer, she'd be the sort of fighter to rush into the ring before the bell finished signaling the beginning of the round. Anyway, Cat, I'd better get back to the bag. I'm going for three rounds. I don't know why you might want to listen to something like this, but I'll leave the tape recorder running. I hope you enjoy the sounds. Talk to you later!

This was followed by footsteps, the squeaking of boxers' boots on concrete, the clink of a metal chain swinging; the jabs, straights, and a one-two combinations connecting with their target.

★

The Housewife with the Exploding Stomach

According to our editor, a psychiatrist friend once told him that certain people have the ability to hear sounds made within their own bodies. But the following case you are about to read about has never been published in any medical journal.

A housewife heard a growling in the pit of her stomach. The growling grew until it sounded like a torpedo detonating right next to her ear. To muffle the noise, she made the valiant effort to keep eating. As a result, she ballooned to more than 200 kg. Her psychiatrist was certain that this was a case of obsessive compulsive disorder, brought on by various neuroses. The lady responded, "What does it matter if it was brought on by neuroses? Or whatever? Everyone's stomach growls when they're hungry, doesn't it? I just need a doctor to rewire my ears so I don't have to listen to it. I can't sleep at night because I'm constantly woken by that growling. At first, it's like snoring. But within minutes the noise is piercing my eardrums. It's like I'm lying with my head in a lion's mouth. Boom! Boom! Boom! The sound keeps going if I lie there without anything in my stomach. I can almost feel my brain shaking. BOOM! BOOM! Can you even imagine what that's like? You think your doctors with their so-called insights can imagine it? It's like having firecrackers shoved into your ears over and over!

From my scrapbook, June 12th

★

Cat, I'm afraid things didn't work out with the competition. Apparently music isn't eligible if it's made using children's recorders, water pipes, and air pumps. I guess that shouldn't come as a surprise. I did feel kind of silly as I stood up there swinging my baton. But like your grandfather says, and I agree, anything that makes a sound in this world is an instrument. If there are people who listen to it and enjoy it, then that sound is music.

Though we weren't allowed to enter the competition, the townspeople all gathered to support us at the grain warehouse. Everyone, including the sailors and their sons and daughters, brought along pots, basins, and whatnot and joined in with our performance. I have to tell you, Cat, everyone seems happier. They didn't just want to listen. They really wanted to play the instruments, too. Even if it sounded terrible, it was such an amazing thing to be able to play together like that! Write again soon and take care of yourself. Everyone in the band is behind you, cheering you on with fanfare in our hearts. We wish you the best of luck with everything.

★

Cat, thank you for the wonderful recording of the cello. I started crying as I was listening to it. All sorts of things went through my mind, and it helped me make some decisions. Starting next month, I'm going to open a confectionery shop on the first floor of the apartment building. Do you remember the baker who brought out a stall on the corner near the bank every afternoon? Well, he's been asking me for a long time if I would open a shop with him. After hearing you and the cellist's music, I found that I couldn't wait any longer. I told him yes a couple of days ago. He's a widower, too.

I'm sorry I had to put so much silica in the box. I know it took up a lot of space, but they told me the package could take as long as a week to reach you by sea. Anyway, I hope you enjoy these. They're chocolate cookies I'm thinking of selling at my store. The shape may be funny for a cookie, but they're meant to look like a cuckoo that just popped out of a clock.

★

The Miraculous Reincarnating Man Visits!

The Miraculous Reincarnating Man, known for his popular interview column has been invited as a special guest at the opening of a department store on the 26th of this month. This year, in this life, he turns twenty. But twenty years ago he was a renowned musician who was first violin in the National Orchestra (he lived to be 55 then). Perhaps your parents, or perhaps you yourself, may have heard him perform. The Miraculous Reincarnating Man is sure to recount his memories from that time like a movie. For a week starting the 26th, he'll be at a special booth set up in the first-floor exhibition space. Please note that a large turnout is expected, so each encounter will be limited to five minutes.

The Boxers

It was only after we had driven a half hour that I realized our destination wasn't the Mirrorless Palace. Instead the car drove past the port and headed closer into the center of the city, where the buildings stood as tall as ocean liners and the sidewalks were bustling with people. All the while the cellist remained silent, as did the driver. Before I had the chance to figure out what was going on, the car slipped into the basement parking lot of a dark building where it found a space between a red car and a white sports car.

"Follow me," said the cellist.

Which I did, his cello in my arms. We took the elevator to the fourth floor, where we were greeted by the smell of carpet and varnish. The cellist made his way down the hall at his usual fast pace. Everyone seemed to know him.

"Open it," said the cellist, pointing at a heavy-looking door that looked like it was the entrance to cold storage in a butcher shop. I positioned my hands on the door and pushed. Immediately, to my surprise, the sound of xylophones and marimbas spilled out. The cellist, first, and then I stepped into to the sound, through the folds of a black curtain, through semi-darkness.

Rays of white light suddenly streamed down on us. I froze, the cello in my arms. A plump woman in short sleeves came over to greet the cellist. One side of the room was lined with percussion instruments, five musicians standing behind them. When they began warming up on the marimba and the xylophone, the sounds hit me like an avalanche. There was, also, something familiar about the rhythm.

"Very nice to meet you," said the plump woman, walking over to me, her hand outstretched. "I'm the director of the National Orchestra. We very much look forward to working with you."

"Excuse me," I said, "did you say working with me?"

"Oh, I see," said the director, turning to the cellist. "You like to keep things to yourself, don't you!"

"I told him," the cellist said. "But I can't help it if everyone's got garbage clogging their ears!"

The director sighed at the cellist and smiled. She then told me, as if it was the most natural thing in the world, they were hoping that I would conduct a few numbers to open the program of the National Orchestra's concert next month.

"Could you repeat that, please?" I said in disbelief.

She repeated it.

The shock of it made me drop the cello case, causing the cellist to leap beneath it to break its fall.

The latter part of the concert had already been decided—a cello concerto to be performed by the cellist and the orchestra. But because it was the 400th anniversary of the city, the director had been looking to incorporate something innovative into the evening. It was around that time that the orchestra's main percussionist handed her a tape that, upon her listening to it, was like being hit on the head with a drumstick. Even the concertmaster was excited, saying he'd never heard music like it before. He went so far as to smash his coffee cup on the floor in delight! When they played the tape for the cellist, however, the cellist was unimpressed.

"I listen to that stuff every day," he'd said. "The one with the cat voice lives with me, and it was one of the members of his band who wrote the song."

Now the director brought out a tape player and pressed PLAY. I don't know which performance the recording was of, but I knew in second that it was the intro to *Fanfare for the Fighting Kids*, with the clarinet's melody, the caretaker's drum roll, and a piercing *Meow! Meow! Meow!*

"I hear you have other pieces by the same composer," said the director, a twinkle in her eye. "And, if I can trust the cellist, your conducting is supposed to be quite something."

"No way. I...I couldn't possibly..." I said, stuttering, backing away. "In front of people? On such a prestigious stage? No way! Impossible."

"No, it's not, Cat," the cellist said, suddenly interjecting himself into the conversation, and yawning. "You can do it. Besides, you've got two whole weeks before the performance."

The caretaker had died less than two years earlier, but in that short time his music had become legendary among percussionists around the world. *Fanfare for the Fighting Kids* was the only full recording of a piece by him in existence. All other recordings were incomplete and had been passed from one band to another on old tapes that were probably sold to them by Town Hall. Despite this, the unique rhythms of the composition had made their mark on all musicians—not only percussionists—whose ears they reached. And, in fact, the actual music score had become a very highly sought item. All efforts to get their hands on it were in vain of course.

On the first day of rehearsal, I stuffed my scrapbook into my bag and set off to the National Orchestra Hall. There was a crowd sitting in the dim space in front of the auditorium. Five percussionists were standing at the highest part of the stage in the rear.

"You look big even from up here," said the timpanist, who was bearded. The four other percussionists nodded.

For the pieces I would be conducting, the director decided, at the cellist's request, that I wouldn't stand on the platform conductors usually stood on. That way, the musicians would be used to my height—that is, they wouldn't need to strain to look up to see my baton.

The percussion section was very well-equipped. In the center were timpani, a snare drum, a base drum, and a gong. To the left were the xylophone, marimba, cowbells, whistles, and various other noisemakers. The cymbals, triangles, and woodblocks were hanging from a stand to the right. The five best percussionists in the city were ready to strike as the music required.

"I once heard a passage that went like this," the bearded timpanist said, proceeding to drag his mallet across the skin of the kettle drum, almost rubbing it. "Do you know it?"

"I do," I said. "It's from a composition by the name of *It's All Thanks to the Lever and Pulley*. And I actually have it here." I opening my red file of sheet music, pulled out the caretaker's scribbled score, and handed the pages to the director.

Impressed, she had the score photocopied straight away and distributed to the percussionists. The musicians puckered their lips as they tried to decipher the notations, like students struggling to understand a formula in a mathematics text.

"Ready?" I said, raising my baton in the air. With the five percussionists focusing their attention on me, I brought down the baton and out emerged the beat of a precise rhythm. But before we reached the twelfth bar, I started to feel like something wasn't right and I stopped swinging the baton. The music stopped perfectly in sync.

"Is something wrong?" the director asked.

"Just tell them," the cellist shouted sharply from the corner of the stage. "Those five will get it immediately."

So I did. I told them that the caretaker had written this piece of music while imagining the rhythm of the pyramid workers dragging the stones and singing. I told them that this was even mentioned in an article in a well-known gossip magazine.

"More, more, that's not enough," the cellist shouted.

I imitated the caretaker's unique movements, bending my body like a robot and letting my arms and legs move willy-nilly. I told them that the caretaker hadn't been born that way but that he'd gotten sick on an island in the South Seas where he was struck by lightning. I described how it wasn't easy for the caretaker to pick up the case with the small drum in it, so there were four small wheels on the case attached by Grandpa. The caretaker had smiled, saying, "Fantastic! That makes it so much easier to carry." Then off he went, bashing the corners of his case against everything in sight, stumbling and swaying right and left. But he made it all the way from one end of the warehouse to the other, thanks to his slick new wheels that went *korokorokoro*.

The five percussionists listened to me in utter silence.

"This is that kind of music," I said, finishing up. Then I slowly lifted my baton.

As soon as the performance ended, the director leapt up on stage and wrapped her arms around my waist. It was only a rehearsal, but the audience behind me exploded in applause. The cellist seemed to be the only one to keep his cool, and he kept looking toward me with a grin on his face. The five percussionists were red in the face.

"Another! Another!" the cellist now shouted, stomping the floor beneath him. So I pulled another score from the file, looked up at the five percussionists and said, "Why don't we try this one. It's called *Serenade for the Weeping Dinosaur.*"

During our break, I got to talking with the percussionists. In a way, we shared variations of the same story. When they were youngsters, they joined their local orchestras hoping to play the violin, piano, guitar, or clarinet. But because they were slightly bigger or slightly slower than the other children, the leader of the orchestra assigned them the large, heavy instruments. The large, heavy instruments were the drums.

"And then," the timpanist went on, sipping his coffee, "my children say, *Dad, why do you always just stand there at the back of the orchestra? You get paid the same as the other musicians, don't you? Looks like you got an easy job!*"

The other four percussionists burst into laughter. I did, too.

"I guess we can't help that it looks that way," the timpanist said. "You know, I sometimes envy the violins. It's got to be easier playing all the way through a piece rather than waiting for the one moment to bang the drum. I mean, talk about pressure. You mistime the cymbal once and you ruin the entire thing!"

"It's happened to me," laughed the bald percussionist, who was responsible for the cymbals and whistle. "I was just starting out. My mother was sick in the hospital, in critical condition, and I was up all night looking after her, so my mind was a blur. I had to strike the cymbals once in a spectacular coda. I completely missed it."

"What happened then?" I asked.

"I was kicked out of the band. But on the positive side, my mother got better. At least I think that's the positive side. Last night she made me eat an awful garlic stew."

It was my turn, and I began to tell the percussionists about the blind boxer. He has a butterfly tattoo on his neck. He had the talent to make it to the finals of the rookie tournament. He lost his sight in an accident in the ring, but he continues to hit the punching bag every day. He can't not do it. "Why do you think he does it?" I asked.

"Hmm," said the handsome, thin guy of the group, "perhaps he was frustrated?"

The timpanist shook his head and said, "Doubt it. Cat, what's the real reason?"

"Well, the boxer said he did it because he was scared," I said. "As long as he was punching the bag, he wasn't in danger of falling down a manhole or getting run over by a bicycle."

"Something tells me maybe you've got a composition about that boxer," the timpanist said coyly.

Hesitantly I pulled another couple pages of music from my red file. The percussionists leaned over one another to read the music, then passed it around to study it further. Then they looked up at me, seeming very impressed.

"This isn't bad. Not bad at all!" said the timpanist, stroking his beard.

"Why don't we add it to the program?"

"Wait," I said. "There's one part I want to add to it first." I took back the score and jotted these instructions:

> This part represents the excited breathing of a dog. But it's a silent voice because the dog is a seeing-eye dog, so it's been trained to be quiet. So it has to call out to the boxer from its heart. Play the passage to make it seem that the sound is intended for the ears of the boxer only.

"How do we do that?" asked the handsome percussionist. "Do you have an instrument for that?"

"No," I said. "But I have somebody in mind." That somebody was the cellist's daughter, Green, whom I told the group about.

After they'd heard her story and heard my idea, the five musicians clapped their hands together in full agreement.

It took me a little longer to convince Green to say yes, however.

"The daughter of the master cellist!" she kept saying, "Making her debut at the National Hall? Just the thought sends shivers down my spine. I can't do it!" Green kept refusing while glaring at me, moving her green-framed glasses up and down on her nose. It was the dogs that changed her mind.

When I put on the tape of the percussionists playing the piece, the seven dogs not only sat still, they began to listen. When the piece got to the part where I'd written the notation in last, the dogs started whistling in symphony! Then they looked at their owner's face beseechingly. Green was almost literally struck silent.

Finally, with a wide smile on her face, she said, "You need to be fitted for a black tuxedo." She flipped through the composition. "By the way, Cat," she said, "there's one thing that's been bothering me."

"What's that?"

"Why is the dog 'red' in the title?"

That was the day before yesterday. Two days before I would find myself lying flat on my back.

It took only two days for Green's dog-whistling and the percussion section to come together perfectly, like two pieces in a jigsaw puzzle. Green, interestingly, had worn a light purple blouse to rehearsals. This was a bit of a change.

Ten days before performance. After rehearsal, Green said we needed to go shopping in town. "We need to get you a smart black suit for your debut," she said. "And a new pair of shoes, too!"

"Shoes?"

"If you get on stage in those raggedy things, you'll slip and fall!" she said, purposely stepping on my feet in the back seat. "You need something serious and sturdy. Proper black shoes with a thick sole."

From the car, I looked up to see the early summer sun shining through trees that seemed to stretch all the way to the sky.

On the ground there was the steady flow of a stream of people. In the middle of town, we got out of the car. Green had one hand in mine and in the other held onto Purple-Green's leash. Off we went, weaving through the crowds.

Purple-Green had ruined her rubber toy the night before, Green said. It was a chew toy in the shape of a mouse that squeaked whenever the dog bit it. Perhaps Purple-Green expected to get a new one anyway. Today Purple-Green was being exceptionally playful and running up to strangers. Since her leash was being held by Green, who was wearing thick, dark sunglasses, Purple-Green must have seemed like a seeing-eye dog that needed to be trained a lot better.

Ton, Ta-tan

Suddenly I heard footsteps that brought mine to a standstill.

Ton Ton

Ta-tan, Ta-tan

Kutze's footsteps were resonating through the crowd of people around us. The steps were loud and clear, and they sounded so incredibly close. Occasionally, they'd fade, then a moment later they'd return until they were as close as could be. I wondered if they were trying to lead us somewhere.

Ton, Ta-tan!

"What's the matter?"

I came to my senses. I was holding Green's hand. She was looking up at me, perspiring slightly. I couldn't hear Kutze's wheat-stepp'n anymore. But I could hear Purple-Green panting, her tongue sticking out, looking a little anxious.

"It's nothing," I said with a laugh. "Nothing. Let's go."

We found ourselves at the department store that had just opened. You could smell the fresh paint. It was enough to make Purple-Green sneeze twice. The store was packed, in part because everything in the store was at half price for the week. There was a large truck parked by the door. The driver and one of the store staff who were arguing loudly. The back of the truck was slightly open and inside were hundreds and hundreds of houseplants.

"If I don't get these out quickly I'll be late for my other deliveries," the driver shouted. "It's not my problem if the store's not ready yet."

"You'll just have to wait. We're almost done," said the elderly staff member in uniform. "Just take the truck around back for now, will you."

"You're not our only customer, you know. I need to make a lot of other deliveries today, too."

"Like I said, just go around back," the elderly man repeated. Then he smiled at us and gestured toward the store. Green, who'd been looking at the back of the truck, whispered, "They all have such healthy leaves. Young summer leaves. It's a shame they have to be kept in the shade!"

When we got inside, the store was absolutely packed with shoppers and there was a large crowd of people waiting by the first-floor elevator. A clerk with a megaphone was shouting hoarsely, "Come meet the Miraculous Reincarnating Man!"

A woman bumped into me, clucking.

"Please, no pushing!" shouted the clerk with the megaphone. "Everyone gets five minutes with the Miraculous Reincarnating Man! Come hear incredible tales from the Miraculous Reincarnating Man himself! Line up, everyone. Line up!"

The Brief Memory of the Miraculous Reincarnating Man

At first, the head of the men's department was adamant they wouldn't be able to finish the tailoring in ten days. He shrugged his shoulders, looking apologetic. "Because you're not a standard size, we'll have to start from scratch. That'll take at least one month."

Green explained the situation. Immediately the head of men's department changed his tune. He whistled and five clerks immediately came rushing over.

"Take this gentleman's measurements right away," he said, flipping through his sample book of fine fabrics. "We must finish his suit within a week!"

The word "National Orchestra" seemed to work like a spell in this city. The same thing happened at the shoe department. As the clerk was measuring my enormous feet, he went on about taking his whole family to see the performance. The only shoes in stock that would fit me, however, were the 35-centimeter pair on display in the storefront, and they weren't really for sale. But the clerk let me try them on anyway.

"They're very simple. Oh, they're classic," said the clerk. "They're very well made, they'll never lose their shape, and—it's unbelievable—they fit you perfectly! You'll feel like you were born in them!"

No one had described a pair of shoes like that to me before. And he was right! The shoes were indescribably light, and were as comfortable as a pair of socks. I got the feeling I could wear them my whole life without my feet ever getting tired again.

With my shopping needs accomplished, Green and I parted in front of the elevators. "I'm going to go look at some clothes for myself. Then I'm off to the toy section for Purple-Green. Let's meet in an hour at the entrance," she said. "We'll go buy food for dinner in the basement market."

"See you then," I said, as Purple-Green sniffed at my new shiny shoes. Green gave her a playful slap on the head before they went on her way.

The girl and her dog took the elevator up while I took the stairs down, listening to the nice dry sound my new shoes made on the polished marble floor while I hummed *All Thanks to the Lever and Pulley* to myself.

An elderly woman resting on a chair by the stairs looked up at me and said, "Someone's in a good mood."

On the third floor, everything was covered with white plastic sheeting. A weary worker was on his break, taking a final drag on his cigarette.

"This is the children's clothes department," he explained. "The boss made the rounds last night and decided the place needs more pizzazz. So on opening day we're redoing everything—the lights, the paint, the floor, the racks.... We've been working all night. And it's not like we get paid overtime!"

"Oh," I said, peeking where other workers were busy toiling away.

"Personally, I don't see the point," the worker said. "I mean, the brats will only go mess it up again." He paused to put another cigarette between his lips and pull out his lighter.

"Where did you get that?" I gasped.

"This lighter, you mean?" he replied with an embarrassed smile. The lighter had the shape of a skunk doing a headstand. "It's sort of a toy, a gag. The keeper at the zoo gave it to us when we were doing a job there. I was repainting the skunk cages with some special stink-free paint."

"So it's not a foreign antique?"

"Nope," he said. "It was just a novelty the zoo got in when they first got the skunks. Always good for a laugh, but not a very good lighter. Cheaply made."

He pulled the skunk's tail down for me, and a small flame popped out.

I turned and carried on down the marble steps one at a time.

Ton Ton Ton

When I reached the ground floor, a line was beginning to form near the elevator bank, people waiting for a chance to ask the Miraculous Reincarnating Man a question. They were holding things like a clock, photos, and letters. The sign hanging from the ceiling read:

> Come right up to hear a miraculous tale from the Miraculous Reincarnating Man. From ten this morning to four this afternoon. Five minutes per person. Ask a question for free when you purchase a copy of At That Moment, by the Miraculous Reincarnating Man.

If it was five minutes per person and ten people were standing in line, then I'd get my turn in fifty minutes—even I could figure that out. Perfect for killing time while I waited for Green. As I stood in line, I stuck my hands in my pockets and jiggled my loose change. Then I lifted my feet, one after another, and confirmed the comfortable fit of my shoes.

"That's right!" came a sudden teary voice from the booth where the Reincarnating Man sat. "Yes! There was an embroidered bicycle on that lost blanket!"

From my place in line I was able to steal a glance at the Reincarnating Man, who was sitting with his elbows propped up on the table. I gulped. The article had said he was twenty, but he looked no older than an elementary school kid. He had a pale bluish face and musty silver hair. I'd never seen such a beautiful, sad person before. He seemed to have innocence of a girl born and raised in paradise who wandered by accident into this world.

The Reincarnating Man kept his eyes down, avoiding the glare of the person facing him. The man who'd apparently lost his blanket listened intently as he wiped tears from his eyes with his sleeve. Then a staff member tapped him on the shoulder and pointed to the clock indicating that his five minutes was up. The man stood slowly and said, "I'll try looking there. Thank you." Then he left, and the line moved forward.

Suddenly, I was overcome by anxiety, as if I shouldn't be standing in line. I considered leaving, but my feet wouldn't let me. My shoes stood their ground, moving forward a step every five minutes.

Ton Ton

I tried to look away from the Reincarnating Man as I got closer and closer to him, but my eyes were glued to his beautiful face.

"Go ahead," the staff member said, when my turn came. "You have just five minutes. Don't waste them!"

I gulped as I took a seat. The Miraculous Reincarnating Man lifted his gray eyes at me and asked, "What would you like to know?"

I felt faint as I took out my wallet and pulled out the group picture of the band when we took first prize at the competition. It was something I always carried with me.

"This is my grandfather," I said, squeezing out the words. "Before you were reincarnated into your current life, when you were first violin in the National Orchestra, my grandfather was there too, playing the timpani."

The Reincarnating Man rubbed his eyes and studied the picture.

"I was told that life in the city was very hard. Do you remember anything? Anything about my grandfather or my father?" I asked.

"Ah!" A hint of warmth spread across his blank expression. "Yes, there was a son. But you seem to be confused. The son was a student of mathematics. I remember he seemed very hard-headed."

"Yes. Yes!" I said, eagerly. "He *was* hard-headed."

"That was a horrible sound," the Reincarnating Man said after a few moments of silence.

"What do you mean?"

"The sound was dreadful. I was completely taken by surprise. Such a horrible noise from such a well-built stage. No one expected it."

I was clueless as to what he was talking about. The Reincarnating Man was focusing on the photo, so I turned my attention to it, too. Standing next to me was the caretaker—that was who the Reincarnating Man was referring to!

Grandpa, in the photo, was standing behind us, with a grim expression on his face. Newly curious, I asked, "How was Grandpa as a timpani player? He must have been amazing."

"Your grandfather on the timpani?" the Reincarnating Man said, seeming taken aback. "I've never heard him play."

I felt dizzy. I was sitting in a chair, but I felt like I was on top of the bell tower with the ocean winds blowing hard against me from all directions. When a staff member gave tapped me on the shoulder to say my time was up, I found it impossible to move. The Reincarnating Man looked at the photo again.

"But his ability with hammers and planes was really impressive."

"What are you talking about?" I said.

"You don't know that your grandfather was a carpenter?" The Reincarnating Man spoke in a low voice that seemed to come from far away. "Your grandfather wasn't the timpanist. He didn't play the timpani. He was the woodwork specialist who built the stage."

Impatient, two staff members were now tapping me on the shoulder.

"Please," I cried to the Miraculous Reincarnating Man, "I need to see you later! I could come back tomorrow. But I have to see you. I must!"

The Miraculous Reincarnating Man looked very sad. "I'm sorry," he said, "but there is no tomorrow, not for me."

As another person now took the seat before the Reincarnating Man, one of the staff members asked if I wanted to buy a copy of the book. "If you do, the consultation is free," he said.

I dug into my pocket, gave him a handful of coins, and stumbled away from the crowd.

Grandpa not a timpanist? A stage carpenter? The Miraculous Reincarnating Man was a fraud. Three thousand years of memories—hah! This guy couldn't even recall the past twenty years with accuracy! I was about to throw my copy of the book in the trash, when all three elevators opened and a crowd burst out in a cloud of white smoke. People person holding handkerchiefs to their faces. Then an avalanche of people came pouring down the stairs, too.

"Everyone, please stay calm." It was a woman's voice coming over the speakers in the ceiling. "There is a fire in the construction area on the third floor. The fire is small and has been contained. Please do not panic. All the fire doors have been secured and there is no danger of the fire spreading further. I repeat: Please do not panic. Beware of the smoke. Use a handkerchief. Keep your head low. Do not use the elevators or escalators. Take the stairs. There are three sets of stairs, in the north, south and west ends of the store. I repeat: The fire is small and has been contained. The fire department has been notified and will be here shortly to take control of the situation. In the meantime, please use the stairs. And please exit the building calmly."

Almost immediately, the crowd of people rushed to the stairwells. There was the sound of hundreds of shoes clicking on the marble floor. I, however, started making my way to the center of the store, past displays of hats, umbrellas, and cosmetics until the scent of all those perfumes was replaced by the smell of smoke.

"Here come the fire trucks!" someone yelled from near the main entrance. "There're loads of them!"

The fire department had responded quickly. Within three minutes of the announcement in the store, the trucks were approaching the department store—red lights flashing, sirens blaring. Moments later, teams of firefighters spilled out of the trucks and ladders were hoisted all around the building. Other sirens joined in the fray, until the street outside was bustling with police cars, more fire trucks, and ambulances.

But I was worried about Green and her dog. I was worried they were trapped in some smoky corner of the store several floors up.

I dashed up the non-moving escalator without hesitation. Beneath my feet, I felt the soles of my shoes bouncing off the marble as if they had a life of their own. The higher I got, the louder the sirens, the thicker the smoke. The smoke, in fact, got thicker and thicker until I could barely see where I was going.

Dark Mice Once Again

On the third floor, the fire didn't look too big. Actually, I could hardly see fire for all the smoke, but at least it didn't seem to be too hot. I crouched down on the floor to get out of the smoke and saw paints of all colors—red, orange, blue, and yellow—splashed all over the floor. But none of the paint lent any color to the billowing white smoke the shade of a dripping sky.

As the smoke began to fill the floor, I heard a crackling noise. For the briefest of moments, the image of a skunk doing handstands flashed across my mind. But this wasn't the time to wonder about the cause of the fire. I had to find Green. I dashed up the escalator through the clouds of smoke to the fourth floor, then the fifth.

If I remembered correctly, the fifth floor was the men's department. I could just about make out the blurry figure of a mannequin with good posture amidst the smoke.

"Please proceed calmly, please proceed calmly!" came the same woman's voice from the speakers. I kept on going to the sixth floor, which was filled with white smoke. I didn't know and I couldn't tell if this floor was for women's clothing or pet goods. Clasping my hand over my mouth, I stepped forward, immediately hitting my knee on something and sending it crashing to the floor. A drinking glass. This had to be kitchenware. I needed to backtrack, get to a higher floor, but pain pierced my chest. I dropped to my knees and breathed what little air was left in the room.

It was my heart. That's where the pain was coming from. My heart that had always worked so hard to keep blood pumping through my outsized body for eighteen years. But now, of all time, it was giving up. I couldn't believe it. Desperate, I pounded my heart then massaged it firmly as if kneading a ball of dough. Slowly, the pain subsided.

Carefully, I proceeded to the seventh floor, where the faint outline of another mannequin came into view—this time dressed in summer's latest fashions. I tried to call out, but my voice was gone! I swallowed a mouthful of saliva and tried to call out again, but my voice was barely there. My throat was hoarse and burning.

"Green!" I gasped, squeeze out her name, with the smoke dancing around me, mocking me. "Green!"

Another stab to the heart. I clenched it again.

Slowly, I made my way along the gray floor, straining to find Green somewhere. It was unbearable. I got down on the floor, lay on my stomach, held my breath, and pulled myself along with my elbows. Pain banged at my chest.

That was when I heard it—that peculiar sound—coming from the white clouds of smoke. It was the dog's squeaky call! And it seemed to be coming from above. I crawled back to the escalator, where black and white swirls of smoke intermingled, staying low to the ground, my heart thudding. As I got closer to the squeak, the squeak got weaker. Finally I was on the eighth floor. I could hear the dog's voice. I tried my best to call out, but my throat had almost entirely closed up. Again and again, I opened my mouth and tried to scream, but no sound would come out. "Please!" I begged my throbbing heart. "Please! Please!"

Suddenly, an amazing thing happened.

Meeow! The call of the Cat leapt from my mouth. No, that's not really what it felt like. It was the cry of a cat that leapt from my entire being—from my throat, my brain, my head, my heart, my gut, my back, my everywhere. And when I pounded my heart again, once more the call came out!

Meeow! Meeow!

The smoke around me seemed actually to vibrate.

Meeow!

I understood. This is what I'd been waiting for. A moment for a whole life in the waiting. Like a conductor waiting to bring down the baton at the precise moment in time. Until this moment, I'd been standing in the back, like a fool, sticking out in the highest place, waiting for the moment to bang my drum.

Meeow!

My voice rang out, more cat-like than ever. Like a majestic cry from a cat's paradise, the cry that rang out through the floor, bouncing against the walls and filling every corner.

The dog's squeak came from somewhere directly in front of me. I planted my hands and knees on the floor and maneuvered my way through the maze of the toy section, all the while pounding at my chest as I drew closer and closer to the sound.

Meeow! I cried, as if searching for the last of my own species.

Eeek! came the dog's voice, like a ship's whistle cutting through fog. Then I saw them: Green and Purple-Green huddled together, cowering in the sporting goods corner of the store, along with swimming goggles and rafts. Green lifted her head me and smiled with colorless lips. Her hair was wet. There was a tank filled with floating dolphin toys near her. Purple-Green looked up at me without dropping the plastic mouse in its mouth.

I was still on my stomach. I was so happy to have found them, but orange flames were now rising from the floor below us. The speakers continued to blast the same announcement: "Please proceed calmly. The fire is small and has been contained! Please proceed calmly. The fire is small and has been contained!"

The escalator was no longer an option. I poured the water from the tank on my head and carried Green on my back. With Purple-Green by my side, we climbed the stairs, which were very hot, to the ninth floor. We headed for the exit to the roof deck, but were met by a metal gate and a sign that read:

ROOFTOP PLAYGROUND UNDER CONSTRUCTION
PLEASE COME AGAIN

I would have kept on throwing myself against the metal gate if Green had not stopped me by pulling my ears. She pointed in the opposite direction, back where the smoke was thickening.

A dead end, I thought.

I could hear the sound of the crackling fire on the floor beneath us. I didn't want to go there. Green shook me and pointed again, urging me to head for the smoke. I let go the metal gate, and we slowly made our way back in.

We pushed on through the thick curtain of smoke, uncertain what lay before us. Every time I stopped, Green urged me forward again with a sharp tug on my ears—sometimes pulling the left ear to steer me left, or the right ear to steer me right. She was like a ship's captain navigating through rough seas, but she was smarter than any ship's captain—pointing the way without a compass, map, or telescope. She was able to see the current of the smoke and see the way it was flowing. It was a colorless world that she could understand, her unique vision allowing her to see the differences in shades of smoke. It must have looked like a living thing, scurrying in desperate search for an exit.

We continued across the floor as if led along by a pack of floating Dark Mice. My shins knocked into chairs—this must have been the food court. Green tugged again, this time to the left and we entered what had to be a kitchen, though I still couldn't see a thing.

Purple-Green made off ahead of us, jumping through a wall of gray. There was the sound of claws against tile. Purple-Green let out a familiar squeak and I placed my hand on the wall and held my breath. Green, still clinging to my back, pointed directly upward and my eyes followed her hand to a ventilation fan struggling to churn fresh air into the choking building.

Unseeing, in the smoke, I felt around until I grasped a stew pot so large I could hardly lift it with both arms. I hoisted it above my head, mustered all my strength, and hurled it against the fan. Then again. Again. And again. With a loud crack, the frame of the fan broke and the fan fell outside the building, pulling a stream of thick smoke behind it. Then I hooked my fingers around the edge of the hole and pulled myself up to my waist. I looked around—occurred to me this was just like I used to do when I popped my head into the attic as a kid.

There were two firefighters on the platform connected to the ladder that extended upward from the fire truck. I waved to them. Even from a distance I could see their astonishment. I took a deep breath and filled my lungs with fresh air. The burning lump in my throat eased a little.

"The ladder!" I managed to scream hoarsely. "The ladder!"

One of the firefighters spoke into his radio to give instructions to his colleagues on the ground. Then I squeezed my body back in, hoisted Green onto my shoulders, and pushed her upward through the hole. When—before too long—I could feel the weight on my shoulders being lifted, I crouched down, picked up the timid dog, and pushed her out of the hole. A firefighter bundled her up in his arms.

I crouched down once more to pick up the mouse toy. It was new, but already covered in teeth marks. I stuck it in my pocket, stretched, and got a grip on the edge of the hole. It took all the strength I could muster to hoist myself up to where a firefighter's hand was just inches from mine.

"That's it. Keep coming!" he said.

I looked around. The sky was a perfect summer blue, and the clouds were translucent. Cheers came roaring up from below, and I sighed in relief before grabbing the firefighter's hand.

"What's the matter?" the firefighter asked. "Hurry!"

"Something's wrong." I said, suspended in mid-air. "Something's stuck."

My body wouldn't budge. It was like the lower half of my body was being swallowed by an enormous mouse. That's when it occurred to me! My shoes—my new 35-centimeter shoes! They were caught on something; they were holding me down.

I wriggled and squirmed as the color of the smoke changed. I could picture the flames lapping against my feet. Enough! Then I made a fist and gave my chest a mighty punch.

Meeow! One shoe flew off.

Meeow! Off flew the other.

Then all at once my outsized body popped through the hole. The firefighter called out to the men below. I looked down. I could see the truck packed with plants and next to it, six men standing in a circle, each holding the edge of a big, outstretched sheet. Big, but probably not big enough. I had no choice. I jumped.

Healthy green leaves came closer and closer until they filled my view.

That was the last thing I saw.

In the Operating Room

Strangers in white coats were milling around the operating table, their eyes cast to the floor as they spoke in an undecipherable language. I was lying on my back. I had no other choice.

Ton, Ta-tan, Ton
Ta-tan, Ton, Ta-tan

"Hey, Kutze!" I said in my mind. "Is that you wheat-stepp'n?"

Suddenly, the strangers in white started to raise their voices. They were saying something about my pulse. Something about camphor. Then the voices faded again, like waves crashing against the docks and sinking into nothing.

Was Grandpa really just a carpenter? What was the "horrible sound" the Reincarnating Man was talking about? I needed to ask him about so many things. Maybe I could ask Kutze? But then, he wouldn't answer. He'd just stomp, sending out a steady rhythm in the dark.

Ton, Ta-tan
Ta-tan, Ton

But then I began to understand something. There were oddballs holding onto various things in the world, and they were all working hard to hone their skills, wanting to take pride in being odd, to take it seriously, no matter how silly they might appear.

Ton, Ta-tan, Ton

It's like everything in this world is a percussion instrument, each making its own sound, its own unique sound. A timpani, a gong, a base drum, a snare drum. Each one makes a different sound to accompany the music of this world.

Ton, Ta-tan, Ton

I didn't understand a lot of things. But that didn't matter. I could cry like a cat, and I could save Green and the dog from the fire.

"Hey, Kutze, how's Green doing?" I asked in my mind. "Think we'll find Purple-Green another one of those toys?"

Ton, Ta-tan, Ton

Just a rhythm. Not a response.

As the soft sound of his stepping echoed through the dark, those careful moves told me that at least one thing was certain. It was something Kutze had told me—something he'd tell people even long after I was gone.

There is no good or bad to it. It's just wheat-stepp'n.

Suddenly, loudly, an urgent voice: "ECG!"

The whispers around me fizzled and faded to the corners of the room.

ECG

"Make them stop!" a voice said. "Make them stop that racket!"

I couldn't hear any racket. I couldn't hear anything. In fact, I couldn't sense the sunlight on my tightly clenched eyelids. And I couldn't—not really—sense the sounds I was hearing, which felt like letters written in invisible ink slowly dissolving into my brain.

"Damn! Any change in that ECG?"

"No. No change."

In This World, You Have to Learn to Wait

I hear the sound of dogs and turn to see three of them prancing on the shore of a lake. A straw hat has washed up on the bank. The reflection of the late afternoon sun in the lake makes the dogs red and yellow.

I hear the timpani. I see a wooden stage in a dark warehouse. But there are no instruments. There's someone standing at the very back, in the highest spot, with mallets in hand. I can't see the person's face. Is it Grandpa? Or a percussionist I don't know? All I know is the timpanist is standing with his back straight and his head high as he waits for the right moment to bring down his mallets.

I hear bells. I see a fight come to an end and the audience recede like the tide. I see a boxer from the red corner being taken away on a stretcher, and I see the ring surrounded by sailors and their kids as a referee stands in the center looking like the caretaker.

I hear the chime announcing the hour. Ringing through town. A boat whistle piercing the white mist. Tapping coming from the dark of the stairs. Then a whisper: "It's a prime—no question about it."

I hear rain. Not mouse rain, but real rain, drops showering into the canal. A man in an expensive suit, he's not carrying an umbrella, he's staring at the canal that looks about to overflow. I see the raindrops bouncing off the hood of the car behind him. He shrugs his shoulders, climbs back into his car, and drives away on the road that's glistening.

I hear a baby crying.

"I named her Green," says a woman's husky voice. "It's the color I've always wanted to see most."

The baby's cries echo through a damp basement. The cellist plays in celebration. Playing high notes, then low, like waves rising and crashing.

The sound of a shooting star. The words the parrot had really wanted to say. The cry of the seeing-eye dogs. These are sounds I cannot hear. It's not that these things don't make sounds. It's a matter of distance. Perhaps you're only meant to hear some things when the time is right to hear them. Perhaps I need to learn to wait. Like a master timpanist. But it won't be easy. Even if people say I'm stupid or call me names, I'll wait, holding my mallets and standing still at the back of the stage. Listening carefully so I don't miss my moment when it comes.

For a very long time I've been surrounded by sound. And now I still am.

I know now that it takes one simple rhythm in this world to transform random noise into breathtaking music.

Ton, Ta-tan

Ta-tan, Ton

I flinch. Is this Kutze again? Or someone else?

At that moment, my ears open up like a rose blossoming.

Meow, meow!

A sound from the core of me.

Meow, meow, meow!

It is a rhythm completely in harmony with the sounds outside the operating room. Then, again, there's the ocean-like sound of the cello. The dogs' cries. Green's amazing imitation of their cries. The captivating rhythm of shadow boxing. And the ill-coordinated women's chorus. I am definitely hearing it. Hearing. The music of this world.

Someone lets out a shriek. I think it is a nurse.

"Doctor, this patient…" she says, "he's alive, he's alive! Look! His legs are moving. He's kicking the table with his feet!"

The surgeons and their assistants gather around my body. They interfere with me in all sorts of ways—slicing my body with a knife, dabbing it with cotton, injecting it with needles. I lie still, accepting their franticness, tapping my finger in rhythm to the ensemble lead by the cellist.

Ashtrays Aloft

When I was wheeled out of the operating room, the cellist and Green were not alone waiting for me. There was the mistress from the Mirrorless Palace, fifteen of her girls, the music director of the National Orchestra, the team of five percussionists, the housekeeper, Light Green, Yellow Green, Viridian, Grass, Purple-Green, Blue-Green, and Dark Green, too. There was even the Butterfly Man—uncharacteristically wearing a matching top and bottom over his impressive physique.

The Butterfly Man, I later learned, had heard about the concert from the cellist. He'd make the long journey to the city, arriving the day after the fire. He went straight to the cellist's house to see Red (or should I say Green) and her pups and that's when he heard about the accident.

As I was wheeled through the corridor, I was surrounded by these familiar faces: I could have been a boxer surrounded by fans after a fight! There was one week before the big concert. Not a lot of time, but I wasn't worried. All the sounds and rhythms I'd been feeling during my surgery were ringing through my body. And I had Green and the Butterfly man visiting my hospital room every morning and evening to talk to me about this and that. Fortunately, Green hadn't suffered so much as a scratch during the fire.

As I was going into surgery, the cellist had organized a ragtag band that included the five percussionists, Green, the dogs, the

Butterfly Man, the girls from the Mirrorless Palace, the housekeeper who sang in falsetto, and himself, naturally.

"Make noise! Make music! Save our friend!" he'd roared. "Remember all those stories he told us. Sing them!"

And they did.

Now, as I was in recovery, the head of the hospital wasn't too pleased when he saw the dogs being led in, but as he was a fan of the cellist he made an exception for this occasion. The Mirrorless Palace closed for three days (it was the first time the place had closed, ever!), and the girls brought items (except for mirrors, of course) to the hospital to make everyone feel at home.

The Butterfly Man had come with a nurse guiding him by the hand. Before anyone could say anything, he ripped off his shirt and started shadow boxing in the corridor as the dogs danced and jumped around him.

"I wish I could have seen everything," I said later. "It must have been amazing."

"It was," said Green. "You should have seen the girls in their black and white makeup. Their makeup—when you see it in black and white like I do—it looks like they've been done up for a festival!"

"I've been blind for twenty years now," the Butterfly Man said, "but I've never been so disappointed that I can't see."

Green had brought a pile of newspapers and letters for me. The fire was big news, and all the stories seemed to describe me as an incredible idiot who'd fallen nine stories after saving the life of a girl and a dog by getting his enormous shoes stuck. Green and I chuckled as we read the articles to the Butterfly Man. And then I cut them out for pasting later into my scrapbook.

The fire had been caused by cigarettes. The remnants of a skunk-shaped lighter among the debris. The Miraculous Reincarnating Man died as he was helping lead the customers to safety. He acted as calmly and professionally as a proper security guard, guiding the sales clerks and office staff safely out of the main entrance, then stopping right outside with a mysterious smile on his face. Right then, a large billboard came crashing down on him. He'd said there was no tomorrow for him. What must it be like to know when you were going to be reborn?

I picked up the most recent letter from the pile and read about the band giving their first performance for in a long time. It was from the postmaster, who chatted on:

> *Everyone is very excited, but we need a new venue because we now have a few dozen percussionists. And your grandpa is still working hard repairing the brass products and playing the timpani.*
>
> *I have one piece of sad news. My sister passed away last night. It was a stroke. Her new husband found her on the floor of the confectionary kitchen at five in the morning. There were strawberries and baked apples scattered across the floor. And they found the new pie crust she had been working on in her mouth. The husband says it was probably the shock of how good the crust tasted that gave her the stroke. So, you see Cat, this is a sad thing, but we can find solace in the fact that she was able to die eating something that gave her tremendous pleasure rather than to die cooped up in a small, dark room. In fact, there's more than solace in that. It's almost proof that God took a special liking to her.*

I slowly folded the letter. I didn't understand much about God. But I wondered if, like the Miraculous Reincarnating Man, the postmaster's sister might have known that her moment was coming. And I wondered what kind of sound it made when she bit down on that pie crust that fateful morning.

Finally, three days before the concert. I was discharged from the hospital. My surgeon was amazed by my swift recovery. As I was about to leave, he warned me about journalists waiting for me out front.

"Would you like to exit via the back door instead?" he asked.

"I don't mind them," I replied.

"Well, okay," said the cellist to the Butterfly Man, "but if any of those journalists so much as touch Green, there's no need to hold back. Go ahead and swing! And if you accidentally break somebody's jaw, then they're already in the right place to get it fixed, aren't they?"

I had a question for my surgeon, a question that had been playing on my mind: "Is there such a thing as an illness where a person hears their own heartbeat as if it were footsteps?"

"No," he said firmly after a moment. "I've never heard of anything like that. Nothing physical, and nothing psychological. In fact, it sounds rather silly to me."

I thanked him and walked over to the elevators. When the doors opened on the ground floor, I was surrounded by journalists. So I glanced over my shoulder to where the cellist had clambered up on the sofa, flinging steel ashtrays at the reporters and sending them scurrying in every direction.

From my scrapbook, July 6th

★

Tomorrow is the day of the concert at the National Orchestra Hall commemorating the exciting history of the city that stretches back over 400 years.

Here is the program:

Percussion Ensemble
It's All Thanks to the Lever and Pulley
Serenade for the Weeping Dinosaur
The Waltz of the Red Dog and the Blind Boxer
(All world premiers)

National Orchestra
Cello Concerto No. 2

The world-famous cellist will be performing in our hall for the first time in a year. First- and second-tier tickets have been sold out, and there are only a few seats remaining at the back of the third tier. The performers politely request that each member of the audience come with something that makes a sound (it can be an instrument, a toy, or any household object. Sirens, however, are prohibited).

From my scrapbook, July 8th

★

Yesterday's 400th Anniversary Concert turned out to be a most peculiar event. The master's cello performance was outstanding and the orchestra followed his lead with a passion. In fact, it was the most spectacular cello concerto I have ever heard in my life.

    The percussion ensemble that opened for the cellist wasn't bad either, with a variety of percussion instruments coming alive with every passing moment. In a way, it sounded like children playing, but at the same time it was perfectly orchestrated. The young conductor making his debut showed great poise and confidence with his baton. As well as being possibly the tallest person in the city, it seems he may be one of its brightest talents as well.

    What was peculiar, however, was the encore that followed after the cello concerto. In the midst of a wild applause, the lights were suddenly turned off, enveloping the hall in darkness. Then a voice, probably belonging to the young conductor, instructed the audience to take out whichever sound-making item they'd brought with them (personally, I brought a stapler). The darkness was then filled with myriad sounds including cowbells, plates, toy whistles, bicycle bells, air pumps, and even scissors. Once all the noise had subsided, the cellist launched into a pizzicato piece, with each note coming out crystal clear and the rhythm held perfectly steady. I felt as if I could go on listening to it forever, when all of a sudden all the instruments on stage joined in, playing loudly, then quietly—all at the same tempo, with the timpani, violin, oboe, horn, and even the meowing of a cat and the squeaking of a toy mouse resounding through the hall to the same constant beat.

    The next thing I knew, the whole audience had joined in. Dishes were banged; door bells went ding, ding, ding. Scissors went snip, snip, snip, and I found myself going kachuk, kachuk, kachuk, with my stapler. Even those who hadn't brought anything joined in by stomping their feet, and there was even several people who got up and began to shadow box. Not one person said a word as everyone concentrated on making their own noise. Then eventually the cellist's pizzicato subsided and the lights came back on. Amazingly, everyone on stage had disappeared and the audience looked at one another in a stupor before quietly making their way home.

I'm still rather baffled by the performance. The many sounds echoing in the hall had somehow felt so soft and intimate. It was as if all of us sharing noises were friends sharing secrets. And even now, as I write this article, that rhythm, that pizzicato still rings in my ears.

It occurs to me now that the hall itself became an instrument that night. That I'd been hiding in that instrument listening to the sounds at their very origin. And though I've been writing about music for more than forty years, it was only last night that I realized something that's essential in music—that performing together can actually be fun.

It may sound like I'm joking, but I'm really not. There is so much joy to be had in listening to music. But somewhere along the way, I'd forgotten what sheer fun it is to play. I'm sure anyone would understand what I mean, even if they weren't part of last night's performance. Just think back, if you will, to when you first laid hands on an instrument as a child.

I imagine that even the first people to play music in the history of this world would agree with this statement. That so much of the fun of music is about playing together. We play instruments, and will continue to do so because we want to believe and confirm, over and over again, that we are connected to something.

The Woman with the Very Large Body

"Let's go with the same program for the next concert," the director said to me. "Two of the caretaker's pieces and one of yours." The concert would be in October.

Since our big performance, the cellist had gone back to visiting the brothel and Green had gone back to school, while the Butterfly Man had taken Purple-Green (who simply refused to leave his side) and returned to the crescent-shaped city where he was soon to begin teaching at the school for the blind which was scheduled to reopen soon.

As for me, I was cooped up every day in the reference room at the National Music Hall where so much information was filed away about the 300-year history of the orchestra, although I wanted only to know about the past several decades. As it turned out, the manager of the reference room had known Grandpa, as did several others who had been there for a long time. The journalist who'd written about the performance and several professors at the university had known him, too. They were all eager to tell me about the time when they lived in the city, in the days before I was born.

When I read the Miraculous Reincarnating Man's book that I bought just before the fire at the department store, I was surprised to find Dad, Grandpa, and Mom all mentioned in it. I learned that Dad and Grandpa hadn't been born here at all. But that they'd moved to the city from a very cold region up north when my dad was still a child. Grandpa had been an excellent carpenter, and he became well known as a stage specialist after working on the interiors of numerous halls. He'd even done the floors of the National Orchestra Hall!

"It wasn't just his ability with the hammer and plane," said the manager of the reference room. "He had an incredibly good ear, too."

It seemed that people who knew music knew that the acoustics of a stage improved significantly after Grandpa had worked on it. In fact, all he had to do was nail in some boards backstage and the violinists performing upfront would suddenly feel as if their skills had taken a leap for the better. So in a sense, Grandpa was actually a stage tuner. He was also known for offering his expert opinion during orchestra rehearsal. If the horn or oboe was even slightly out of tune, Grandpa would tap the floor of the stage with a wooden hammer or the handle of a saw from under the floorboards.

"Don't you play an instrument yourself?" the director had asked Grandpa one day.

"Play an instrument?" Grandpa had said shrugging his shoulders. "To me the stage is an instrument. A very large percussion instrument. Though if I ever have trouble finding work, I'm hoping an orchestra somewhere in the world will let me in."

"Nobody took more pride in his work than he did," said the now elderly director as he puffed on his cigarette, a distant look in his eye.

After finishing a job, Grandpa would stand on stage—keeping his back straight and take steps on the stage floor to check the reverberations. Then he'd lift his feet straight up and bring them down in rhythm, like some old countryside dance.

Ton, Ta-tan, Ton
Ton, Ta-tan, Ton

"What kind of beat is that?" someone had asked.

"It's just a boring folk song from my homeland," he'd replied, continuing to step away.

Dad's interest in mathematics, I learned, had been awakened by a toy instrument that Grandpa made for him when he was young. It consisted of five silk strings stretched across a wooden slab and could be tuned by shifting the bridge for each string.

"It's about ratios," Dad would say to his colleagues.

When Dad was about to turn thirty, he was teaching at an elementary school while doing research at the university. He was already known for his awkward social skills and for being a little pig-headed. But nobody could doubt his talent for mathematics, especially not his professors. Those same professors were perplexed one day when Dad sat in a daze and had no comment to offer about recent research findings. And they were even more perplexed when a woman showed up at lab the next day and handed him a lunchbox saying, "Hey, you forgot this!"

"She started coming to the research lab two or three times a week to bring him lunch," the assistant professor at the university told me. "She was a very large woman. I remember she always had a wonderful, very contagious smile. A smile like a wildfire."

This large woman was from the same northern village as Dad and Grandpa. She wore colorful clothes in outrageous combinations, but they looked great on her. She couldn't find anything in her size in a store, so she made her own clothes by stitching different pieces of fabric together. She spoke her rural accent with pride.

I was surprised when the assistant professor told me that it was Dad who had approached her while she was waiting at a bus stop, her hands full with shopping bags. He'd thought her body was a magnificent combination of ratios, that from a mathematical perspective, she was perfectly balanced. She immediately recognized Dad's accent as her own, and without hesitating she dropped her bags of tomatoes and onions to the ground, scooped Dad up into her arms, and held him tight to her bosom.

In time, she made lunches for the young researchers and the professors, too.

"But it wasn't just the way she looked," said the assistant professor. "Your mother was a woman of perfect harmony in every way. She was like a fertile farm on the horizon where the sun shines every day without fail."

Mom and Dad lived together for nearly a year, and Grandpa came to visit often.

"Your grandpa must have been very fond of that woman," said the manager of the reference room. "He never said so, but it was obvious. One day he was yawning, saying he hadn't gotten any sleep. I asked him what happened, and he grumbled about being forced to tell stories about his village until daybreak at his son's house. He looked very pleased."

I learned that Mom was in perfect health on the morning I was born. And that as soon as she had given birth to me, she got up, marched into the eatery next door, and ate three omelets. Then she returned home, gave her right arm a couple of slaps, and tied me to it.

Every morning, she'd dangle me from her arm as she walked, swinging me gently back and forth. In the afternoon she worked at the port, lifting heavy items. Not a soul there forgot her.

"I'm sure she could have easily walked with five, even ten kids hanging off her arm!" said the owner of the eatery. It turned out she often ordered three omelets whenever something made her happy. The same owner also remembered one occasion when he saw Dad peeking into the kitchen.

"Can I help you?" said the eatery owner.

"Erm..." blinked Dad awkwardly as he stood with his notebook in hand.

"Do you have a sort of secret to cooking eggs?"

A lot of kids at the elementary school where Dad had taught were the children of wealthy parents, several of which contributed funds for the construction of an auditorium for winter concerts. It was decided that Grandpa would be in charge of the project. Three months after I was born, the auditorium was completed. The kids of the school were knocked out by the sparkling new stage, and they stared in awe, mouths wide open, as if seeing a snowy mountain too majestic to climb.

"Go on," Grandpa told them. "I made this stage for all of you to make noise on. This is your stage. So go on! Go make some noise!"

Slowly, the children inched forward. At the front, a girl tapped the heel of her shoe against the floor, and the sound echoed around the hall. Then the sound of another tapping heel followed. Then came the sound of all the children slapping their hands on the wooden stage until the music hall was completely filled with the sounds of children.

"He looked so happy," said the principal. "Your grandpa had his eyes closed, just soaking up the sound. But I was so surprised. Usually the shrieks and jokes of the children can be hard on the ears. But in that hall, they combined into beautiful music."

The inaugural concert was to include an ensemble by the elementary school's trumpet and drum corps, a piece by the string section, and a solo by a soprano from the National Orchestra. People would be coming from all over to commemorate the official opening of the hall.

Mom brought out a special dress she'd been keeping deep in her closet. It was a purple ball gown with gold tufts that she'd sewn—it had taken her many years just to collect enough of the right fabric for it.

"I'm going to my first concert!" she'd laughed, delighted, as she went around showing the dress to people in our neighborhood. Everyone remarked how beautiful she would look in it.

At seven o'clock on the big day, Dad, his university colleagues, and Mom holding her baby entered the concert hall. Their seats were toward the front in the center. The seats around them were filled by children.

"The back of the hall is fine for me," said Mom. "If I sit here, people behind me won't be able to see."

"But this is where your seat is," said Dad, who was inflexible where numbers were concerned. "Here it is—K17—in the eleventh row." Mom just frowned and did her best to fit her soft, large frame into the seat.

Band members were blowing their trumpets excitedly as they waited their turn in the wings. The elite members of the National Orchestra who were sitting in the audience couldn't believe that such a fine facility had been built expressly for children.

The soprano was warming up when the recording staff hurried into the wings and whispered, "The mics aren't working properly. The sound keeps cutting off."

"What?" Grandpa said, poking his head through the curtain and gazing upward where an old sound reflector was attached to a beam. It was a square black box the size of a trunk. Above it, you could see a tangle of twisted cables dangling down. "Another case of shabby workmanship," he grumbled. "You know, I was sure I smelled alcohol on those workmen who put the finishing touches on that thing. I'm going to have a look."

A minute later, Grandpa was balancing on the beam making his way to the sound reflector, with all the grace and agility of a master carpenter.

"There was exactly five minutes before the start of the performance," said the soprano, with a slightly trembling voice.

Later, the recording staff, the school officials, and even the boys blowing their trumpets in the wings all agreed that the master carpenter could not be blamed. They'd all been watching Grandpa up on the beam. Just before his fingers were about to grasp the box, the sound reflector fell loose and started to sway, dangling in midair. Grandpa wrapped his legs around the beam and did his best to grab it. But he was a second too late—with an ear-piercing screech, the sound reflector started to swing beyond his reach, then plummeted straight into the audience. And Grandpa came falling at the same time.

On hearing that terrible screeching, everyone in the audience had looked up. Of course, most people had no idea what was happening. Mom, however, jumped out of her seat, grabbed the children around her, and put her arms around them, positioning her body over them.

From more than ten meters above, that heavy old sound reflector fell—crashing down on Mom's head with such an awful sound that you could feel in the pit of your stomach. The microphone picked up the sound, which reverberated throughout the auditorium. The auditorium was frozen in the sound and its mournful echo.

Dad was lying on the floor holding his head. He'd try to throw himself on top of Mom, but Grandpa, who fell with the sound reflector, clipped him on the forehead with his knee. Under my mom were ten elementary school children and me. She had broken Grandpa's fall; he was holding his knee and moaning in pain.

Mom said, "It was my first concert ever," as she lay heavily concussed in the ambulance. Dad was in that ambulance with a bandage on his head, as well as the elementary school principal and Grandpa with a splint on his leg.

"Are the children safe?" my mom asked.

"Not one suffered a scrape!" the principal told her.

Mom strained to smile. Then, just as they were about to arrive at the hospital, my poor mom drew her very last breath.

Dad told the undertaker that there was no need to change her fantastic purple dress with its gold tufts. Grandpa kept shaking his head throughout the funeral, as if trying to shake away the dark cloud that hovered above him.

Dad never blamed Grandpa for what had happened. Nobody blamed Grandpa.

The music director was concerned about Grandpa's knee and urged him to go to an orthopedist. "He told me that's what he was doing," said the director. "Three days later he had the same splint on. I later learned he'd been going to an ear doctor instead."

I went to visit the eye clinic Grandpa had gone to and was surprised to find there the very same doctor who'd attended to him.

"Your grandfather said he had a terrible ringing in his ear," he explained. "An awful echo that wouldn't subside. I remember it to this day. It was like he was on fire. He was screaming, *If you can't fix it, just punch a hole in my ears. It'll be better than this!* He was a desperate, scary patient."

After a week, Grandpa's right knee had stiffened in the shape of the splint holding it, and he could no longer bend it at all.

The elementary school principal from those days told me that late one afternoon he happened to notice that a light in the auditorium was on. Looking through a crack in the door, he saw my dad with his messy hair—half of which was now gray—sitting in a seat on the 11th row. It was seat K18, where Dad had been sitting the moment of the accident, and he was staring at the empty seat next to him. He was totally still. Didn't move. He didn't blink. The principal himself was frozen as he observed Dad's grief. Then, after a bit, Dad leaned back in his seat and let out a sigh that seemed to stretch to the ceiling before echoing throughout the hall.

"It gave me the shivers," the principal said, in a whisper. "I've never heard a sigh like that. It was like a breeze blowing in from a fetid beach. He seemed to breathe through a hole in his throat, and he kept sighing over and over again. To be honest, I felt more scared of him than sorry for him."

A few days later, Dad handed in his resignation. He told people that a foreign university had offered him as a lectureship in mathematics, though nobody in the research lab had ever heard of the university. Grandpa made some changes too, and he began selling all of his tools.

"He wouldn't have been able to continue with that leg of his," said the music director. "It was obvious they were both in a hurry to leave town. At least, that's the way it seemed to me."

Lots of people showed up dockside to send the three of us off—Dad, Grandpa, and baby me. Elementary school students were lined up wearing black arm bands, and as we were boarding the boat a student representative presented Dad with a notebook and Grandpa with a sturdy silver cane. Both Dad and Grandpa had received their gifts with a shrug of the shoulders and quickly walked up the gangplank. As the ship's whistle blew, the band started playing the song they'd planned to play at that fateful concert—puffing out the sounds with rosy red faces.

Grandpa paused on the deck, listening to the drums booming and the triangle letting out a high-pitched *ting*. He couldn't help himself: he spun around, banged his new cane on the railing, and yelled, "You call that music?"

Nobody in the band knew how to respond, and several students even dropped their instruments. But Grandpa carried on yelling while banging away with his cane.

"Triangle! Have you no ears? Raise your arms more. It doesn't matter if they fall off! Don't rest! Third base drum! Stretch your arms! Snare drum! What are you doing? No one can hear you like that!"

Some students burst into tears. But that didn't stop Grandpa. He kept pounding his cane down, yelling at them not to stop, to keep on playing. Dad had been the children's teacher until just a few days before, but now he backed away and vanished into the crowd on deck without a word. The boat slowly churned away from the dock until the children could see nothing more than a manic silhouette banging his cane in the distance.

Despite this very mixed moment, nobody had anything negative to say about Dad or Grandpa. Everyone was very nice when I asked about them. I hadn't found the sweets and the sandwiches of this town to be too bad either, contrary to Grandpa's warning. Until now how they could have had such a "horrible life" was beyond my comprehension.

But of course, the accident in the auditorium tainted everything. The awful echo of the sound reflector hitting Mom in the head did not stop haunting Grandpa. The same awful sound gnawed away at Dad's soul. At last, I began to understand them. I began to understand how a single horrible sound can drain the colors from life and blast away the beauty from even the most accomplished music. These are the things that happen in this world.

Wheat-Stepp'n Kutze

An old bus trundled along the dirt road, with bare farmland stretching into the distance on either side. It was a little past noon and the sun was shining down from the cloudless sky. Here in the far north the sun sets very late in summer. I was seated at the back and I leaned forward to ask the farmer in front of us if we were nearly there. He was an old but sturdy-looking man, and he pulled at his white beard as if it was a piece of cotton string. Then he glanced out the window and said, "Yeah, we're nearly there."

I huffed in frustration. He'd told me the same exact thing more than an hour ago! Green, sitting beside me in a short-sleeved blouse, was trying not to laugh. It was just the three of us on the bus—Green and me in our new dark brown shoes, and the farmer in his muddy boots.

As we rode through this vast landscape, I looked out of the back window to where the wheels kicked up yellow sand and dust in our wake. Green turned around too, holding her binoculars to her sunglasses and gazing at the horizon. Every so often the driver would give a friendly honk to the women walking along pushing wheelbarrows.

At some point, I asked the white-bearded man about farming, and he (who'd previously seemed to be a man of few words) began to talk with such enthusiasm that a small spray of saliva punctuated his words. He told us that in this region, wheat is planted each year in the first week of October and harvested the following May. The winters are severe, the air is as cold as ice, and snow falls by the meter. To protect the land, the farmers cover it with matting made of woven wheat.

"Wheat stepping?" The farmer stroked his nose. "People use rollers these days. I bought the latest one myself recently."

"No, I'm talking about the kind where you move along sideways stepping on wheat. Don't people do that here?"

"Hmmm," the farmer said, taken a little off guard. Then he started speaking with a passion, telling me all about the tradition of wheat stepping—becoming more and more animated until he eventually stood up and showed us.

"You choose a clear day after the frost has settled. The frost lifts up the dirt, lifting the wheat seeds with it. We stand along each row of wheat and move along it, stomping the wheat into the dirt."

"Actually stomping on the wheat?" I asked.

"Yes," the farmer said, kicking the floor of the bus. "The young buds and all. You push them back down into the frozen dirt."

"Why?" Green asked with wide eyes. "If the wheat has already grown, why push it back down into the soil? I feel sorry for the poor wheat."

"Poor wheat? It makes the wheat grow stronger," said the farmer with a laugh. "If you don't step on it, then it will become weak in the winter. You see, they don't yield much during the spring. It's funny you think it's such a horrible thing, young lady. That thought never occurred to me. To us farmers it's all about the yield."

"But doesn't some of the wheat just get crushed and die?" said Green, unconvinced.

"I guess so," the farmer said. "But no one knows until harvest time whether it's good wheat or bad wheat. Even the ones that die fertilize the land. So no wheat is really bad wheat. Wheat is wheat. It's our job come winter to step on it all the same. Except now, of course, that we use rollers."

"So there's no such thing as good wheat or bad wheat?" Green asked.

"That's right," the farmer replied. "And there's no such thing as good or bad when it comes to wheat-stepping either."

The farmer then went off at a tangent about a particularly large potato he'd once grown. Green and I sat back in our seats, slipping in and out of sleep.

"Come on then, hurry up if you're getting off!"

I opened my eyes to the driver looking at us with a cigarette hanging from his mouth. We'd come to a stop in the middle of farmland.

"I'm pretty certain this is near the village you were talking about," said the farmer, tugging at his beard.

So we stepped off the bus and onto the road. The sun was stronger than I'd expected. Green put on her sunglasses and a hat on her head. The bus shuddered before engulfing us in a black exhaust and waddling away into the distance.

There was absolutely nothing on the road to indicate that this was actually a bus stop. There was just flat, yellow land that stretched out in all directions, like some infinite dry sea. In fact, the only things between us and the horizon was a small cluster of about four or five farmhouses. We started along a narrow path that led through the farmland. There wasn't a tree in sight, but the sound of cicadas was everywhere. We may have been in the northern lands, but by the sound of it, summer was still summer.

When we at last approached the village, we saw a dozen farm wives washing jars by a well. They were singing together. All wore the same purple shawl on their heads; it must have been the local tradition. It was the same kind of shawl on the head of the mother who was leaving the city with her daughter on the day I first arrived. I wondered for a moment what that girl was doing now.

As we came closer, the farmers' wives stopped their singing, shooting each other a glance before turning to look at us rather intently. They had, I noticed, more than a purple shawl in common. They all had very generous figures.

One of the women smiled, and then made room for us to join them. Green and I sat in front of one of their buckets, and another woman offered us a drink of well water from a jar. Its coolness felt good on my tongue and soothing to my throat.

Summer afternoons in this part of the world were slow. While the men were at the cannery and the children were in school, the women prepared the earth and washed the jars for pickling fruit. Preparing the earth meant fertilizing it and leaving it to bake in the sun—all in readiness for the long, harsh winter to come.

I opened my scrapbook as the farmers' wives bundled up their shawls to peer over my shoulder.

"It's Kutze," one of the older women said without hesitation.

"You're right! It *is* Kutze!" another exclaimed.

"Let me see," said the gray-haired woman who'd given me a sip of water. "It's him all right. Hasn't he aged!"

I was completely at a loss for words. "That..." I finally said, "isn't my grandfather's name."

"Not saying it's his name."

One of the women explained: Kutze was the word traditionally used here to describe a person who was very unusual. For example, people would say, *That guy is a real kutze!* Or, *Stop being such a kutze!* But nobody knew where the word came from.

"Anyway," said the gray-haired woman, "this one here—he was a true kutze!"

According to these farm wives, Grandpa had raised his son all by himself. But he never dirtied his hands with farm work. Occasionally he might help repair a farm tool or climb up on a roof to pound a nail in here or there. But other than that, he spent his time singing with the children.

"Whenever he went out in the field, all he did was step on wheat," said the gray-haired woman, causing a ripple of gentle chuckles. "And he did that all year 'round."

"All year 'round?"

"Yes," said the one of the older women. "On snowy nights, on spring mornings. The seasons—they didn't matter. He'd be out there with his son, stepping on the dirt, moving along sideways, steps at a time. Such a Kutze he was!"

This brought laughter to the women, whose bodies swayed like flowers in the breeze.

"What about that farm?" asked Green. "Is it still there?"

One of the women, who was exceptionally tall, led us to the back of a barn and pointed in the direction of a tattered old scarecrow. Apparently, all the yellow land that spread out beyond the scarecrow had been part of Grandpa's farm. Now, in keeping with Grandpa's wishes when he left the village, this was a wheat field that was shared by everyone.

As the tall woman strolled back toward the well, we heard the singing start up again, accompanied by the sound of the glass jars knocking into each other as they were washed.

Green and I stepped off into the empty wheat field. On the bus, we'd learned that the seeds were planted in October, so there was another two months to go.

If we hadn't been told that a scarecrow was there, I would have mistaken it for the remains of a broken fence. But as I got nearer, I saw the yellow hat plopped on top—it was full of holes and perched on head made of a bundle of straw. The body of the scarecrow was a wooden cross, and from the horizontal piece dangled assorted junk—rusty forks, walnut shells, sticks—all clinking and clunking in the breeze.

"Cat, look!" exclaimed Green, who'd gone around to the back of the scarecrow. There, carved into the wood, in big letters was:

KUTZE

"And touch the dirt!" she said. "It's really warm!"

I grabbed a handful. She was right. It was really warm, surprisingly so. Perhaps it was because of the fertilizer? Or maybe it was the rays of the warm summer sun? Soon there would be seeds planted into this dirt. Which would later it would be covered in frost. Then it would be stomped on. By spring, the land would turn green as far as the eye could see and golden ears of corn would begin to reach for the sky.

I opened my fist and let the wind carry the dirt from my palm, sprinkling it across the field, like golden rain, like seeds of light. I took a deep breath, filling my lungs with the clean air of the country, and I began to step along the dirt as the rays of the sun warmed me. With a precise rhythm I stepped steadily sideways. Just as Dad had done. As Grandpa had done. Then Green joined me and we stepped along together, sharing the same rhythm as our shoes turned to yellow.

Ton, Ta-tan, Ton
Ton, Ta-tan, Ton

On the other side of the barn, we could hear the farm wives singing. Carried by the wind, the sound of the familiar song came drifting towards us.

Step, step, step, wheat-stepp'n Kutze

We stepped in time. Taking a step in our city shoes, then raising our feet to the sky before taking the next.

White, black, brown. Step till they're flat.

At that moment, I promised myself that I'd take Green and the cellist to my island hometown the next year. I imagined Grandpa would keep a stern face when he met her. Then he'd probably ask her what instrument she plays. I imagined her performing a dog's squeak for him and Grandpa tapping his cane in response.

"Your tone's not bad," he'd say, "but your rhythm is a little unsteady. I don't think you've quite mastered the breathing of a dog yet. But I can give you a lesson tomorrow. Be ready to work hard!"

Ton, Ta-tan, Ton

Green dabbed at the beads of sweat on her forehead. Then it was back to stepp'n, the sound of our shoes echoing high in the sky before melting into that soft summer sun.

Ton, Ta-tan, Ton

We were the perfect ensemble, Green and me.

Ton, Ta-tan, Ton

Together we kicked the golden dirt around our feet.

"Hey, you two, nothing's been planted there yet!"

We turned around to see the gray-haired farm wife behind us.

"Don't you know the first thing about wheat-stepping? What a pair of kutzes you are!"

As we looked back in her direction, the scarecrow seemed to be dancing in the wind. Its trinkets clinking and clunking and flying into each other. It sounded like children laughing in paradise.